Infinite Dendrogram
3. Clash of the Superio
Sakon Kaidou
Illustrator: Taiki

Figaro
Figaro
One of the Kingdom of Altar's Big Three and the one sitting at the top of the country's duel rankings. He's the reigning champion of the Colosseum and has the ultimate job of the gladiator grouping — Over Gladiator. His nickname is "The Endless Chain."

Xunyu
Xunyu
A Superior occupying the second place of the Huang He Empire's duel rankings, Xunyu was summoned to participate in a certain major event. Has the daoshi grouping's Superior Job — Master Jiangshi. Xunyu's nickname is "The Yinglong."

A player and an active Journalist affiliated with the information organization known as DIN. Knows a lot. Currently accompanying Ray due to his habit of getting involved in all kinds of incidents.

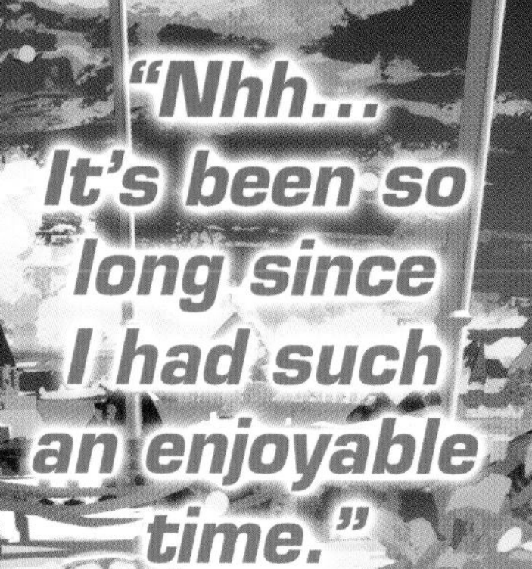


"That's good to know."

**Elizabeth**

Elizabeth S. Altar

The second princess of The Kingdom of Altar. An innocent hoyden of a girl who doesn't hesitate to act based on her curiosity. Often sneaks past her guards to go and play around the city.

SIDE STORY **A Day Off in Gideon**

# Infinite Dendrogram

## 3. Clash of the Superiors

**Sakon Kaidou**

**Illustrator: Taiki**

Infinite Dendrogram: Volume 3
by Sakon Kaidou

Translated by Andrew Hodgson
Edited by Emily Sorensen


Illustrations by Taiki

First published in Japan in 2017
Publication rights for this English edition arranged through Hobby Japan, Tokyo.



President and Publisher: Samuel Pinansky
Managing Editor: Aimee Zink

ISBN: 978-1-7183-5502-6
Printed in Korea
First Printing: November 2019
10 9 8 7 6 5 4 3 2 1

# Contents

## Prologue One of the East's Mightiest

*Western Caldina, Valeira Desert — an area bordering the Kingdom of Altar*

Before the break of dawn, a wind was blowing through a dimly-lit desert, gently shifting its sands. It was an east-bound sea breeze that came all the way from the western ocean, crossing the entire Kingdom of Altar in the process.

Caldina was a country of sands. 99% of it was desolate wastelands, while the remaining 1% contained oases.

A land so lacking — if not downright deadly — wasn't a good environment for any country to thrive, but Caldina was located in the middle of the continent. It prospered due to being in the center of all transactions between the two eastern countries (Huang He and Tenchi) and the three western countries (the kingdom, the imperium, and the fairyland). But it was also abundant in underground resources, ores, and ruins full of various magic items. Any food problems it might've had due to lack of fertile land were easily fixed by trading such riches.

Caldina could be summed up with the words "sand," "wealth," and "trade." The deserts that comprised its territory became a road that connected the east and the west, creating an immense flow of riches.

It was similar to what people of Earth had once called the "Silk Road."

On one such road, there was a row of about ten sizeable dragon carriages, so called because they were drawn by Demi-Dragons.

From their design, it was obvious that the carriages had come from Huang He rather than Caldina. Though it was uncommon for the eastern country to make deliveries to the west without stopping in the desert country, it definitely wasn't unheard of. However, there were two things about the carriages which many would find odd.

The first was the fact that each and every single one of them was flying the flag of Huang He. While some merchant dragon carriages bore patterns that indicated what country they belonged to, none of them ever hoisted a flag.

The second oddity wasn't with the carriages, but with the person sitting on the roof of the one carriage at the very back. The person was looking at the trails the wheels left on the road and the predawn desert scenery passing by. Enjoying the scenery, the person blew into the tobacco pipe-looking item at the edge of what passed for a mouth and continuously released soap bubbles into the wind.

If that had been the only notable thing, many would have passed off the person as merely "eccentric" rather than "odd." However, it wasn't any conduct that warranted such a description, but a matter of overall appearance.

The person's limbs were far too long. Though the long, daoshi-like clothing did a good job covering them, it did nothing to conceal their abnormal length.

The eccentric's total height was above four metels, and the legs made up more than half of it. They were reminiscent of the classic stilt-walkers you might see at a circus. However, the person's arms were inappropriately long, as well. There was more than length to them, though — the five "fingers" grasping the pipe looked more like thin, sword-like blades than anything else.

The arms were far too long and had to be bent in a peculiar way just to let the person keep the pipe in the mouth and blow into it as they enjoyed the passing scenery.

The state of the person's face was quite bizarre, as well. The hat they wore had a talisman attached to it, which hung downwards and hid the eccentric's visage. When combined with the daoshi clothes, it made the person look like a jiangshi from Chinese movies.

The palpably strange appearance made this person stand out from the rest of the world. At the same time, the person emitted a shapeless aura of intimidation that had nothing to do with what you could see with the naked eye, yet was definitely there for those who could feel it.

This eccentric was both abnormal and awe-inspiring enough to appear like a threat to the world just by the virtue of existing. Despite being so menacing, however, the person did nothing but silently enjoy the desert scenery and the bubbles floating in the wind.

"Master Xunyu!" Soon enough, someone called out to the jiangshi-like character by using that name.

The source of the voice was a boy who looked about ten years old. He was trying to get on the same roof Xunyu was sitting on. Since the dragon carriage had no ladder, the youngling found it to be a particularly hard task.

In fact, with the vehicle moving, him falling off was a perfectly plausible scenario.

Noticing that, Xunyu used one of those long arms to take the boy by the nape and pull him to the roof. And thus, the child got safely onto the same platform as the eccentric jiangshi. Though the fingers that held the boy were like blades, neither the boy's luxurious-looking clothing nor his frail skin were damaged in any way.

"Ah! Thank you very much, Master Xunyu!" he said.

"You sure are eaRly, Cang," the jiangshi replied.

Though Xunyu's intonation was peculiar, the boy referred to as "Cang" didn't seem to care about it and spoke his response with a smile. "Not as early as you, Master Xunyu."

"...Ya know, having you call me 'master' makes me feel pretty uncoMFOrtable."

The boy looked at the jiangshi with gleaming eyes, which made Xunyu exhale a heavy sigh and blow some more bubbles.

Cang's real name was "Canglong" — meaning "Azure Dragon." In the Huang He Empire, the only people allowed to bear names with references to the sort of dragons that Masters would refer to as "oriental" were the direct male descendants of the emperor, meaning that this Cang boy was of imperial blood. Specifically, he was the third child of the current emperor.

Indeed — the reason why these dragon carriages were so unlike those belonging to traders was because they were a mission escorting the empire's royalty to the kingdom.

"We're about to reach the boRDer," said Xunyu.

"Indeed we are, Master Xunyu!" said the boy with glee. "Speaking of which, have you visited the Kingdom of Altar before?"

"Can't say that I haVe, but the guy in the alien costu— the 'Spirit Turtle' or 'Linggui' or whatever he wants to be called — said that he's been there onCe."

"Master Gray α Centauri? What did he say about it?"

"...Apparently, and I quote, 'There was an interesting costume there.'"

"Costume?" The boy looked reasonably confused.

As they were having such exchanges, the row of dragon carriages eventually reached the border of the Kingdom of Altar.

The kingdom's officials went through the necessary formalities to allow their entry into the country. They looked seriously tense through the entirety of it, while the two people on the roof seemed completely unaffected. The tenseness was present even among the empire's own officials and chamberlains. It was obvious that they wanted to say something, but their reverence for Cang's royal status and Xunyu in general made them hesitate.

Cang was an upfront boy brimming with curiosity. Due to that nature of his, he often addressed non-royalty in a highly nonchalant manner. However, not many of them replied the way Xunyu did. Most would turn humble and abase themselves, and considering the boy's status, they were completely right to do so. Xunyu, however, was special — even among Masters — and thus was allowed to respond differently.

About an hour had passed since they had crossed the border between Caldina and Altar and begun traversing the Cruella Mountain Belt.

The kingdom's people had already told them about the Gouz-Maise Gang that had their hideout in this area. They'd said that the group was led by a powerful undead-gladiator duo, and that — though they focused primarily on kidnappings — the possibility of them attacking dragon carriages wasn't zero and suggested that they be on their guard.

The problem clearly wasn't something that could be ignored just by upping their alertness, but the kingdom's officials had said nothing more. Still, it hadn't been negligence on their part. They simply hadn't said anything more because "being on their guard" was *more than enough* for this group of carriages.

"...Something reeKs." Xunyu suddenly spoke up while sniffing. "It's not undead stench, thoUgh Cang, get down for a biT."

"All right!" The boy listened to the jiangshi's words and slid down prone on the carriage's roof. A moment later, Xunyu's long arm released a flash.

Two seconds after that, they both heard the sound of something sinking into the damp ground nearby.

Those with the appropriate knowledge would instantly know that the object was a rifle bullet.

Not saying a word, Xunyu glared through the talisman covering the visage that passed for a face and observed the rocky area several hundreds of metels away from them.

Caldina was a land connecting the east and the west, creating an immense traffic of gold and other riches.

Also, with the encroaching possibility of the Kingdom of Altar's demise, many wealthy merchants had begun abandoning the country for the eastern nations and Caldina itself. Whether they were heading towards or out of the desert country, those going through the border always had treasure on them.

Due to that, many hungry wolves with a taste for wealth would bare their fangs at those passing the area.

"First bullet failed to land on the target. I'm sorry. It seems I missed."

In the rocky area Xunyu was looking at, a woman was lying down with a large, scoped rifle in her hands.

She wasn't alone, for over twenty other people were hiding in the rocks around her. Each had their weapons at the ready as they fixed their eyes on the dragon carriages several hundreds of metels ahead.

They were outlaws. That alone didn't make them special by any means, but this particular group all shared a certain feature.

On the backs of each of their left hands were unique crests. They marked the people as Masters — players of the game known as *Infinite Dendrogram* and immortal beings commanding special powers known as "Embryos."

The group's name was Goblin Street. It was the very same PK clan that had taken part in the blockade surrounding the Kingdom of Altar's royal capital, attacking anyone trying to go through the Wez Sea Route leading to the harbor town to the west of the city. That incident had been caused by someone who'd hired three PK clans and one solo player killer to do it. Though the four — Goblin Street, K&R, Mad Castle, and the Superior Killer — all focused on player killing, their motives were different.

Mad Castle's goal was to rob and exert dominance over other players while role-playing as villains.

K&R's goal was to hunt other players.

The Superior Killer acted as a hired hit man who gave players the death penalty according to people's requests.

And finally, Goblin Street was a band of bandits that attacked and robbed *anyone.*

During the blockade incident, the only one of the four areas where tians were harmed, robbed, and killed was the Wez Sea Route

— the one handled by Goblin Street. Due to that, the clan was the only one of the four guilty entities that had gotten on the kingdom's wanted list.

In *Infinite Dendrogram*, murder and robbery between players wasn't considered a crime. That was because tian laws had no power over Master disputes.

However, the same couldn't be said about cases where Masters committed crimes against tians.

Just like criminal NPCs, such players were put on the country's wanted list, or — provided the crimes were severe enough — the wanted list of every country in the game.

If a Master's respawn points were all in countries that had them on the wanted lists, getting a death penalty would cause the player to respawn at the save point in the gaol.

That was the reason why Goblin Street's activities now took place near a border.

Once they had become unable to use the kingdom's save points due to being on the wanted list, one of the kingdom's Superiors — Lei-Lei the Prodigal of Feasts — had given the death penalty to everyone who was online at the time. Though some went on to respawn in other countries, many didn't have save points outside the kingdom and got sent to the gaol, causing about half of the clan's members to leave.

Obviously, the damage the group sustained was severe, and it wouldn't have been strange for it to have ceased its activities or split up altogether. In fact, that was exactly what happened to another clan that had taken part in the blockade: Mad Castle. Despite not being on the wanted list, the group had split up after they'd been annihilated by Figaro.

Goblin Street, on the other hand, had simply moved their save points to Caldina and still continued their hunt in the kingdom. They'd sneaked through the eastern border of the country and begun their activities once again. Due to how close the area was to Caldina, it was far more convenient than the Wez Sea Route from last time. In fact, the Cruella Mountain Belt was so good for bandits that even the infamous tian group, the Gouz-Maise Gang, had had their hideout here. Truly, finding a more bandit-friendly environment would be no small task.

Of course, with Goblin Street being a band of player killers and criminals, there was the possibility of them getting hunted down by adventurers or attacked by other nearby gangs such as the aforementioned Gouz-Maise Gang. However, Goblin Street wasn't the type of group to be afraid of such scenarios.

"Hey, what the hell?" one of them said. "Didn't you say that switching your job to Sharpshooter turned your effective range into 1,000 meters?"

"I seem to have miscalculated the carriage's movement speed," the woman replied. They were talking about the sniping that she'd attempted on the person on the dragon carriage. Everyone — including herself — thought that she'd missed.

No — not everyone. There was one exception.

"You're wrong there, Neeala. You didn't miss. The bullet just got deflected."

"What do you mean, boss?" she asked.

The man who had spoken up was young and had red hair. The upper half of his body was covered by a similarly-colored jacket that had lion mane trimming on it. However, while the red of his hair seemed natural, the crimson on his jacket made it seem as though it was merely showered in something of such a sanguine color.

"You shot a bullet, and that freak deflected it," he said. "There's nothing more to that."

"But that's impossible," replied the girl. "The bullet was faster than sound."

"*I* can do it, you know? And it just so happens that there's someone else who can," the red man said in a nonchalant manner.

His words caused a stir among those surrounding him. It wasn't caused by the claim that the boss himself could do it, but by the assertion that the opponent was capable of it, as well.

They believed and were well aware that their leader could deflect bullets. He was King of Burglary, Eldridge. Having the throne of the burglar grouping's Superior Job as his own, he was considered to be one of the kingdom's strongest player killers.

When his clan had been purged by the Superior, he had happened to be offline. Due to that, he'd survived the event completely unharmed. However, the members of Goblin Street were absolutely certain that not even a Superior could defeat their leader, and that things would've turned out differently if he'd been online back then.

In fact, Eldridge's strength was the sole reason why the clan still continued to function, despite being forced to change hunting grounds. The members were confident that Goblin Street would remain alive and well as long as they had him.

Eldridge looked at the group of dragon carriages hundreds of metels ahead.

"That freak probably has one of Huang He's Superior Jobs," he said. "We're not letting that stop us, though. I can handle that one by myself. You guys attack all the weaklings that come out once I'm done. That'll be enough."

He then opened his hands and extended them behind him. Soon enough, his palms were filled with power and murderous intent, making it seem as though he was drawing a bowstring to the absolute limit.

His muscles creaked as he closed and opened his hands. It was a subconscious, habitual action that was nothing but a show of his innate desire to grasp and rob his targets' belongings.

"Greater Pickpocket… Greater Takeover… set!" he shouted.

The King of Burglary had three unique skills, all of which used his hands.

In his right hand, he set a skill that robbed people of their items: Greater Pickpocket. It allowed him to pick any transferable items within the effective range, a radius of 100 metels, and forcefully store them in his own inventory. Even a dragon carriage was a viable choice, making it a particularly fearsome skill.

In his left hand, he set a skill that robbed people of their lives: Greater Takeover. As long as they were within the effective range, he could use it to remove his opponents' body parts. Anything that fit into his hand could be plucked from a distance and end up in his possession.

*I've gotta aim for the dragon carriage with that long freak sitting on it,* Eldridge thought. Due to his maxed-out Identification skill, he could easily tell that that particular dragon carriage was special. *It's a mobile save point.*

The Huang He Empire was highly advanced when it came to the creation of magic items, but this vehicle stood out even when that was considered. For Eldridge, who had lost his save points in the kingdom, it was something that he was simply compelled to rob.

The dragon carriage was about three hundred metels away. From its speed, he calculated that it would take between one and two minutes for it to get into his effective range.

Eldridge planned to take the dragon carriage the "long freak" was sitting on, forcefully ruining the tall eccentric's posture and giving him a window of opportunity to take the *head*.

He was confident that it would be over with just that.

It had to be noted that Eldridge's calculations weren't off the mark.

If the conditions had been as he'd set them to be, things probably would've gone exactly as planned. However, there was a certain condition he'd gotten wrong.

He'd assumed that Xunyu was merely an owner of a Superior Job from Huang He.

Alas, there was a decisive difference between his assumption and the reality.

"The freak got off…?" he said, raising an eyebrow.

Just as he'd said, Xunyu was no longer sitting on the dragon carriage.

The jiangshi's limbs appeared to be even longer than they had seemed back when Xunyu had just been sitting.

From a distance, the overall impression the eccentric gave off was closer to "utility pole" than "person."

"Are we about to get attacked?" one of the bandits cried.

"Did the first attack give off our position?!" another yelled.

"Be on your guard! The jobs you can take in the east of the continent are different than those in the west! You don't know what to expect!"

As his clan began making a fuss about the change in situation, Eldridge silently observed Xunyu.

*...This might be bad,* he thought, and not without reason. Whether it was caused by the Danger Sense skill he'd acquired or the instincts he'd been born with, he felt that he was in peril.

However, he'd felt the same way about many a boss monster, Master, or tian he'd encountered during his entire playtime, and on countless such occasions, he'd come out on top.

Even with the danger considered, Eldridge — owner of the Superior Job known as "King of Burglary" — didn't think that the eccentric could emerge victorious.

*Now that the freak is off the carriage, it's safe to expect an attack,* he thought. *Still, I just have to wait until the shithead enters my effective range and take their head before anything happens.*

With that in mind, he instantly switched the skill on his right hand to Greater Takeover.

Due to the jiangshi's long clothes, Eldridge couldn't tell how the body looked under them, but he figured that Xunyu would die the moment he removed the head.

There was nothing wrong with that line of thinking. Losing their vitals meant death to just about anyone. Having killed countless people like this, Eldridge knew that better than most.

And so did Xunyu.

"The freak's not mov— Ghuh... Ah?"

Eldridge began to speak his confusion about the lack of activity from the jiangshi. But before he could finish his sentence, his voice was replaced by a powerful flow of blood.

In fact, the sanguine liquid began to flow out of every orifice on his head — mouth, nostrils, ears, and eyes.

The blood trailing down from the seven holes painted his face crimson.

"U-UAAAHHH!" one of his underlings screamed. "B-BOSS?!"

"Hey! Where's our healer?! Wait, no, someone get him an Elixir!"

As his clan members began to panic, Eldridge was surrounded by a mysterious silence. He could barely make out even the most loudest of sounds anymore. Tilting his head to the side, he touched his chest.

*...Oh, I see,* he thought as he shifted his gaze to Xunyu. In the jiangshi's right hand — which was more like a menacing, metallic claw — there was a dark red object.

It looked very much like *a heart.*

*...I've been robbed.*

A moment after he realized what it was, the man known for being one of the Kingdom of Altar's greatest player killers was reduced to particles of light, and vanished.

"B-BOOOOOSS!"

"Wha...? E-eh?!"

The sudden and mysterious death of the man they so relied on made the remaining members panic and scream.

"Too slOw."

Before they could even finish doing that, however, Xunyu — who had been about three hundred metels away just a moment ago — suddenly stood in the center of their group.

A woman hastily tried to aim her rifle, a man quickly brandished his sword, and others hurriedly tried to use their Embryo skills, but the jiangshi acted faster than anyone present.

The action was a simple spin. Xunyu bent that tall frame and spun those long arms. A second later, the people surrounding the jiangshi were *sliced into fine discs* and fell to the ground like tinned chunks of pineapple.

Some of them were wearing accessories that prevented fatal damage, but Xunyu made sure to slice them so thoroughly that it meant nothing.

The immense damage quickly killed them, and the severe destruction of their bodies left no time for resurrection, almost instantly making them vanish.

With them gone, all that was left was the sound of trees dancing in the wind and the ridiculously long shadow made by Xunyu standing in the morning light.

That was how the PK clan known as Goblin Street experienced their second annihilation.

All of it happened in less than two minutes after Xunyu got off the dragon carriage.

"Man, that was boRing," said the jiangshi while taking the familiar pipe out of the inventory and putting it in the mouth again. "Is this the par for the kingdom's SupeRior Jobs?"

Blowing bubbles and sighing, Xunyu used those sharp claws, the Superior Embryo that had just sliced over twenty people, to skillfully scratch their head. "This makes me wonder if I should expect much from the country's SuperiOrs."

Yet again sighing from boredom, Xunyu, the Huang He Empire's Superior, returned to the dragon carriage.

"Well done, Master Xunyu!" said Cang.

"What a splendid display!" said one of the chamberlains. "A Geomancer said that the bandits were a group of dozens of Masters, and yet you were able to take care of them all by your lonesome!"

"I would expect nothing less from one of the Huang He Si Ling — the empire's greatest four!" added one of the country's officials. "Truly, only Master Xunyu is deserving of the nicknames 'Landmine,' 'Divine Speed,' and 'Yinglong.'"

Upon returning to the dragon carriage, Xunyu was showered in such praise. Despite the positive appraisals, however, everyone besides Cang seemed to be somewhat afraid of the jiangshi.

"It ain't muCh," said Xunyu. "Still, though, a job's a job, and with it being so early, it made me pretty sleEpy." Those words made the chamberlains and the officials hastily leave Xunyu's dragon carriage. Cang, too, lightly bowed and excused himself.

Left alone, Xunyu sat down on the custom-made, long sofa and sighed yet again. "With Cang being so genuine, the way he flatters has a certain chaRm to it, but the shameless brown-nosing from the adults is just unSightly."

However, no one could really fault them for their behavior. They were delivering royal blood — Cang — to the Kingdom of Altar for a mission so important that not even Xunyu had been told about it. They had expected the journey to be filled with many attacks such as the one that had just happened, and the jiangshi's protection was invaluable.

However, Xunyu was a Master — one of the wielders of unique powers due to which their very existence in this world was fickle.

If Xunyu happened to leave this realm — to "log out" — for a long period of time, they could never complete their task. Not to mention that their heads would roll the moment something bad happened to Prince Cang.

Originally, the role of protecting this mission hadn't been anywhere in Xunyu's schedule, and the eccentric would've surely left them to their own devices. The only reason why the jiangshi had accepted the role was the fact that the mission had headed out for the kingdom's royal capital at the same time Xunyu had some unrelated business in the same country. Of course, it would've been a lie to say that the jiangshi didn't find the reward — this custom-made dragon carriage — to be attractive, as well.

"HmPh." Still lying on the sofa, Xunyu reached for the inventory and took out two pieces of paper.

The first was a written request directed to Xunyu, while the other was a leaflet.

The written request had come through the adventurers' guild in Huang He, and displayed a reward good enough to make the journey to the kingdom worth it.

It asked Xunyu to have a match in the arena of the duel city known as Gideon. The requester was Count Gideon — the ruler of the city.

It wasn't hard for Xunyu to understand why the man had requested that. The jiangshi had the second place in Huang He's duel rankings and was a Superior, a wielder of a Superior Embryo.

According to the information Xunyu had gathered, the situation in Gideon wasn't the best, so the count was probably trying to dispel the gloomy atmosphere with a grand show fit for a duel city.

That was displayed on the other piece of paper — the event leaflet with the words "Clash of the Superiors" written on it. It informed people of the duel between Figaro — one of the Kingdom of Altar's Superiors and the so-called king of the duel city — and Xunyu, another Superior.

A match between two Superiors. It was an unprecedented event that had yet to happen in any duel city in any country, giving it lots of attention from both in and out of the kingdom.

*Count Gideon is probably thinking of having the local hero, Figaro, win and heighten the spirits of his people… Sadly for him, my loss isn't part of the request,* thought Xunyu as a grin spread across that terrifying face.

Though the talisman hanging down from the hat and covering what passed for a face made it hard to see, the grin was brimming with ferocity.

*I don't know whether he just didn't think this through or if he simply trusts Figaro's strength, but I'll do the same thing regardless — fight with all I am, enjoy it for all it's worth, and beat him with all I've got.* Still covered by the talisman, Xunyu laughed in a menacing manner.

"Khahahahah. Here's hoping you can entertAin me, Altar's SuperiOr."

That was how the dragon carriages carrying one of the east's mightiest and the Empire's prince crossed the border and entered the Kingdom of Altar.

The Clash of the Superiors — Figaro and Xunyu — was just a few days away.

Unknown to most, however, the battle would act as a trigger to an even greater happening.

# Chapter One: Lectures and Reunions

*Paladin, Ray Starling*

It was the morning after the hellish day during which I'd fought the Gouz-Maise Gang and the Revenant Ox-Horse.

Before dawn broke, Nemesis and I were dashing through the Nex Fields on Silver's back while talking about what we would do from now on and hunting the local monsters.

Defeating Gouz-Maise had made me level up to level 39, and this hunting had increased that number to 40. My HP now crossed the 5,000 mark.

Becoming able to ride Silver increased my speed and hunting effectiveness with him. What I found particularly effective was firing Purgatorial Flames at groups of monsters as I passed them by.

"A red-black man on horseback releases a stream of fire without as much as a 'hello' and leaves, just like that," said Nemesis. "No matter how you look at it, that seems like a description of a real villain."

"I'm aware," I said.

*Still, I feel that killing a large number of normal monsters is a better way to level up than going through the hassle of killing a single boss monster, but whatever,* I thought.

Momentarily satisfied with my level, I stopped the hunt and decided to do some tests. Specifically, I wanted to see what Silver and the Grudge-Soaked Greaves, Gouz-Maise could do. The stats bonuses on the Greaves were exactly what the item said they were, while the energy gathering caused by Grudge Conversion seemed to work just as intended.

Also, I noticed that it wasn't necessary for the grudge to come from the dead. The negative emotions released by the living were significantly weaker than those of the deceased, but they could still be converted to MP and SP.

That meant that keeping the enemy alive and torturing them was a good way to stock up on both of those stats. As useful as that seemed, however, the idea of actually doing it just freaked me out.

The other skill on the greaves — Rider and Horse, As One — had proven to work just fine yesterday, when I'd begun using its Horse Riding skill bonus to ride Silver. Thus, it was time to test Silver's own skills.

There were a total of three — Running, Wind Hoof, and one unknown skill that showed up as only "???" on there. The Miasmaflame Bracers also had an unknown skill on them, so I could only assume that unknown skills weren't *that* rare.

First up was Running, which — as it said in the name — was a skill that allowed Silver to run while someone was riding him. The speed and quality of the running was dependent on the rider's Horse Riding skill level. *How horse-like,* I thought.

Then there was the other skill, Wind Hoof. It could only be used when the rider's Horse Riding skill level was above 3 or Riding skill level was above 6. The description said that it "Allows air-travel by compressing the air under the hooves" and "Uses the rider's MP to create a barrier of compressed air."

The difference between Horse Riding and Riding was the fact that the former was exclusive to horses and thus allowed better use of them for less levels, while Riding could be used with anything ridable in exchange for needing more levels.

With all the riding I'd done while going back from the Mountain Belt to Gideon and the dashing we did since predawn today, my Horse Riding had reached level 2. The +1 bonus from Rider and Horse, As One made it level 3, allowing me to use Wind Hoof.

I tried it out and… sure enough, we flew. Though it was less like "flying" more like "running on invisible platforms in the air."

"Whoa." I couldn't help but be moved.

"What a view." Nemesis shared my sentiment. It was something that I could never have experienced in real life.

As great as the experience was, however, the act's similarity to riding a horse over glass made me feel a bit anxious and scared. Still, I got somewhat used to it after about an hour or so. Thankfully, Silver himself covered the cost of this air-running ability, leaving my MP completely untouched.

However, the skill could be used in a way that *did* drain my MP.

It was the barrier of compressed air. According to the skill's description, I could use it to protect myself from attacks.

There happened to be a Goblin Archer right below me, so I used it to see how well it worked.

"Go on, shoot!" I shouted. The result was simple — the arrow broke through the barrier as if it wasn't even there and sunk into me.

Slightly panicking, I used Purgatorial Flames to burn the Goblin Archer below.

*Man, I know I'm the one doing it, but hanging in the air and raining fire on those on the ground is pretty messed up,* I thought.

The Goblin tried fighting back, but all its arrows got burned before they could reach me.

Once I overcame this unexpected predicament, I began to analyze what had just happened. The problem was obvious — Wind Hoof's barrier was just way too weak.

I began thinking about why it was like this, and it didn't take too long for me to find the root of the problem.

I simply hadn't used enough MP. With my maximum MP being so low, I had subconsciously used it sparingly and — naturally — hadn't gotten the results I'd wanted.

When trying it again, I used all of my MP. My next opponent was a Goblin Warrior.

"Bring it on!" I shouted.

The result was simple — its ax broke through the barrier as if it wasn't even there. I'd expected there to be a wall-like patch of air, but the ax had cut through it like it would paper.

By a hair's breadth, I avoided getting split in half and began fighting the Goblin Warrior. Naturally, I emerged victorious, but not having any MP made it a harder battle than it should've been.

"It's no good," I said.

"No good, indeed," agreed Nemesis.

Wind Hoof's air-running effect was great and all, but with my meager amount of MP, the barrier aspect seemed completely useless.

"The efficacy seems quite poor, if you ask me," she added.

*Yeah, seriously,* I thought. Miasmaflame Bracers — a special reward — allowed the use of powerful skills such as Purgatorial Flames and Hellish Miasma for far less MP than Wind Hoof. I could only assume that it was a testament to just how great special rewards were, and...

"Ah," I said as an idea came to my head. I had a certain combo available to me.

So I tried it. And the result was simple — a great success. Not only did the barrier stay intact, it increased my defensive ability so much it was immense.

The only problem was an unexpected side effect that got me all covered in mud.

Also, there was something I had to keep in mind.

"I can't use this in the city," I said.

"It's a quick way to get on the wanted list, no doubt about it," commented Nemesis.

This new way of using the skill was so dangerous that we decided not to touch it unless the situation called for it.

After we were done with the testing, we went back to the city, I took a shower at the inn, and then I made my way to Gideon's knight offices. I went there because Liliana had told me to report the destruction of the Gouz-Maise Gang to them.

I entered the offices in Gideon's first district and saw many Knight-like people busily running around. They seemed about five times busier than high schoolers getting ready for a school festival.

It appeared like there was some event coming up soon, and they were hard at work preparing for it.

Trying not to get in their way, I went through the less crowded hallways and made my way to the office Liliana had told me about.

However, before I could get there...

"Ah."

...I ran into a white armor-clad knight whose face I recognized — the one that Liliana had referred to as "Sir Lindos." From the way he stopped and stared at me, it was fair to say that he recognized me, as well.

"Hello," I greeted him. However, all I got in response was silence.

*Well, I already know that he doesn't think too highly of us Masters, so whatever,* I thought.

Not minding his attitude too much, I began heading to the office again.

"I hear that you defeated the Gouz-Maise Gang," said Sir Lindos before I could walk away.

"Yes," I replied. "I can't say that I did it alone, though."

In response, he silently closed his eyes. "Thank you."

Then he left after saying just that.

"Huh?"

*What am I supposed to make of that?* I thought.

"Maybe he just wanted to express his gratitude?" said Nemesis.

"But why him, of all people?"

"I'm not one to know."

Slightly confused at what had just happened, I went towards the office again.

Gideon's knight offices had a free-to-enter area dedicated to the citizenry's appeals and the like. Naturally, there were lots of secretive areas where civilians weren't allowed to enter, but the office I was looking for was in the open area. There were guides to help people get around, so I had no trouble getting to my destination, where I quickly began going through the relevant procedures.

During the process, I was told something about merit or whatever, but I didn't remember most of it. Almost the whole of my visit consisted of me looking at and signing some documents.

Most of them looked fine, and I didn't hesitate to put my signature on them, but I refused to sign the one that gave me "The Right to Acquire the Treasure Plundered by the Gouz-Maise Gang."

There was no denying that I had monetary troubles. Sure, with me getting the Grudge-Soaked Greaves, I no longer had to buy an Amulet of the Equestrian Tribe to get the Horse Riding skill, but the thinness of my wallet was a problem nonetheless. However, I was highly averse to the idea of possessing money the scumbags hoarded by preying upon children. That was why I asked the office to donate that money to charities that helped children.

With Hugo also having a right to those dirty riches, my only regret was the fact that I'd decided this without consulting him. Sure, his letter had said that he needed no reward, but it still didn't feel right to not get his input on this. If he didn't agree with this decision, I was fully intent on giving him the reward I'd get from the guild.

However, I felt that this would never happen. Hugo and I hadn't known each other for long, but I was certain that he'd have done the same thing as me if our positions had been reversed.

We were alike, and not just because we were both Maidens' Masters.

Once I was done signing the papers, I was told that I was probably going to be contacted sooner or later, so I gave them the address of the inn I was staying at here in Gideon. With that, the procedures were done, and we began making our way out of the offices.

Before we left, however, one of the workers there stood up.

Facing me, he bowed and said one thing: "Thank you for avenging my little boy."

I didn't know what to say in response to that.

I'd had such gratitude directed at me back when I saved Milianne and protected Alejandro's people against Gardranda, but the situation was completely different this time.

Specifically, there were two main differences.

The first was the fact that I had only taken part in this incident's end. I had only seen the conclusion of the tragedies surrounding the Gouz-Maise Gang. I hadn't seen anything but the results of what they'd done, and the final end Hugo and I had delivered upon them.

To the people living in this city, the tragedy had been a process that had constantly tortured them. Since they hadn't been able to do anything about it, that suffering had probably extended to the country's knights, as well. In fact, that might've been the reason why Sir Lindos had thanked me. However, I knew nothing about this painful process these people had been involved with.

The other difference was the fact that I wasn't being thanked for saving anyone. I had been thanked for avenging the son the worker had lost. The tragedy had already happened, and many children kidnapped by the Gouz-Maise Gang had lost their lives.

Though we'd successfully saved the boy that our quest had indicated, and a number of other children along with him, the number of undead I'd burned in the dungeon had been at least ten times greater.

Far too many children would never return home. Thinking of that made my heart ache.

I felt unreasonably guilty about all that was lost and the fact that I had been too late to do anything about it. I couldn't forgive myself for that, and felt that I had to make up for it somehow.

But…

"What can I even do about this?" I murmured.

"I certainly don't know," Nemesis responded, with a wry smile on her face. "I can see that you're seriously troubled about this, but there isn't much I can say to you as you are now. If I have to, however, I'll merely suggest that beating yourself up over a tragedy that already occurred and wondering whether it could have been prevented or not is best left to protagonists of time loop stories. It's better to be troubled by what has yet to come. After all, you don't have the power to go back in time. You are only human… and my only Master."

"'What has yet to come,' eh?" I asked.

"Things will probably be the same as they always were," she said. "You'll happen upon an incident, and if you feel like letting it happen will give you a bad aftertaste, you'll intervene and help those you feel should be helped. I am fully certain that this will keep happening to you."

After a moment of thought, I realized that I'd been doing primarily that ever since I'd entered *Dendro.* No, in fact, such events had been with me ever since I was a child.

"That makes me seem like a highly haphazard individual," I said.

I didn't have a plan most of the time, and I often let the flow lead me to all sorts of trouble, which I'd often dive into headfirst. It never came to me when the incidents actually happened, but when I looked back, it often seemed like I'd gone straight for them of my own accord.

My words made Nemesis smile.

"There's a number of things I like about you, and that's one of them," she said.

"'That,' as in...?" I raised an eyebrow.

"You don't run away when you feel like you have to save someone."

"You like me for being foolhardy?"

"No, I like you for not hiding your courage, no matter how fearsome your opponent is. That part of you makes you very cool, if you ask me."

I was silent.

*Well... You're gonna make me blush,* I thought.

"However, even if it's par for the course for you to face opponents far greater than you, it would be far better if *you* were the stronger one," Nemesis said. "So, if you feel like you *must* do something, you should start by raising your base power."

"Base power, eh?" I said.

It was obvious that I'd become stronger than before, but I was still among the weaklings of this world. Even with my trump cards Vengeance is Mine, Like a Flag Flying the Reversal, and my special rewards, I'd still needed lots of luck to emerge victorious against all the formidable foes I'd fought so far. After all, the PK, the Superior Killer, had ended me as if I was nothing.

"However, if you want to talk about becoming stronger in that regard, you have a far better person to turn to than myself," said Nemesis. "Look, you have a friend that's far more experienced than us. If we ever want to give the Superior Killer what's coming to him, we should ask her for advice."

Nemesis pointed at the café where our group agreed to meet. The "her" she was referring to was the woman sitting in the café's open terrace as she waved at us — Marie.

"So you want to become stronger. I see, I see," Marie said as she nodded in a pondering manner.

While I was telling the Journalist about what was troubling me, Nemesis got herself a pile of sandwiches for breakfast and dug into them.

*Well, there goes the money I made during this morning's hunt,* I thought.

"Indeed we do!" said Nemesis. "We need your advice if we ever want to give the Superior Killer what's coming to him."

"...Right," Marie said. She covered her face for some reason.

"Since you've played *Dendro* far longer than me, I imagine you're pretty knowledgeable about it," I said.

"Oh, believe me, I am," she said. "I'm unemployed, and I've been doing this for more than a year now. Been going hardcore, so to speak."

*...Is your life all right?* I thought.

"Anyway, you want to know what you must do to become strong enough to win against the Superior Killer, correct?" Marie asked. "Hmmm." She put her hand against her mouth and pondered something before speaking. "What do you think are your weak points?"

"Weak points?" I asked.

*I feel that I'm still weak in many ways, but if I have to converge on something specific, then...*

"My range is too short, and also everything goes to hell if I mess up Nemesis's skills," I said.

"Indeed, that's more or less right," nodded Marie. "Can you explain why?"

The problem with my range was obvious. Vengeance, my trump card, was limited by the reach of my greatsword, and though my Purgatorial Flames went a bit farther, the distance still wasn't particularly notable.

Given that, it would be hard for me to do anything about those who used guns or magic and attacked from hundreds of meters away. Sure, I could defend myself against such opponents by using Counter Absorption, but the skill's maximum stock was very limited. The tough enemies I'd defeated so far — Demi-Dragon Worm, Gardranda, and Gouz-Maise — had all been close-range fighters, just like myself.

Meanwhile, the Superior Killer, who stood at a distance and shot monstrous bullets at me, had killed me without getting as much as a scratch on him. If that wasn't a weak point, I had no idea what was.

There was also the lingering possibility of me failing to use my skills properly. That included scenarios where I used Counter Absorption against the weakest of attacks — basically wasting it — or where the enemy stopped the damage conduction from Vengeance is Mine by removing the part of the body I'd landed it on, which was something I'd thought about during the Gouz-Maise fight.

If my enemies were aware of these possibilities, they could easily nullify Nemesis's unique skills. It wouldn't usually be a problem on the first fight, but that would change the moment they figured out how my skills worked.

"Yes, you seem to know why those are big problems," said Marie. "However, you forgot another weak point."

"Which is?" I raised an eyebrow.

"The lack of speed or toughness."

*Yeah, I'm gonna need an elaboration,* I thought.

"All right, Ray," she said. "You want to get stronger, so I'll tell you what you must do from the game's perspective," she continued. "'Raise your AGI or END.' That's it."

...*What?*

"Now wait just a second," I said. "That can't be all there is to it, is it?"

"Of course," Marie nodded. "There are job and skill builds to consider, not to mention their synergy with your Embryo. However, when looking at the way the game works, you simply *must* raise either of those stats."

"'Must'?" That word seemed kinda off in this context.

"Now, Ray," she spoke up again. "Have you ever felt that the surroundings slowed down when you were fighting?"

"...Yeah, actually," I answered. That sensation was especially palpable when I was strengthened by Reversal. The world seemed to be in slow-motion, making it far easier for me to evade the enemy's attacks.

"That happens because of the greatness in difference between AGI in normal situations and battles," she explained.

"'Difference'?" I repeated.

"Yes. First of all, when you don't have a job, you're much like a standard person on Earth. You know how your stats were at about 10 or 20 back then?"

"Yeah, I remember them being around that range."

"So, as you already know, when you raise your job levels, that number can go to 100, 200, or even break the 1,000 mark if you pick a high-rank job with a focused stat growth. Those numbers become ten times greater when they're about HP, MP, or SP."

"I'm aware."

By the time I maxed out my Paladin job, my HP would likely be far above the 10,000 mark. But it wasn't like this job was focused *only* on HP, and from what I could tell by looking at Liliana's stats, standard Paladins didn't get that much of it, so my stat growth was probably greatly influenced by Nemesis. It was fair to assume that other Masters could easily get to those numbers with their own Embryo bonuses.

"All right, so," Marie continued. "The amount of time experienced by a person with 10 AGI is different to that experienced by a person with 100."

"Hm?" I raised an eyebrow.

"Right now, when we're not doing any fighting, we're experiencing time the same way someone with normal AGI does," she said. "However, when you enter a battle or merely make a conscious decision to switch it, that stat instantly changes. Why not try it?"

"Hm..."

With the bonus from the Grudge-Soaked Greaves, my AGI was about 100. Just like Marie suggested, I consciously changed my stats. In that state, I looked down the street and, sure enough, the people there were walking at a slightly slower pace.

It was the first time I'd experienced it outside of battle, and the results slightly impressed me.

"It's not like the time perceived scales directly with AGI," Marie added. "However, this function is a part of the game's system, and no Master, tian, or monster is an exception. I think it works like this because a constant slowing down would affect people's day-to-day lives."

"So AGI affects the amount of time experienced during battle, huh?" I said as I pondered.

By now, it made sense why Marie had suggested that it was a "must." Experiencing more time gave those with greater AGI a huge advantage in battle.

"It doesn't matter all that much to rear guard roles," she continued. "Vanguard roles, however, *must* have enough AGI to allow them to act faster than their opponents or enough END to survive their attacks. Those focusing on the latter also need to find ways to fight back."

With me being a Paladin, my build was leaning towards END. However, it still wasn't high enough for me to survive attacks from those more powerful than myself. Also, Paladin was my very first job, so I didn't have the stats that most people would normally have after maxing out low-rank jobs such as Knight.

Clearly, my situation wasn't the best.

"By the way, riding fast mounts and the like has no effect on the time you experience," Marie added.

I was fully aware of that. Riding Silver had increased my movement speed, but I didn't feel like there was much of a change in the time I'd perceived.

I said, "But man, I'm surprised I was able to win such tough fights without being aware of this difference, and..."

Suddenly, I realized that the tough enemies I'd fought against so far hadn't had that much AGI. The Demi-Dragon Worm, Gardranda, and Gouz-Maise had all excelled in endurance rather than agility.

"Remember that you can take six low-rank jobs and two high-rank jobs," Marie spoke up again. "Your overall power is greatly affected by how many of them you have."

"So, with me being on my first job and my level not being all that great, I still have a long way to go, huh?"

"Yes," she nodded. "Oh, just so you know, AGI-focused Superior Jobs can get their AGI to five digits."

"Five?!" *Superior Jobs seem to have a serious stat inflation problem,* I thought.

"People with such jobs can move at supersonic speeds and even block or catch bullets mid-flight," Marie continued. "Also, this is merely something that I happened to hear through gossip, but they say that the so-called Superior Killer has an AGI-focused Superior Job, so you should really raise your AGI or END if you want to stand a chance against him."

*Well, if that guy's an AGI build, getting my stats up is pretty much a necessity,* I thought. *Wait, speaking of stats...*

"What if I focus on STR?" I asked. Increasing offensive ability seemed like a very simple, reliable way of becoming powerful.

"STR build?" she asked. "You'll die."

*D-Die?!*

"Focusing on STR would have you sacrifice AGI and END, after all. No matter how hard you hit, you won't be able to dodge or bear many attacks, leading you to dying pretty quickly. The fate of all glass cannons."

"So that's how it works..."

"There are some well-balanced builds that merely happen to have high STR, and there are people such as the King of Beasts — the 'Physically Strongest' — whose *every* stat is so high, it's stupid. However, your average STR builds are just fodder."

*I see,* I thought. *Also, if I recall correctly, the King of Beasts is one of the imperium's Superiors. I didn't know he had "Physically Strongest" as a nickname.*

"That just about settles the talk about the basic power relations in fights," said Marie as she took a cup into her hand. "Now, let me tell you about player skills."

After gulping down some of her tea, Marie took a breath and began talking again.

"There's so much to player skills that I'm not sure where to begin. Well, for example, if you're good at martial arts in reality, you can use those techniques in *Dendro* just fine. Or if you can draw, you can do it here without getting the skill for it."

"Martial arts, huh?" I said.

Naturally, with him being a person who had won Un-kra, the one that came to mind was my brother. However, instead of applying those skills to his *Dendro* fighting, he used a minigun and even rode a tank.

*Can he even do any martial arts in that suit, though?* I wondered. *It sure didn't look that comfortable to move in. And hell, bears are usually the targets of martial artists, not the other way around.*

"Well, the subject of real skills involves too many person-to-person differences, so let's leave it aside for now," said Marie. "In battle — especially against other people — there are three main things one must always consider."

"Which are?" I asked.

"One: you must know the conditions in which your opponent is strongest; two: you must know the conditions in which you are weakest; and three: you have to be able to predict your opponent's ultimate attack."

"Hm..." I could understand the first one. Basically, I had to avoid being where the enemy wanted me to be. The thing that came to mind was my fight against the Demi-Dragon Worm. Though I'd emerged victorious, there had been the lingering possibility of me getting pulled underground, like my brother was. Even with Nemesis with me, the chances of me winning while fighting in absolute darkness — their natural habitat, at that — would have been extremely slim.

The second one made sense, too. It reminded me of the time I'd gotten killed by the Superior Killer. While being outside my attack range, he'd attacked me with countless bullets against which I'd been able to do absolutely nothing. With my only defensive option having limited uses and my offense being exclusively melee, it was only natural that I'd died back then.

By now, I could move far better than before and my range was slightly greater. However, it would be hard to say that I'd stand a chance against a long-range fighter such as him.

All that said, I didn't know what she meant with the third point.

"'Ultimate attack'?" I raised an eyebrow.

"Just about every strong battle-oriented creature has one," said Marie. "Masters, tians, bosses such as UBMs... They all have some trump card which they have absolute confidence in. Enough to think that the battle would be over the moment they use it."

The term "trump card" reminded me of my and Nemesis's Vengeance is Mine skill.

"So, it's basically a strong skill?" I asked.

"It could be a skill, a weapon, or maybe even a tactic. The stronger the creature, the more of these they have. Embryos even have skills that are actually called 'ultimate skills.'"

"'Ultimate skills'?" I repeated.

"Oh?" Nemesis' eyes lit up, and she momentarily stopped eating sandwiches to join our conversation. Apparently, the subject of ultimate skills had caught her curiosity.

"Ultimate skills are the greatest, strongest skills of an Embryo, and they're always named after the Embryo itself," continued Marie. "All of them — without exception — have a powerful effect that strongly expresses the Embryo's dominant characteristic."

*Well, that sure makes them sound intriguing,* I thought.

"Actually, you saw one in one of the videos I showed you — the one where Figaro fought against the leader of Mad Castle," she added. "It was the last skill that the leader used."

*Yeah, I remember that,* I thought. It had been a rush of attacks that the leader had done after momentarily binding Figaro in place. In the end, Figaro had evaded it, but the skill had left a giant crater where he'd stood.

"Hmm... So my ultimate skill would be called 'Nemesis,' correct?" asked Nemesis.

"Yes, that's exactly how it would be," nodded Marie.

"Nemesis" worked pretty nice as a skill name.

"But I feel like some Embryo names wouldn't really work as skill names," I said. "For example, 'Momotaro.'"

"Oh yes, such cases definitely aren't unheard of," said Marie. "For example, one of Granvaloa's Superiors, 'The Great Seven Embryos of Granvaloa,' has an Embryo called 'Abura-Sumashi.'"

"A-Abura-Sumashi..." I repeated the name and, sure enough, I didn't feel a hint of power behind it. If I recalled correctly, it was just the name of a yokai with a big head.

"Oh, the name probably makes you think it's weak, but just so you know, Abura-Sumashi is actually among the top ten strongest Embryos I know," said Marie.

"Are you serious?" I asked.

"Very," she nodded. "After all, it turns any liquids it touches into explosive material. Seawater, bodily fluids — you name it and it can turn it into an explosive that makes nitroglycerin pale in comparison. There was a time when the Master used it to turn all the seawater in a radius of 500 meters into explosives and blew a horde of monsters to bits."

*That's just freaky,* I thought.

"Also, I've heard that back when he had a dispute with a certain pirate clan, he fought one of its members, changed the pirate's bodily fluids into explosives, let the pirate run away, and then *used* him to blow the clan's hideout to bits."

*Savage.*

"Due to that, Abura-Sumashi's Master got the nickname 'Human Bomb'..."

*Sounds like trauma material,* I thought. *I feel like I won't be comfortable looking at abura-sumashi illustrations ever again.*

"Well, just keep in mind that a name has no relation to strength," concluded Marie.

*Yeah, you don't need to tell me twice.*

"Anyhow, I'm really looking forward to the time I get my own ultimate skill," said Nemesis.

"As you should," said Marie. "However, at the earliest, you would get it after becoming high-rank, so it might take a while."

"I imagine it will," I nodded. "Wait. Marie, you said you've been playing *Dendro* for more than a year, right? That's three years in this world, isn't it?"

"Yes."

"If you've been at it for that long, you should have your ultimate skill already, right?"

"Hm? Now that you mention it, I've yet to see Marie's Embryo," said Nemesis.

Marie's reply to that was silence. Though she was smiling in the same way she always did, for one reason or another, a great amount of sweat was running down her face.

*I guess wearing a suit in this spring-like weather made her heat up a bit,* I thought.

"Uhh… I, umm… my Embryo is… it's called uh… Arc-en-Ciel and, uh…"

"French for 'Rainbow,' huh?" I said. "That's pretty cool."

*So Embryo names aren't limited to myths and fairy tales, huh?* I thought. *Of course, rainbows are common in legends, so maybe it's not actually an exception.*

"As for what kind of Embryo it is, well… uh…" muttered Marie, for some reason showing hesitation about saying it.

"Hello! Sorry we took so long!" Rook cried.

"I'm sooo hungry! Let's have some food, Rook!" Babi added. At that moment, the other people we were waiting for arrived at the café.

"Now, wheeere aaare they?" asked Babi while looking around.

"Oh!" exclaimed Marie. "If it isn't Rookie and Babi! Good morning! Are you hungry?! You are?! Let me get you something, then! The sandwiches here are really good! I'll go and order some right now!"

After saying all that in one breath, Marie stood up and ran to the café's counter.

"Ah ha ha! Looks like Marie is in high spirits today," said Rook.

"She was nowhere near like that until just a second ago..." I commented.

*Well, it's not like being in a good mood is a bad thing,* I thought.

Marie, still in that weird state, came back with even more sandwiches than Nemesis had eaten, and we all had to do our part to make sure the food didn't go to waste. However, the exchange of information continued even as we ate, and I ended up telling them about what had happened yesterday.

"Eh? Ray, you can use the Purifying Silverlight?" Marie cried.

"Well... yeah?"

Marie looked absolutely puzzled. Rook heard me, as well, but with him not being the type to eat all that much, the sandwiches he'd forced himself to consume had made him drop his head on the table and thus not take part in the conversation. Nemesis and Babi were merely too focused on eating.

Anyway, the current subject was the Purifying Silverlight. It was the skill I'd learned when I'd cremated the undead children in that underground hallway.

Purifying Silverlight was an anti-undead skill, and a ridiculously good one, at that. It had been simply invaluable in the grueling battles I'd won yesterday. After all, it had not only made my attacks do holy damage, which worked even on spirits, it had also multiplied all damage done to undead by 10.

Again — 10 times greater damage on undead.

Though it hadn't worked with Vengeance due to its damage being fixed, it was still an insanely good buff for my standard attacks. And that wasn't the end of it, either. If an undead was hit by Purifying Silverlight, the wound could never be healed.

Though Gouz-Maise — the affront to sanity that it was — had been able to heal by removing the entire injured part, all the other undead had vanished before they could even exhibit the toughness unique to their kind.

Yesterday's battles wouldn't have gone nearly as well if I hadn't had Purifying Silverlight at my disposal. As useful as Vengeance and Purgatorial Flames were, it was doubtful if they would have been enough for me to even live long enough to face Gouz-Maise.

Marie silently stared at me. That reaction weirded me out. She looked seriously surprised about something.

"*How* did you become able to use Silverlight?" she asked.

"Well, I got a message saying 'Eliminate 100 appropriate monsters...'" I answered.

"Can you show me your counter?" she asked.

"My counter?"

...*Of what?* I thought.

"Open your menu window, go to the battle history screen, and you'll find the creature type kill counters among the extras."

"Oh, this, right?" I opened it and, sure enough, there were creature types such as undead, beast, avian, dragon, devil, elemental, demon, human, etc. with appropriate numbers beside them. My greatest one was undead: 158. It was followed by beasts and demons.

"So, are these the total numbers of monsters I've defeated?" I asked.

"Yes," Marie nodded. "Supposedly, the condition is 'defeat a certain amount'... but this number seems way too small."

As she muttered things like that, I shifted my gaze back to my kill counters. "There's one for humans, too, huh?"

On the window, my human kill count was 0. Apparently, though originally being human, the Lich Maise had counted as undead.

"What kind of creatures does the human counter cover, anyway?" I asked.

"A human is any creature that can have a job," answered Marie. "So if you see someone with a job, it's a human. Or 'humanoid,' as they're technically called."

"Then why didn't the Lich I killed count as human?"

"Oh, that's because the job comes with the effect of turning the human that takes it into undead, so he stopped being human the very moment he became a Lich. It's one of the very few exceptions."

That made me assume that there were scenarios where unfortunate humans that merely happened to look like monsters got attacked for that very reason, and I didn't know how to feel about that.

"Oh, but it's not like a Lich is *completely* like your usual, monster undead," added Marie. "You know how monsters have their names hanging above their heads? Well, with them originally being human, that doesn't apply to Liches."

*Oh yeah, I totally forgot about that,* I thought. *Guess those scenarios are pretty rare, then.*

"But man, it actually keeps track of the number of humans you kill," I said.

"Just so you're aware, it includes the kills made within the barriers of duel cities such as this one," Marie explained. "So a high human kill count doesn't always suggest that the person is a murderer. After all, once the duel is over, things go back to being the same way they were before."

"Oh, I see," I nodded.

"So many of those who frequent this city have probably killed hundreds of people," she added.

*Well, that sure is a grim way to put it,* I thought.

"I have a question." Rook raised his head and joined our conversation. "How do kill counters for tamed monsters work?"

"When they're used under the minion capacity, their kills are counted as the owner's kills," answered Marie. "When they're used as party members, however, their kills are counted as their own. You can see it for yourself by looking at their stat windows. Oh, also, kills done by autonomous Embryos such as Guardians are automatically counted as the Master's kills."

"Then what happens when a Charmed creature kills something?" Rook asked again.

"Umm... Those count as the Charmed creature's kills. The kill count of the one who did the Charming stays the same. Also, in scenarios where someone Poisons the opponent, escapes the battle, and merely waits for the Poisoned enemy to die, it still counts as the poisoner's kill." Apparently, it was dependent on who landed the finishing blow. Tamed monsters within the minion capacity were considered to be like the limbs of the owner, so their kills went to him. While in a party, however, their kills went to their own kill counters.

With status effects such as Poison, the kill went to the one who was directly responsible for the poisoning. Indirect kills, such as the ones done by Charmed opponents, went to those who had done the killing, rather than the Charmer.

"So, if I want to, like Ray, fulfill a condition that has me defeat a certain number of something, I have to avoid using Charm or party slots and instead fight with my own strength or with those that fit in my capacity, right?"

*I see why he was curious,* I thought. I recalled that Guardians used 0 minion capacity, so he would have been able to use Babi to increase his kill counts even if she hadn't been his Embryo.

"This is so strange," muttered Marie after a while of serious pondering.

"What's strange?" I asked.

"This is the first time I've seen a Master with Purifying Silverlight."

"...What?"

"The skill's existence itself is quite well-known due to tians, especially the famous users such as the previous knight commander or the current vice-commander. However, there hasn't been a single case of a Master getting it. Which is really strange. It's right next to Grand Cross as one of Paladin's greatest skills, and there have been tons of people who've tried to get it, due to its great effects."

"Huh? But you only have to kill 100 undead," I said. *That's what the message said, anyway,* I thought. It definitely wasn't a hard condition for your average Paladin to achieve.

"That's true," nodded Marie. "Tians were asked about it and said that it was unlocked by the undead kill count. However, there are Paladins who have killed over 5,000 undead, yet still don't have it.

They even finished leveling all their low-rank jobs before they got the skill and… huh?"

Realizing something, Marie put her hand on her chin and slightly tilted her head.

"Ray, what's your Paladin level?" she asked.

"41," I answered. I'd leveled up during the testing I'd done in the morning.

"And your total level?"

"41, as well." I didn't have any other jobs.

"That's probably the answer. This is only an assumption, but I think the condition only counts undead of the same level range as yourself. Total level range, to be precise."

"Level range, huh?" I murmured.

*Now that I think about it, there was also a message saying something about the requirement being "Undead of the appropriate total level,"* I thought.

"It likely goes by 50, based on low-rank and high-rank," Marie continued. "Meaning that, if your total level 50 or less, the condition's target is low-rank monsters — those under and including level 50. And if you're in the 51-100 total level range, that changes to high-rank monsters — those who are also in the 51-100 range."

"I see," I nodded, fully understanding why I'd been able to learn the skill. After all, my total level was below 50. However, that condition didn't seem like it was unachievable by other people.

*I mean, they simply have to max out Knight, switch to Paladin, and fight against undead over level 51 and, uh…*

"…Huh?" Something didn't seem right about that thought of mine. The person's total level would be 51, but it was questionable whether they could put up a fight against high-rank undead while their Paladin level was so low. The High-End Skeleton Warriors that had popped out of the hallway while I was fighting the Lich had probably been among such high-rank undead, but I felt that I would've had no chance against them if I hadn't had Silverlight and Silver. I'd completely crushed them exactly because I *did*.

"This is pretty awful," said Marie. "To get Purifying Silverlight, you basically have to throw away everything else."

"It's *that* bad?" I asked.

"Normally, high-rank jobs have you max out one, sometimes even two or three low-rank jobs. Paladin is a prime example of a difficult-to-acquire high-rank job."

"You might be right," I nodded. Not only did it require you to have the gold for it, you also needed to do a certain amount of damage to a Demi-Dragon class boss monster. I'd been told that a Demi-Dragon's power was equivalent to a full party of people with low-rank jobs.

There was also the recommendation you had to get from a member of a knight order. Anyone trying to clear these job conditions in a normal manner would probably max out more than one low-rank job in the process.

"And by the time the person is a Paladin, fulfilling the conditions for Purifying Silverlight would be difficult... no... impossible, actually," said Marie.

"Is there something about monsters with a level above 100?" I asked.

"100 is actually the maximum level for all normal monsters — including bosses," she said. "The only ones that go beyond that are SUBMs, Superior Unique Boss Monsters, such as the Tri-Zenith Dragon, Gloria... but that's irrelevant to the subject at hand. The fact is that the level problem makes acquiring the skill completely impossible."

"Wait, wouldn't it be impossible to the tians, too, then?" I asked.

"The tians that become Paladins are most often the sons and daughters of influential people. They have no money problems to speak of, are well-trusted, and get tons of support when going out to defeat the boss."

"I see," I said.

A high-level person would act as a tank and keep the boss busy while the one wanting to get the Paladin job — perhaps assisted by support magic — would slowly chip away at its HP until it died. Clearly, it wasn't impossible. If luck was on their side, they could probably fulfill the Paladin job conditions before maxing out Knight.

"But wait," I said. "Can't Masters get such help, too?"

"It's very hard for us to gain the trust of the knight order's top people," answered Marie. "They're really picky about who they let in. Most who get accepted have really long lists of favorable deeds under their belts."

*Deeds during which they reached a total level that was too high to let them acquire the skill, eh?* I thought. *Man, I don't even know what to make of all the luck that was involved in me getting Paladin and the Purifying Silverlight.*

With its conditions being so strict, I could totally understand why it was so powerful.

"Playing normally makes it impossible to acquire the skill, but there's a way that would allow you to get it pretty easily," said Marie.

"Which is...?" I asked.

"Resetting every job besides Paladin."

My brother had told me about job resetting back when I was choosing my first job. Just as it said in the name, it was a function that allowed people to reset the jobs they didn't like or need.

Marie was right — it was a very easy way to get the skill. After becoming a Paladin, a person could reset all the other jobs to cause their total level to drop. Then they could spend some time killing low-rank undead in the Tomb Labyrinth to acquire the Purifying Silverlight. In fact, that might even be the reason why Paladins were allowed to enter there without the need for a Permit. However...

"Resetting the jobs means losing all their stats and skills, right?" I asked.

"Oh, yes," nodded Marie. "It would even include Knight — a job from the same grouping."

*Daaamn,* I thought, summarizing my reaction quite perfectly.

"I'll put this info on the wiki, but I can only wonder if anyone will be willing to go through with it," she said. "Considering how long they will have spent leveling those jobs, the risk involved is just too great."

Though Silverlight was unmatched in usefulness when fighting undead, it was pretty meaningless in just about every other scenario. Also, though we knew that this info was true, the people on the wiki wouldn't, and a scenario in which they dropped all their other jobs for nothing would probably leave them crying. When that risk was considered, it was obvious that there wouldn't be all that many people who would go through with it.

On a related note, I later asked Liliana about how she'd gotten Silverlight, to which she replied, "I reset all my jobs besides Paladin, acquired Purifying Silverlight, and then raised my other jobs — such as Knight — from square one."

When I considered the fact that tians weren't exactly in a position to reset their jobs so willy-nilly, I was quite impressed by her resolution.

"I must say, though," Marie spoke up again. "The path you're walking is quite something, Ray. People who go through the things you do are few and far between. Yesterday was quite a day for you, wasn't it?"

"Seriously. I thought I was gonna die," I said. "The whole thing was worse on my nerves than the time I got the death penalty in Noz Forest."

Though, unlike that time, I'd actually come out alive.

*Speaking of which, I wonder what the Superior Killer was doing after escaping the King of Destruction?* I thought.

"'Thought I was gonna die,' you say?" Marie repeated my words. "Well, you *are* a Maiden's Master, after all."

"From the way you're saying that, I assume you know about our common characteristic," I said. "Maidens' Masters..."

"'Maidens' Masters don't think of this place as a game,' correct?"

*Yeah, that,* I thought.

"Weird, isn't it?" I said. "In my head, I'm fully aware that this is a game, but..."

*...my heart just doesn't agree.*

"I wouldn't call it 'weird,'" said Marie. "Many long-time players share that sentiment, after all."

"Really?"

I would never have expected there to be enough for someone to use the word "many."

"After all, though this place has countless things that don't exist in reality, the five senses work in the exact same way," Marie continued. "Not to mention all the tians living here."

That was true. Aside from pain, the bodily sensations experienced here were the same as in reality. In fact, it was possible to turn pain on by going into the options window, so even that could become real.

There were also interactions with tians, something that no player could avoid. It was only natural for there to be people who had been in the world and watched its inhabitants for so long that they'd stopped thinking that it was just a game.

"At the same time, there are people who treat this place as a game all the way to the end," said Marie.

"Well, of course there are," I nodded.

*It's sold as a game, after all,* I thought.

"Stances on tians, their civilizations, and even *Infinite Dendrogram* itself differ based on who you ask, but there are quite a lot of people who take its status as another reality, or as merely a game, for granted."

"I see," I said.

"The ones who see it as another reality are 'worlders,' while those who see it as just a game are 'ludos.' To the former, the latter are inhumane, while to the latter, the former are just cringy."

*So that's how it is,* I thought. As I was now, I could somewhat relate to both sides.

"What other kinds of people are there?" I asked.

"Well, there are tons of those who just aren't certain about which side they're on," answered Marie. "Oh, and let's not forget those who try *Infinite Dendrogram* and then quit it for one reason or another."

"Like?" I asked.

"Well, many think that it's just not worth the trouble. *Dendro* encourages players to interact with people, move their avatar as if it were their own body, and make some serious decisions, all of which can be pretty taxing. It makes them feel like, 'This isn't what a game is supposed to be.'"

That seemed like a perfectly reasonable stance. Regardless of whether it was a world or a game, taking part in *Infinite Dendrogram* was a radically different experience from playing with a controller while looking at a screen.

"There are also those who quit after being emotionally scarred by some painful event," said Marie.

I was silent.

"Those two are the primary reasons why people who've been in *Dendro* for longer decide to quit, but some people stop right after starting. Specifically, right after their first battle. After all, fighting other living beings can be really scary and stressful. There are many of those early quitters among those who didn't chose anime or CG as their visual setting."

"Well, I can see their point," I said. My first fight against the Demi-Dragon Worm had been a terrifying experience, and I already knew what it was like to die in this world. There was nothing strange about there being people who distanced themselves from *Infinite Dendrogram* after getting to know the fear of being eaten or murdered.

Some of those who'd stayed regardless might quit after experiencing something painful. And those who continued their existence here after going through such filters would all look at this world in their own way.

"I wonder if the Superior Killer is a worlder or a ludo," I said. With him being the player killer responsible for my only death so far, I couldn't help but be curious about his stance on this world.

"Who knows?" Marie shrugged. "If you don't know, it's best to think that he's somewhere in between."

"That's true."

I knew far too little about him. He'd killed all the newbies, including me, in Noz Forest. Then he'd gone on to help me out in the Gardranda fight when things had gotten dire.

I didn't know what motivated him to act the way he did. In fact, due to the mist that had been covering him back then, I didn't even know what he looked like. His personality, height, and even the age of his avatar were all a mystery to me.

I was silent.

"Hm?" Suddenly, I realized that Rook was staring at Marie for some reason. His gaze was reminiscent of the one my brother would adopt when solving a crossword puzzle.

*Thinking about it, I wonder why the crossword was in Arabic,* I thought.

"Oh, I just remembered," Marie spoke up again. "I have something to give you two."

Marie reached into her inventory, took out two tickets, and handed them over to me and Rook. On them, there were flashy letters saying "Clash of the Superiors," along with some numbers and a precise date. The day was today, and the time was tonight.

"And these are...?" I asked.

"Well, you know how I asked you to leave the use of the remaining money from the Gardranda reward to me, right?" said

Marie. "This is the result — box seat tickets to today's event in the central arena."

"Event?" I asked. "Is something happening?"

"...Oh? You're unaware?"

"Yeah." Way too many things had happened since I'd arrived at Gideon. Although I would've been lying if I'd said that I hadn't seen any leaflets with the same title as on the tickets here and there.

"I see," Marie nodded. "Just so you know, this is not something you'd regret seeing. After all — it's a match between Superiors."

"Superiors?" I asked.

"Yes. Though battles between Superiors aren't a new thing, this is actually the first public match ever."

"Who's fighting?" I asked.

"Naturally, one of them is the king of the duel city — Super Gladiator Figaro — while his opponent is the one with the second place in Huang He's duel rankings, Shi Jie Xian. Or as he's better known: Xunyu, the Master Jiangshi."

*A match involving Figaro, eh? Now I'm intrigued,* I thought. I'd yet to go to him and say hello due to all that had happened after I'd arrived at Gideon. I felt kinda obliged to thank him for taking care of the player killers that were blocking the way here.

"This is where most of the pooled reward money went to. Are you two okay with this?" asked Marie.

"Of course," I said. "I'm sure it will be worth it."

A clash between Superiors — the greatest of players — was surely something I wouldn't regret seeing.

I was sure that just seeing it would have little effect on my overall strength. And it would help me gauge just how powerful we — Masters — could become.

"I am okay with this, as well," Rook approved of Marie's decision. "I've wanted to learn more about battles against people."

"Good to know," said Marie. "Make sure to be there when the time comes."

"All right," he said.

And so, we split up. We would be doing our own stuff until the event started, at which point we would meet up again.

I still had to go to the adventurers' guild and report to them that the Gouz-Maise Gang had been eliminated.

Apparently, Rook had something he wanted to talk about with Marie. I tried asking what it was, but all I got was, "It's a secret." He then whispered something into Marie's ear, making her face turn stiff as she muttered something along the lines of "How did you know?" Naturally, I was curious, but a secret was a secret, and I didn't want to pry.

By the way, about 90% of the vast number of sandwiches bought by Marie had ended up in Nemesis's stomach. The blatant increase in the amount she could eat in a single sitting made a chill go down my spine.

"What do we do with this?" I wondered.

"What, indeed," Nemesis agreed.

Nemesis and I were sitting at a table in the adventurers' guild's bar. Our faces were close as we discussed something, making it obvious that we were troubled. With all that had happened since yesterday, I was becoming quite familiar with trouble. However, one would think that a person would get a break every now and then.

"This is just *way* too much..."

"But we can't just refuse it, can we...?"

The thing troubling us this time was the window I had opened.

It was my item screen, but the important thing about it wasn't an item. It was the field displaying the money in my possession. The amount displayed there was a whopping 80,000,000 lir.

Needless to say, it was a real fortune. In fact, it was equivalent to 800,000,000 yen. As to why I'd come to receive such a great amount of money...

It had happened when I'd arrived at the adventurers' guild to report the elimination of the Gouz-Maise Gang.

Unlike how it had gone in the knight offices, showing the special reward wasn't enough. I'd also had to answer a few questions and explain how it all went, making the whole process seem strangely long and thorough. Though I'd found it to be more annoying than the basic marking and signing I'd had to do with the knights, I didn't hesitate to give them the answers they'd wanted. Sure, I'd hid the fact that my comrade in this event, Hugo, had been a Master belonging to Dryfe, the enemy of Altar, but I'd said nothing but the truth.

As a result, I was recognized as the one who'd eliminated the Gouz-Maise Gang and received the reward. Before I'd gotten the money, I'd thought something along the lines of, *I should find Hugo and split it. With me getting the special reward, his portion should be bigger and...*

However, such thoughts were completely overshadowed by the 80,000,000 lir that'd been placed in front of me.

*Excuse me? 80,000,000 lir? Not 800,000 or 8,000,000? Eighty times more than we got for Gardranda?*

30,000,000

As confusion overwhelmed my brain, the person at reception began explaining why the reward was so great.

Originally, the reward the adventurers' guild had set for the Gouz-Maise Gang's two leaders had been 1,000,000 each, while its normal members had gone for 10,000 each, making the total about 3,000,000 lir.

However, each and every person that had gone to eliminate the gang had gotten killed. Due to that, it had become known as a highly fearsome group that couldn't be underestimated.

There was also the fact that each and every failure to defeat them resulted in the death of the kidnapped children, so the risks had been too great for any party to attempt it again.

Naturally, there had been many people who were unsatisfied with that state of the situation. That included the families of the kidnapped children and even Count Gideon himself — the ruler of the city.

With Gideon being so prosperous, many of the kidnapped children's families were wealthy. A number of them had paid the ransom, but only received their children's corpses. Driven by grief and anger, many such people had wished for revenge and added money to the adventurers' guild's reward.

Due to the Gouz-Maise Gang's many crimes in his domain, Count Gideon himself had grown to hate the group with a passion and had wished to eliminate them by using the local army. However, with them having their hideout at the eastern border, he wouldn't have been able to go through with it because using the army might have been considered an act of war against Caldina.

Thoroughly upset with the state of the situation and hoping for a strong party to defeat the scoundrels, Count Gideon had used his own riches to increase the reward. Due to such reasons, the money had reached the great amount of 80,000,000 lir.

"It's surprising that nobody did anything until now," I said.

A fortune such as this would've attracted many people to this quest. Especially Masters, since there were few risks for us in getting involved in such perilous business.

"Any failures would reduce the chances of the children returning home, so the guild decided not to show any wanted posters for the gang and instead chose to hand-pick the people that looked like they could certainly do it," said the receptionist. "Specifically, the Superiors."

*Ah, so they kept it a secret to not make the situation worse,* I thought.

I wasn't completely sure if that decision had been a good one.

"The guild expected the great event happening in the central arena today to attract lots of powerful people from all across the land, so we were aiming to use it as a chance to find our person..."

*...and have them do the quest, huh?* I thought. From what I'd heard the Lich say, the gang had seen that coming and planned to leave yesterday.

"That is why we were quite confused to find out that the Gouz-Maise Gang was eliminated before we found someone to do it..." she added.

They'd been watching, waiting for an opportunity, and then Hugo and I had come out of nowhere, saying we'd already taken care of the problem. I could see why it was hard for them to believe.

In the end, the fact that I wasn't lying was proved by my Grudge-Soaked Greaves, Gouz-Maise. Anyway, that was how I'd ended up with a reward that was way too big for my pockets.

"I have to meet up with Hugo," I said.

"Indeed," nodded Nemesis.

Though he'd said in his letter that the money was mine for the taking, I couldn't let myself accept these riches without consulting him. I also wanted to talk to him about the decisions I'd made back in the knight office. However, I had no means of contacting him and had neglected to put him on my friends list, so I didn't even know if he was online.

"Whatever the case, I'll decide where the money goes after I meet him," I decided.

*Sure, I have monetary issues, but still,* I thought.

"They said that the reward for the horse undead was 1,000,000 lir," said Nemesis. "Why not let yourself use that much, at least?"

"...You have a point."

That was completely reasonable. 1,000,000 lir was the same amount we'd gotten for defeating Gardranda, and it was more than enough for shopping done by a newbie such as myself.

However, I wasn't quite sure about what to buy. Due to level restrictions, it was far too early for me to get new equipment.

*My only real shopping options are accessories and... weaponry, I guess,* I thought.

"Are you thinking of cheating on me?" demanded Nemesis.

"No, damn it," I answered. "Remember what Hugo said? About how Maidens can get skills after fighting in their human form?"

"That he did say, yes."

"So yeah, I'm thinking of getting a weapon for you and for me when you're in your human form."

"Well, that certainly sounds like something we need," Nemesis nodded, fully understanding my point. "All right, if you're to wield a weapon that isn't me, I'll have to make sure that it's fully worthy!"

*...Well, someone's excited,* I thought. *Oh right, if we're gonna go to Alejandro's shop, I should also—*

"Surely you're not about to think that you should pull the gacha again, are you, Ray?" demanded Nemesis.

"Ha ha ha, whatever do you mean, Nemesis? Do I look like someone who doesn't learn from his mistakes?"

"Oh, I don't know. Let me take a better look at you by *looking you in the eye when we talk.*"

"...I'm sorry."

*But come on, I know that it's possible that I'll draw another Permit or an item that's worth less than I put in, but wouldn't it be great to land something as great as Silver or Rook's Touch of the Silencer? I mean—*

"Huh?"

As I was making my way towards the shop, I saw a familiar silhouette standing in the plaza before the central arena. At first, I thought that my eyes were deceiving me, but once I got close, I became fully aware that they weren't.

Black fur covering the whole body, a stature greater than that of the average person, a fat waist and limbs that were relatively short. It was a bear suit, surrounded by a large group of children.

"Ohh! This popularity is so great it's almost unbearable! I feel like a star! Ursaa!"

The one wearing it, obviously, was my brother.

I said nothing.

Again, the one in the bear suit was my very own brother.

Likely due to being in the plaza, he had probably gotten mistaken for some performance artist or a mascot, causing him to be surrounded and jostled by many children.

"I don't even have anywhere to stand! Ah! Climbing on me is fine and all, just make sure not to fall!"

"...Bro, what the hell are you doing?" I asked as he became overwhelmed by children and was about to evolve into a walking adventure playground.

"Hm? Who is it fur whom I am a brother dearest...? Oh! It's Ray!" He greeted me by raising his arms, but his appearance made me feel like I was being menaced by a wild beast.

"Brother dearest" was quite an exaggeration. I had no recollection of ever having that much respect for him, and that included the days before his Un-kra fight.

"I feel like I haven't seen you for a while, Brother Bear," said Nemesis.

"A beary good afternoon to you, too, Nemesis," my brother greeted her as he slowly waved his arm. The reason for the slowness were the children hanging on to it.

"But man, you're as popular as always," I said. "You were in a similar state when I met you back in the capital."

"Costumes like these are beary rare, after all," he said.

"They are?"

"No one wants to wear them because they're terrible as equipment."

"Really?"

"Wearing these things takes up all the slots except the ones fur weapons and accessories," he explained.

*Okay, the lack of popularity instantly makes sense,* I thought.

"Suits that make up for that huge minus are unbearably rare," he continued. "I don't even know five Masters who wear them on a regular basis."

"...So you're saying that you know four?" I said. With my brother Shu included, that number became five.

*Sounds like a wacky hero group,* I thought. *...Oh yeah, he was actually a part of one once.*

"What do you mean?" Nemesis asked telepathically.

*It's no big deal. He just had a role as a member of a hero group in a certain tokusatsu show.*

"I can't say that I am knowledgeable about that world, but based on the common sense I received from you, isn't that quite impressive? Wait, wasn't he a martial artist?" she asked.

*Oh yes, he was during his middle school and high school days. In his elementary school days, however, he was a child actor and a singer. That was when he got the role as an extra — the sixth — in a certain hero group. But that ended before I could even think properly, so I don't know the details.*

"Just *what* is he?" she demanded.

My big brother. Currently unemployed.

"So, bro, did you come to Gideon to observe the Clash of the Superiors?" I asked.

"Bearily, yes. I came to see my buddy Figgy fight."

*Figgy? As in, Figaro?* I thought. *I didn't know they were friends.*

"Well, I'm planning on watching it, too, so maybe we'll meet there?" I said.

"Eh? You bear a ticket?" he asked.

"Yeah. A friend of mine got me one," I answered as I reached into my inventory and showed it to him.

"Oh, it's for a box seat, too. I'm impressed you… Hm?" After glancing at it, he focused his eyes — the eye parts on the suit, anyway — on a certain part of my ticket.

"What?" I asked.

"Look here," he said as he took out his own ticket.

I looked at it and noticed that it said "L-001."

The L referred to the box itself, while the 001 was the number of the seat inside the box.

It was relevant because my own ticket was L-004.

"We're in the same box?" I asked.

Different seats, obviously, but we were still next to each other.

"A pawsitively amazing coincidence," my brother declared. "We'll be watching it together!"

"I didn't even think this could happen."

"Your friend probably bought it from the same scalper as me," he said.

That seemed entirely plausible.

"But oh, the fact that you've already made some friends here in *Dendro* makes me oh-so-beary happy," he said as he took out a handkerchief and pretended to cry while putting it against his suit's eye parts.

*…I'm quite sure that no tears are coming out of there,* I thought.

"Also, by looking at your gear, I see that you've already been on some big adventures," he added while looking at my bracers and boots — the Miasmaflame Bracers and the Grudge-Soaked Greaves.

"Well, things happened, all right," I said. "I kinda want to talk about it, but this doesn't seem like the situation for long chats."

Shu had been surrounded and jostled by children for the entirety of our conversation so far.

"Good point," he said. "All right, children! This bear has to go now! Here's something to help you bear this farewell!"

He reached into his inventory, took out a huge amount of candy, and began tossing it around and at the surrounding children. Naturally, the kids were overjoyed, expressed their thanks, and went away from him, one by one.

"You did this back in the capital, too," I commented.

"Heh, it's a bare necessity when wearing this suit."

I was about to suggest that he take it off, but then I remembered that he couldn't. The face under it was his real face, after all.

"Why aren't you wearing some sort of mask or a disguise instead?" I asked.

"I don't want to look like a weirdo."

*...Do you really think that wearing a bear suit isn't weird?* I thought.

"Then why not do what you're good at and use the appearance of a hero, instead?" I asked.

"There's a clan focused entirely on that, so things could get beary annoying."

"...There's actually a hero group clan?"

"And a masked hero clan, too."

"Well, *Dendro* sure doesn't seem to lack freedom," I muttered.

Soon enough, Shu finished distributing the candy, and there were no longer any children around. Indeed, the *children* had left, but...

"Isn't there something on your head?" I asked.

"Well, I'll be. There actually is," he said.

Something was holding on to the top of his head. It definitely wasn't a human child. Though caricaturistically distorted, it looked somewhat like a hedgehog or porcupine.

The way it clung to Shu made it look like some sort of mascot, but I was fully aware that my brother didn't come with any such extras. It had appeared seemingly out of nowhere.

*There's no name above its head, so it's clearly not a monster. Is it an Embryo, then?* I thought.

"Oh, sorry about that," I heard someone say.

I turned to the direction of the voice and saw a woman. She looked like she was in her early twenties. Her clothing, despite fitting the fantasy setting, gave her the appearance of a secretary. The crest on the back of her left hand was proof that she was a Master.

"Apologies. My Behemot seems to have troubled you," she said.

"Behem…? Oh, this thing," my brother said.

"Behemot" was one way to refer to Behemoth — a creature from the Old Testament. That meant that it was an Embryo and that the lady here was its Master.

"Go on now, little lady. Big lady's here to pick you up," said Shu as he took the hedgehog, Behemot, and tried to remove it. But it didn't show any signs of letting go.

*"Little lady?" It's a girl?* I thought.

"xD!" Behemot emitted a strangely irritating chitter of joy and grabbed hold even harder. Apparently, she had taken a liking to Shu's head.

"Behemot, get off the bear's head," said the lady. "We have to go or we won't make it. We're in the standing area, so we have to hurry up."

Behemot complied, jumping off my brother's head and into her Master's chest.

"Now, if you'll excuse us, we will take our leave," the woman said and began walking away.

"Oh, wait a second," said Shu before reaching into his inventory, taking out some candy, and giving it to them.

"I bear gifts for all!" he exclaimed. "Enjoy it to your heart's content, you two."

"...Thank you very much."

"thx!"

With that, Behemot and her Master walked away from us. From the mention of a "standing area," it was fair to assume that she was going to see the event in the central arena.

"So it's not just children, eh? You seem to be popular with small animals, too," I said.

My words made Shu tilt his head for some reason. Though it wasn't too noticeable, with him not being a real bear and all.

"Well, I guess you can just say that I'm beary popular among the little ones," he said. "Everyone loves bears!"

"Whatever you say, bro." Though he'd said that he'd started wearing it because it was necessary, he seemed to enjoy it quite a lot.

"In fact, this bear suit is so popular that I don't really feel up fur wearing any other suit," he added.

"You have other ones?!"

"You don't have enough fingers to count the number of suits I have, and that's just for special rewards."

"That many?!"

I didn't know what was more surprising — the fact that he had that many special rewards or the fact that they were all suits.

*Man, my brother is quite the barrel of laughs,* I thought.

"Let's go and have a nice chat somewhere," he said.

"Sure. Let's go, Nemes— Wait, what's with that face?"

For some reason, she was just standing there. I suddenly noticed that she hadn't spoken a word for a while. I didn't know why, but she was looking at the direction where Behemot and her Master had gone.

"What's wrong?" I asked.

"Oh, it's nothing," she said. "I'm probably just imagining things. She has an Embryo, after all…"

I couldn't make out what she was so concerned about.

"Hey! Why are you just standing there?! Don't make me wait fur you!" exclaimed Shu.

"Oh, he's right. Let's go, Ray."

"Yeah."

We caught up with my brother, and we all decided to go to a café. He let us choose the place, so — by Nemesis's suggestion — we ended up go to the same sweet-focused café as yesterday.

*I dread to imagine how much she'll eat,* I thought.

"Well then, Behemot. Are you quite satisfied?" she asked.

"lol…"

"Excellent. You did say that you found the bear cute and wished to hug him. Though I found it a bit improper, it's good to see that you had your fill. Now, let's hope that you can also get what you want from today's fight, as well."

"yeye."

"Truly, I hope the Superiors in this nation are powerful… It would be great news indeed."

"git hype."

## Chapter Two Catching up

*Paladin, Ray Starling*

"Gardranda and Gouz-Maise, huh?" said Shu. "Looks like you've been through some beary strange things, Ray."

"You think so?" I asked.

At the familiar sweets parlor, my brother and I were having a little talk about what had happened so far. Since I was still full from the sandwiches from before, the only thing I ordered for this chat was tea.

Nemesis, on the other hand, was eating as she always did.

*What the hell is up with your stomach?* I thought.

"Encountering UBMs is rare, and even Epic ones are damn tough," he said. "It's not every day you get someone who fights and kills them not too long after entering *Infinite Dendrogram*."

Shu put some honey-covered pancakes into his mouth. Of course, he didn't neglect to use a fork. I was impressed that he could do it with those bear hands of his, but then I figured that it was probably easier than using a gatling gun.

Also, the overall image of a bear sitting on a chair and eating honey-covered pancakes was quite lavish. It seemed kinda cute, as well. At least, to anyone who didn't know that the person inside the suit was a man in his late twenties.

"Well, I'm probably not the one to talk, considering I killed my first UBM when I was on my first low-rank job," he continued.

"Huh?"

"It was also the time I met Figgy," he said. "We happened to get lost in a certain field and had to fight two UBMs..."

"TWO?!"

I instantly began imagining myself fighting both Gardranda and Gouz-Maise at the same time.

*Nope, it'd be hopeless,* I thought. *Even as I was now, they'd kill me easily.*

"So you and Figaro went two-on-two against them?" I asked.

"Nope," he answered.

"Oh, so Figaro wasn't the only who helped, then."

"Wrong again. We both went against them one-on-one."

*Excuse me?*

"Separating them was a real pain, and I really had to use my head to beat mine..."

"Wait. You said you were still on your first low-rank job, right?" I asked.

"Yeah."

"What about Figaro?"

"He, too, was on his first job — Gladiator. Not even level 50, either."

"...What about your Embryos?"

"Both were in their third forms. And no, neither of them had any giant-killing abilities like your Nemesis does."

I was stunned into silence. *I'm probably not in a position to think this, but how the hell did they do it? I mean, they didn't even have the support I did. Also, he says it happened when he — one of the first players — was on his first job. Doesn't that mean that they were among the first Masters to have beaten UBMs?*

"Anyway, going any deeper into this would mean revealing Figgy's Embryo's abilities," he said. "I'm beary averse to the idea of giving this info away myself, so I'll only explain it to you after you more or less understand it yourself."

"Well, then I guess I won't push it," I shrugged.

This duel city was Figaro's hometown, and with him being the local king of the arenas, the people here had lots of info about him.

However, there was a decisive lack of knowledge about his Embryo. Its powers, shape, and even category were all a great mystery to everyone. The other two in the Kingdom of Altar's Big Three weren't like this in that regard. The King of Destruction's Embryo was assumed to be a battleship, while the High Priestess's was widely known to be the moonlit night. However, there was absolutely nothing known about the Embryo of the Over Gladiator.

I had seen Figaro fight the player killers in the video that Marie had shown me, but even then, I hadn't seen a hint of his Embryo's abilities.

If the event Shu was referring to was linked to the truth behind it, I could totally understand why he didn't want to talk about it.

"But you *do* know it, huh, bro?" I asked.

"Figgy and I have been acquainted fur a long time, after all," he answered. "A whole four years by *Dendro* standards."

"I see. So I guess you also know why he's so fixated on going solo?"

"I do, but going into that would mean compromising his privacy, so I won't explain it," he said.

"All right. I won't push it, then."

It was probably the core of the reason why Figaro had said he wasn't "interested in sloppy battles" and refused to participate in the war. I wanted to know, but if it was something private, I couldn't really delve any deeper.

"I must say, you seem to be quite well-connected, Brother Bear," commented Nemesis.

"Well, it happens kinda naturally when you've been a long-time player," he shrugged.

"This has been bothering me for a while… How many hours a day do you spend here, anyway?" I asked.

Being the unfairly rich neo-NEET that he was, Shu had all the time in the world, so I couldn't help but wonder.

"I know what you're thinking, but no, I'm leading a beary healthy life," he said.

"'Healthy,' as in…?" I prompted.

"I never neglect to have three meals a day, take a bath, go to the bathroom, and spend an hour training to keep myself muscular and aesthetic."

"You're basically saying that you spend the rest of your time here!"

*That's not too different from a basement-dwelling sweaty tryhard!* I thought.

"Well, I don't really have anything I want to do outside of here, so whatever," he said.

"With the time and money you have, you could easily get into a relationship."

*Mom probably wants to become a grandmother by now,* I thought. *I was a high school student until recently, so it was too early for me. As for my elder sister… well… uhh… Anyway, Shu is the closest one to getting married… but from the looks of it, that won't happen for a while.*

An hour passed by as we were talking about this and that.

"Anyway, I have somewhere to go to, so I'll be leaving now," Shu said at last.

"Well, all right," I replied. "See you at the show."

"Yeah. I'm beary excited to meet your friends."

And with that, he left.

On the table, there was a considerably large sum of money. Considering the huge reward I'd gotten, I'd planned to be the one to pay for us both, but he'd wanted to show off and had ended up doing it before I'd even gotten the chance. I gladly accepted his generosity.

Also, about 90% of the money we owed was due to Nemesis's eating. It was quite troubling how the amount she ate seemed to gradually increase. For someone named after a goddess of divine punishment, she sure enjoyed indulging in the deadly sin of gluttony.

"Oh, but you're wrong there, Ray," she read my thoughts and said.

"How?" I asked.

"Gluttony refers to the wasting of food through reckless consumption. I, however, savor and enjoy every bite before it becomes a part of my flesh. Thus, I am not a glutton, but a gourmet!"

"All right, that's fine, then," I said. "However, let me ask you one thing."

"Do go ahead."

"Just how much weight would you gain if it all actually became part of your flesh?"

*Talking to girls about their weight isn't the nicest thing I can do, but seeing your eating habits is kinda troubling.*

"Heh, there's no need to worry," she said. "I am an Embryo, remember? My shape and weight do not change easily."

"Riiiight. Ain't that greaaat."

"What's with the sarcasm?!"

*Your shape and weight change a lot when you go into your other forms, though.*

"So, wait, are all Embryos big eaters or what?" I asked.

"Wrong," said a voice coming from my side. "Being an Embryo has nothing to do with being a big eater. I'm not one, after all. Nemesis being gluttonous is her own problem. Which is good, since I really wouldn't like having such a monstrous stomach as part of my base stats."

"I see," I murmured. *Now that I think about it, despite liking things ridiculously spicy, the Embryo Babi eats normal amounts of food. In all honesty, her blasphemous tastes seem a bit more normal than Nemesis's big eating—*

"...Wait, what?!" I burst out, startled.

"Hm?!" Nemesis added.

"Hellooo," said the fully white girl now sitting at my side. She was Hugo's Embryo, Cyco. "The number of plates stacked next to Nemesis is terrifying. I don't think I could handle even 5% of it," she said before biting into a pure white no-bake cheesecake.

Her tone was as monotonous and disinterested as the last time I'd heard her speak. It seemed as though she'd been in this establishment for a while now, but despite her appearance standing out so much, I hadn't noticed her at all.

*Was I really that preoccupied with my meal with Shu and Nemesis?* I thought.

"You seem confused," she said. "The secret to this is the fact that I have the Presence Manipulation skill. To a certain extent, I can prevent myself from standing out."

"Why did you do that, though?" I asked.

"I surprised you, didn't I?"

"Well, yeah."

My answer made her put on the most smug and self-satisfied smile before she bit into her cake again.

*...Huh? Did she really only want to surprise us?*

"As hard to read as always, this girl," commented Nemesis.

*Seriously.* Though she was a friend who'd helped in the elimination of the Gouz-Maise Gang, I still had little grasp of what kind of person she was.

"Cyco," I addressed her. "Is Hugo not with you?"

"He should be here soon," she answered. "We split up for the search, but I just telepathically told him where we are, so just wait."

As I was about to ask what they were searching for, I heard the door open and the shop's bell ring. The one who entered the establishment was a familiar man wearing a militaristic rider suit.

"Greetings, Ray," he said. "I believe I should thank God for meeting you again, safe and sound." It was Hugo, acting as exaggerated, affected, and pompous as always.

*Man, I'm sure meeting a lot of familiar people today,* I thought.

The shop had entered its peak hours, and the more packed it became, the more Masters and foreign-looking people I saw.

"It's delicious! The wiki was right! The sweets here are great!" a young girl squealed from behind me.

"...I-Io, y-you're too loud..." one of her friends said.

"Peach tart, 80 points. Shortcake, 76 points. No-bake cheesecake... 95 points."

Those young girls were getting noisy at the table behind me.

To the left of me, an Arabian-looking man, wearing a turban and everything, was noting something down. "Oh, there's take-out here. I believe I found my souvenirs for Yumeji and Carl. Though perishable, they will last just fine in an inventory with good preservation ability. As for Albert… I should get him something other than food."

Then there was a crude-looking group with beastly leather armor and a bunch of macho men in bandanas surrounding a girl in a pirate hat. Clearly, the customers were far more varied today than they had been yesterday. I could only assume that they'd all gathered to watch tonight's event. And with this shop being in the same city as the arena, even those who didn't fit in among its usual customers had come to enjoy some sweets.

"This is a pretty popular place, isn't it?" I said.

"Indeed it is," nodded Hugo. "Tians and Masters alike recognize it as a great sweets shop."

"No-bake cheesecake, yogurt mousse, soft serve ice cream… Delicious," agreed Cyco.

They both seemed quite satisfied with this establishment. *Even though it looks like Cyco is only eating white things, for some reason.*

Anyway, since Hugo and I had happened to meet up again, I told him about the reward.

"I never would've expected the bounty to be that great," he said. "Truly surprising."

His reaction was only natural. 80,000,000 was an astonishing amount of money.

"Now, about the split…" I said.

"Like I wrote in my letter, I intend to refuse it… but it doesn't seem like you will agree to that, will you?"

"Hell no," I said. Keeping such vast riches for myself was too much for me to handle. "Let's split it in half."

"No, I'll be fine with just a quarter," Hugo said. "I already refused it once, after all. And even then, it feels too much for me."

"Really?" I asked. When it came to the Gouz-Maise Gang bounty, all I really deserved was the part for Maise, so I really wanted him to take more.

"You're selfless and honest to a fault, aren't you?" said Hugo. "You could've chosen to not inform me and keep the money for yourself."

"Why would I lie to a friend like that?" I asked.

For some reason, my question made Hugo avert his gaze.

*What's wrong?* I thought.

"Oh, also, this is something that happened at the knight offices…" I told him that I'd asked the knights to use the treasures the gang had left behind for charity.

"That's fine by me," he said. "I would've probably done the same."

*Well, that's a relief,* I thought. *Just as I figured, he and I share a way of thinking.*

"Indeed," agreed Nemesis. "You two are quite alike."

*We're both Maiden's Masters, after all.*

With that, the conversation about the bounty was over, and I gave Hugo his share of money.

*Good thing none of it got stolen by a Thief or something… I really hope there are none of them in the shop…* I thought.

"There, I now have my part of the bounty," said Hugo. "Thank you. It will make up for the destroyed Marshall II."

"Oh...? How much are those things, anyway?" I asked.

"10,000,000 lir."

"T-TEN?!" I yelped.

*I had no idea it was so luxurious!*

"With special tuning and extras, it can easily go over 20,000,000 lir," Hugo added. He pointed at the inventory where he'd just put the 20,000,000 lir I'd given him, his eyes still insisting that the Magingear's destruction wasn't going into the necessary expenses and that he didn't actually need any more of the bounty.

"Still, it's quite an expensive piece of equipment," said Hugo. "Also, that is the original pricing, exclusive to us clan members of the Triangle of Wisdom. On Dryfe's standard marketplace, their price is twice as great. That number is doubled or tripled yet again when we're talking about the machines that have gotten leaked to Caldina." I had no idea whether I should be more surprised by the immense original pricing or by just how much greater it could grow.

"The pricing is the biggest problem with a Marshall II, and humanoid Magingears in general," he added. "The machines are generally as strong as Demi-Dragons, yet actual tamed Demi-Dragon monsters cost only about 3,000,000. A striking difference."

*So that's how much Demi-Dragons cost, eh?* I thought. *Maybe I should buy one along with a carriage? Then again, I have Silver, so maybe I don't need it.*

"Still, Magingears are not without their advantages," said Hugo. "For example, they don't use any minion capacity and can be mass-produced as long as there are materials and funds."

Anything "Demi-Dragon" was considered to be equivalent to a full party of people with low-rank jobs. Being able to create such things was quite a big deal. I could totally see why they were so costly.

"Yeah," I nodded. "Monsters are living creatures, and you sure as hell can't produce them just by having the materials and money."

"...True," he nodded.

"Also, you said something about Caldina selling them, as well. Can you elaborate?"

"Sure," he said. "Caldina imports and sells special items from all countries, even if they *aren't actually exporting them.* Dryfe's Magingears, Granvaloa's ships, Altar's Tomb Labyrinth drops, Tenchi's weaponry, Huang He's and Legendaria's magic items, etc. Caldina's main selling point is that, as long as you have the money, you can buy goods from every country. Even your social standing is dependent on how much you're offering."

*"Money is Everything: the Country," huh?* I thought.

"Due to that, many high-end players with fat wallets move over there... which has resulted in them having the most Superiors out of any country," Hugo muttered, clearly troubled by what he'd just said.

"'Most,' as in...?" I prompted.

"Nine Superiors," he answered. "The strongest force at any country's disposal."

"...Damn, that's a lot." The Kingdom of Altar had four, and nine was more than double that number. Thinking about that, I added, "Oh yeah, in the war, Dryfe—"

"Overwhelmed Altar, but was soon invaded by Caldina," he cut me off and explained. "Dryfe's Superiors had to leave the front lines to defend against those attacks, allowing Altar to prevail."

And that was why the kingdom had continued to exist even after a war in which none of its Superiors had participated. Sure, Altar didn't have enough power to retake the land taken by Dryfe, but still.

"Before the war, there was a large feast in Dryfe to celebrate the inevitable victory, yet the result was so inadequate that the one in charge of the country's domestic affairs — Prime Minister Vigoma — was at his wits' end," said Hugo. "Oh, by the way, Dryfe only has enough funds to buy the help of Masters just one more time. Anything beyond that would cause the economy to crash."

"You sure you can say that to me?" I asked.

"That's inside info that's readily available to Masters as lowly as myself. You see it quite often on online message boards, too. Me revealing it to you doesn't mean much."

"Oh, I see..."

"Anyway, to win this war, Dryfe has to either occupy the Kingdom of Altar before Caldina intervenes or merge with the country through peaceful methods."

*Well, the latter case isn't impossible, considering that the kingdom has been weakened and is certainly not in a good shape to participate in a long-lasting war,* I thought.

For better or for worse, Caldina had acted as a stopping force to prevent Dryfe from doing whatever they wanted.

...Still, I wasn't too fond of them, considering their involvement with the Gouz-Maise Gang.

"Oh, by the way," Hugo spoke up again. "Caldina was also the reason why Legendaria — Altar's ally — didn't participate in the war. Being south of Altar, the country is far from Dryfe while being extremely close to Caldina, which covers the entire desert area in the center of the continent. If Legendaria had sent its Superiors or tians with Superior Jobs to help in the war, Caldina would've used the opportunity to take it over. The reason why Caldina interfered in the war was to prevent Dryfe from merging with Altar, thereby stopping our country from gaining the momentum it needed to conquer the entire continent. However, Caldina itself is planning the exact same thing."

*So there are two countries vying for world domination? These sure are turbulent times.*

"The reason why Caldina only invades countries that show an opening is because it's in the middle of the continent," said Hugo.

Basic geopolitics. Besides Granvaloa, which was on the ocean, the countries of the world could be vertically split into three parts, like a French or an Italian flag. To the left were the three western countries: the Dryfe Imperium in the north, the Kingdom of Altar to the south of it, and Legendaria even further down. In the middle, there was the City-State Union of Caldina. And off to the right, there was the Huang He Empire and Tenchi — the island nation that was relatively close to the continent.

The central country, Caldina, shared a border with every nation except the far-east land of Tenchi.

"Dryfe, Altar, and Legendaria to the west and Huang He to the east, not to mention the sea-based nation of Granvaloa," said Hugo. "It's surrounded. If Caldina focused on attacking something, the other countries would use the opportunity to take its land. They have plenty reasons to do so, after all."

"A bit of a deadlock there, huh?" I said. And the only real way for the situation to move out of this stalemate would be the war between Altar and Dryfe.

"...This might be a bit belated, but why are you so casual about looking like that?" I added.

"Like what?" Hugo asked.

"Isn't that Dryfe's military uniform or something?" I asked.

Hugo was wearing the exact same clothing as yesterday — the ones that looked like a military uniform mixed with a rider suit. Considering Hugo's affiliations, it needn't be said what military the uniform belonged to. Thus, wearing it in this country didn't seem like a good idea.

"No, this isn't Dryfe's official equipment," he said. "It's the suit from GodFrame Grand Marshall."

"GodFrame Gra… what?"

"GodFrame Grand Marshall."

*Well, if that doesn't sound like a name for a mecha show…*

"When did this anime air?" I asked. Assuming that Hugo was French, it might've been a western cartoon…

"It's not an anime," he answered. "It's a manga drawn by a Painter belonging to the Triangle of Wisdom."

"Drawn… here?"

"In this world, yes."

Hugo began explaining how the manga had come to be.

After troubles too many to count, the Triangle of Wisdom had finally finished its first battle-ready robot Magingear, the Marshall II. Being a group of people who'd gathered for the very purpose of creating a robot straight out of a mecha anime, they'd gone absolutely nuts about it.

While most had gotten fired up to continue improving their robots, some had become motivated to do other things. One of the clan members had used the skills from his Painter job to draw a cool-looking Marshall II design.

From that, another member began had begun drawing a manga.

Those who couldn't draw had begun writing novels or creating models, while some had gone as far as composing opening themes and soundtracks.

With the ever-growing number of clan members, this chain reaction had continued until it had become a considerably large production.

The Triangle of Wisdom was pretty much a gathering of mecha anime fans. Having a Marshall II as reference had strengthened their inner fires and urged them to create various creative works. It had gotten to the point where they now dedicated an entire area of their headquarters just for such production. And among the things they produced was the clothing based on the suit of a pilot from the manga — the very same thing Hugo was wearing right now.

"So you're constantly cosplaying, huh?" I asked.

"It was actually made by a skilled crafter, so the stats are good, too," he said. "It's considered to be the uniform of Pilots belonging to the Triangle of Wisdom. Still, that's not well-known outside of our inner circle, so I can wear it in this country with no problem."

"The stats are good?" I asked.

"Not nearly as good as those on special rewards, but it's no doubt among the best things I can wear at my level."

I could only imagine the amount of passion that had gone into the costume. Nothing could really stop a person when they got absorbed in something they liked.

"What about you?" I asked. "Did you join the Triangle of Wisdom because you're a mecha fan?"

"No." He shook his head. "I joined the clan because I know the leader. In fact, I started *Infinite Dendrogram* because he invited me."

*Well now, doesn't that sound familiar?* I thought. *I started in the Kingdom of Altar because my brother told me to.*

"All right, I have some things I want to know, as well," said Hugo. "I'm especially curious about the details of the Gouz-Maise fight."

"Sure, I'll tell you," I nodded. "After you and Cyco escaped with the children, Nemesis and I..."

After that, Hugo and I continued exchanging information or just chatting pointlessly for awhile.

"Oh, it's time," I said. Before I'd realized it, barely over an hour was left until the event began. I no longer had the time to go shopping at Alejandro's, so I rescheduled to tomorrow.

"Is something happening?" asked Hugo.

"Yeah, I got my hands on a ticket for the event," I said. "In the central arena, there's gonna be a match between Figaro and Huang He's Xunyu — two Superiors. Do you know about it?"

"I do. In fact, it's probably what every Master in this city is here for."

"Are you gonna see it, too?" I asked.

"...You could say that, yes."

"Oh, we might meet in the arena, then."

Hugo said nothing. He seemed to be pondering something.

*Did I say something strange?* I wondered.

"Ray, there's something I want you to keep in the corner of your mind," he said before taking a deep breath and continuing. "It's west."

"'It,' as in...?" I raised an eyebrow, not understanding what he meant.

"It's nothing important," he said. "You know how the fighters in the great arena's matches enter from the east and west? Well, today's main deal, the Over Gladiator, Figaro, will go in from the west side."

"Is that how it works? I've never watched a match before, so I didn't know," I said, unable to shake the feeling that Hugo was hiding something. "Anyway, I'm going to the arena now."

"I see," said Hugo. "Cyco and I will wait a bit longer."

"All right, then. Guess this is goodbye for now. Oh, should we add each other to our friends lists?" I asked. If we ever had business with each other, knowing whether the other person was online or not could be a great help.

"Not now," he answered. "Let's do it next time we meet… or the time after that."

"Hmm. Well, that's fine by me." We seemed to have some sort of bond, so I didn't doubt that we would meet again.

"Until then, Ray," he said.

"See you again, Nemesis," Cyco added.

"Yeah, later, Hugo," I said.

"Until our paths cross once more, Cyco," Nemesis added.

"Hey, Hugo. Was it really okay to tell him that?" Cyco asked.

I said nothing.

"Isn't that what they call 'leaking information'?" she prodded.

"It might be," I admitted.

"You don't want the plan?" she asked.

"…Maybe, maybe not," I said. "In all honesty, I'm not sure myself."

"You're not?"

I shook my head. "I certainly want to help fulfill his desires. If I didn't, my very existence as Hugo would be meaningless. However, I also cannot ignore women in distress."

"What an antinomy."

"Antinomy… that's a good word for it. I gave Ray the information, but that's the whole extent of what I did. Whether he acts on it or processes it as idle chatter is of no matter to me. As a piece in the plan, I will only do what I must."

"Then I will help you do whatever it is you do," Cyco said.

"Thank you." I nodded.

## Interlude 》 Before the Festival

*Royal capital Altea, State Guest House*

In a certain part of the royal capital's noble district, there was a building meant to accommodate honored guests from foreign lands. One of its rooms currently had three people in it.

The first of them was a bedridden young boy with a mask covering the lower part of his face. The ice pack on his forehead and the occasional coughing made it obvious that he had a condition similar to a cold or flu.

The second person was a young woman standing by the boy's bed, looking obviously worried. Her thick glasses implied that she was nearsighted, and they made her appear like a fainthearted kind of person.

The third person was abnormally tall, to the point of making someone question whether that individual was actually a person.

The bedroom's ceiling was high — perhaps surpassing four metels — and yet the creature's head was almost touching it. Naturally, it was a weird sight, but the other two people didn't seem to be bothered by it.

The first person was Canglong, third prince of the Huang He Empire. The second was Lan Meihai, Huang He Ambassador. And the third was Master Jiangshi Xunyu, one of Huang He's Superiors.

Canglong coughed and coughed. "I'm sorry, Master Xunyu," he managed at last. "I wanted to watch the match and cheer for you, but I'm clearly not in the state for it…"

"It's fiNe. You just rest till you're healthy aGain," said Xunyu in response. "But man, seeing *you* bedriddEn is just…" The jiangshi heaved a sigh so heavy that the talisman covering the face did nothing to hide it.

"Yes. I find it quite curious, as well…" murmured the prince. "But at the very least, I can be glad that you didn't get ill, as well."

Soon after the long trip from Huang He to the Kingdom's royal capital, Canglong had become part of an Epidemic.

"Epidemic" was a term used to describe any sudden diseases that spread among the weak and strong alike. Masters saw it as an unpatterned, irregular, widespread *Infinite Dendrogram* event. There were many various Epidemics that covered many large areas, creating sufferers among both Masters and tians. Though some went away with the passage of time, some required special healing methods such as vaccines or healing magic available only to Superior Jobs.

Epidemics completely ignored all stats and resistances. Even high-level Masters would become bedridden or simply log out until the disease went away. They were considered to be natural disasters above human knowledge.

Needless to say, it was quite fortuitous that the current Epidemic was more like the common cold or flu than anything else. However, it was an illness nonetheless. Originally, Canglong had been meant to accompany Xunyu to the Clash of the Superiors and observe the battle, but it was clear that he was in no state to do that. The same applied to the first princess of the kingdom, who'd also succumbed to the Epidemic.

"Oh dear... umm... Your Highness, should I change the ice pack?" asked the woman fretfully. "Or would you like an apple?"

Meihai's worry about her country's prince's condition was needlessly excessive.

"Ambassador, you've changed the ice pack five times in the past hour. And I *just* peeled an apPle for him," said Xunyu. "Oh yeAh, this country's queen is sick, too, rigHt? That's the reason why Cang's business got postpoNed, isn't it?"

"M-Master Xunyu!" the ambassador protested. "She's not the queen, but the first princess!"

"...Whatever. She's acting as a queen, anYway."

"She isn't! There are many differences in a diplomatic setting! First of all...!" Meihai began arguing with — or merely lecturing — Xunyu. Though it made her seem quite childish, she was a member a distinguished family and had a lot of diplomatic skill that made her stand out as an ambassador.

Some might have argued that such behavior didn't belong in the presence of her country's prince; however...

"Hee hee. You never change, Mei," said Canglong before coughing again, clearly not minding her inappropriate behavior.

Though he spoke to her in a highly casual manner, Meihai definitely wasn't in a respectable enough position to have the prince treat her like that. The reason he did was because Meihai's mother was Cang's foster mother, making them foster siblings. That meant that the only ones in the room were those who were close to Cang. The other chamberlains and officials were in a different part of the guest house.

"Master Xunyu," said Cang and coughed. "Shouldn't you go to Gideon now…?"

He was looking at the clock hanging in the room. The event would begin in about three hours. Normally, that amount of time was far too small to cover the distance to Gideon, which usually took a whole day and night. However, everyone in the room knew that it wouldn't be a problem.

"You gonna be saFe?" asked Xunyu.

"You've no need to worry," said Cang. "It's true that I'm not at my best, but I'm sure I can manage."

"Don't be stuPid. You'd be overdoiNg it… Give me your hAnd."

Cang did as he was told and Xunyu gave him a gem — a Jewel, to be precise.

"Master Xunyu?" he asked.

"It's a spare Jewel. One of the ones I don't plan to use in this match."

"Are you sure you won't?" the prince asked.

"Duels only allow you to use ones that don't exceed your caPacity. Take iT," said Xunyu and made Cang close his hand around the Jewel. Though it was done by the jiangshi's blade-like claws, the action was strangely gentle, and didn't put a single scratch on the prince.

"Then I shall take it, Master Xunyu," said Cang.

"GoOd," the eccentric nodded in response.

Following that exchange, Xunyu went to the window. After skillfully opening it with those blade-like claws, the jiangshi made them clash.

The resulting high-pitched, metallic sound made one of Cang's chamberlains hastily run into the room.

"Your Highness! Master Xunyu! What is the matter?!" asked one of them.

"After we leaVe, close the winDow."

"Excuse me?"

Ignoring the puzzled chamberlain, Xunyu extended one arm to the side — making it reach more than five metels in length — and made the metallic claw wrap around Meihai.

"Eh?" she sounded a voice of confusion.

"Well, ambassAdor, we're goiNg to Gideon," said the jiangshi. "Don't bite your tongue on thE way."

Then, Xunyu's body bent…

"Umm, Master Xunyu! I-I'm not quite ready yet, so—AAAAAAaaaaahhhh!"

…and they both disappeared beyond the window, leaving behind only the echo of Meihai's scream.

A few seconds later, they were on the walls of the noble district, so far from Cang's room that they looked like ants.

"Goodbye, Master Xunyu and Mei," the boy said as he raised up his upper body from the bed and waved at them.

The chamberlain had no words for what had just happened, so she did as she was told and simply closed the window.

Thus, the Master Jiangshi Xunyu left the capital and went towards Gideon.

*Gideon, City of Duels, ???*

The city of Gideon was full of excitement.

With it being the most prosperous town in the Kingdom of Altar, such a mood wasn't a new thing here. However, the enthusiasm that had enveloped it this evening was on a different level than usual.

The reason for that was the fact that the event happening in the central arena was simply *that* big.

It was a duel between Superiors — something that had never happened in any duel city anywhere.

People gathered from in and outside of the city and even other countries, and everyone was full of enthusiasm and expectations for the event. It seemed as though all of Gideon was lapsing into delirium with excitement.

However, the town also included someone who shared none of that sentiment.

That person was looking down at Gideon with cold eyes, and that was no exaggeration. After all, he was wearing an Adélie penguin suit. Those cold, man-made eyes made it hard to guess what the person inside was thinking.

However, from the way the person was groaning and holding his head in his right hand, it was clear that he wasn't in an optimal state of mind.

"Ohh boy… Ohhh man… Ohhhhhhhhh crap…"

After a moment of writhing, he used the Portable Communication Magic Device in his other hand to contact someone.

Two or so minutes passed before that someone answered.

"Ayy there, Your Excellency," the penguin idly complained to the person on the other side. "There's been a change of plans. One of my boys in the royal capital contacted me and, well… he said that the first princess won't be coming."

The information he was nonchalantly complaining about was a secret that was supposedly only available to a select few officials.

"And when I told it to His Majesty's people... well, just *her*, actually, since she's his contact and all... she actually went, 'Then we will simply enjoy the fight and the sights here,'" he went on. "Ohhhh man..."

The penguin and the person who'd answered the call had a certain plan. That plan was based on the participation of the first princess and the help of another person.

"Well, yeah, with her being the Imperium's strongest, her presence changes a lot. Now we're left without a joker."

The penguin spoke his complaints in a blatantly sad manner. Sad as his tone was, however, he was still smiling.

"Well, it won't be a problem. She was a bit too much for this plan, anyway. Even if I don't have all five of my cards, the other four are more than enough for the job."

He went on:

"From my clan, there's me, Veldorbell, and my favorite. Then there are the betrayers... Yes, the ones that want to switch sides to Dryfe. Sure, they don't want to go to the gaol, so they'll probably fight only Masters, but that's more than enough, honestly. Tians without Superior Jobs aren't a threat... Oh no, I'm definitely not belittling the Imperium's forces. Still, what we have is good enough for a 90% chance of success."

The person on the other side seemed to agree with the penguin's words. However...

"You want the chances of success if there's a Superior that's aware of the plan? 50%." The penguin answered the person's question without a moment of hesitation.

"Ha ha ha! 'Won't it become lower?' you ask?" The person inside the suit then put on a faint smile…

"Have you forgotten who you're talking to?"

He spoke with a menacing voice thick with madness and even bloodlust.

"So yeah, the plan's target will have to be changed, and I'll have to do some other tweaks, but I'm still going through with it. You just sit there and pray for my success."

With that, he ended the call.

"No stops from our sponsor, then. Guess the financial situation ain't the best, so he probably wants it to be over quickly. This means that the plan's failure would likely lead to us doing it the field marshal's way…" The man inside the penguin suit chuckled. "Come what may, I say. Though I have no idea how things would proceed if someone tough showed up. What should I try then? How far should I go?"

As he imagined what would happen next, the suited man's expression changed. It was reminiscent of both an innocent child pouring water or inserting firecrackers into an ant colony, and a cool-headed, calculating adult considering how things could unfold. However, he soon remembered something and reassessed the situation.

*Oh, but anyone tough would probably lose to him before I even got the chance to intervene.* The penguin remembered the Master he'd brought to the city. It was a person that he knew very well, and a rookie who'd started *Infinite Dendrogram* no more than a month ago. Though being a Maiden's Master made him quite special, he was still far from a veteran.

*His Embryo is a joker card in its own right. Anyone who's tough and has a relevant history is at a disadvantage. Honestly, if the situation is right…*

"…I wouldn't be surprised if he killed every Master in Gideon all by himself," the penguin said.

Despite that Master being a rookie, the penguin had unwavering trust in his powers, and in the results he would bring.

## Chapter Three Xunyu the Yinglong

*Paladin, Ray Starling*

Opera halls and the like had a thing called "boxes" or "loges." Half-open, half-closed and fixed to the walls, they were luxury seats which gave the best view of the stage.

Our box in the central arena was much like one of those, but not completely. It was closed off, but the wall facing the stage was all glass, giving us an unbroken view of the fight.

The normal seats in the arena were like those in a soccer stadium. The paths linking those with the viewer benches were all made of a stony material, while those of us in the box seats had a carpet under our feet and some fancy, antique-looking chairs — antique-looking by the standard of this world, anyway.

There was quite a bit of space between them, too, giving each of us the option to ignore the rough duels beneath and just relax. And with the fully-functional air-conditioning, the comfort here was nothing short of perfect.

*Man, is this fancy,* I thought. *I can totally see why it cost a whole 100,000 lir. Of course, this is actually the equivalent of spending 1,000,000 yen to watch real life sports, which is something I'd definitely never do.*

"For someone with a fortune of 60,000,000 lir in his pocket, you sure are frugal," said Nemesis.

*Having money doesn't mean I have to be inconsiderate about how I spend it.*

"Gacha."

"Guahh..." I groaned, unable to say anything back to her.

*...B-But gacha has a charm that I can't resist, and...*

"Ray, won't you watch the match?" asked Marie, who was sitting next to me.

"Oh, yeah, I will," I replied and shifted my attention to the stage.

Before that, though, I took one last look around our box. The ones in here were me, Nemesis, Rook, Babi, and Marie.

Due to Nemesis and Babi being Embryos, the two had gotten in here for free. However, I hadn't known that beforehand, so I'd tried to get in after returning Nemesis to the crest.

"This is not something I like saying, but I felt like a dog about to be carried in one of those portable crates," she said.

*What kind of comparison is that?* I thought.

"Oh, right. *You're* the dog here," she went on.

"Could you not dig up a memory I want to forget?!"

*The dog ears disappeared this morning, and I want them gone from my head, too!*

"They looked quite good on you, though," she said.

*...Yeah, whatever.*

Anyway, we five were the only people here. My brother, the last person in our box, still hadn't arrived yet.

*Did he stop by a shop or something?* I thought. *Oh, well. I'll just wait for him while watching the match.*

There was a semi-event going on in the battlefield below. It was a perfect chance for me to reassess how duels work.

First, once the people stood on the stage, they set and agreed to the battle conditions. Then, they activate a special duel city barrier and begin fighting.

Inside the barrier, any injuries received, including fatal ones and player death penalties, disappeared after the battle was over. That allowed for deadly-yet-safe fighting.

The safety of the spectators was accounted for, as well. Multiple layers of barriers separated the audience and the duelists, letting through only sound, light, and the fighters' enthusiasm.

Of course, dangerous light like lasers or dangerous sound like destructive sonic explosions were blocked, too. Though apparently, players under level 50 — like me — could pass through the barrier unhindered, which was the reason why I couldn't participate in duels yet.

Also, the box we were in had come equipped with various devices. For example, there were monitors imbued with farsight magic, letting us observe the battle from numerous angles. The battle's sounds reached us, as well, including the words of the participants and the names of the skills they used. All of it made for a highly simple and convenient viewing experience.

These boxes were used by wealthy tian nobles, traders, and Masters who wanted to analyze the fighters on the stage.

"But many are just enjoying the duel, right?" I said to myself.

Due to no one's life being in danger, there were a lot of people who participated in duels. It was a popular activity among Masters and tian fighters alike. However, the main attraction of the arenas was the duels between Masters, and after seeing the fight before me, I could totally understand why. It was simply on a different level.

"Hhaahhhh!" shouted one of the Masters in the fight before me.

She was a black longsword-wielding, gothic-looking girl with black wings reminiscent of fallen angels sprouting from her back, and she freely flew around the space inside the barrier while leaving black feathers all around her.

"Blackwing Orchestra!"

Each and every one of the innumerable scattered feathers released jet-black wind blades. They formed a dark lattice which rent the air as it surrounded the enemy, fully intent on slicing her apart.

However, the opponent, a girl wearing a pirate hat and swinging around a giant golden ax as if it was no big deal, tightly gripped her weapon and forced it into the stage's stony floor. "World Reversal Waterfall!"

A moment later, the seemingly-empty stage's surface released a great flow of water with a force far more immense than a flash flood's.

The jet surrounding the girl was much like the skill's name: a reverse waterfall. It made the surrounding black wind blades completely vanish.

However, at that moment, the black-winged girl broke through an opening in the waterfall caused by the clashing between the water and the feathers, and slashed straight at the pirate girl, who still had her ax stuck in the stage.

The pirate girl used her left bracer to block the attack, but it wasn't enough. It broke through the material and damaged her regardless. But at the same time, the gothic girl bent her body due to injury.

Right as the pirate girl raised her left hand to protect herself, she used a blind spot created by the enemy's attack to launch an offensive skill with her right hand, creating a ball of water which hit the gothic girl right in her abdomen.

The winged girl instantly jumped backwards, and the pirate girl's ax cut through the air where she'd just stood. She'd probably been aiming to make use of the gothic girl's loss of posture, but it hadn't worked.

The two spread out, creating some distance between them, then stared at each other, predicted their opponent's moves, and clashed once again.

"Damn, they're good," I said. I was a bunch of tiers beneath them, not just in terms of basic stats, but playing skill, as well. "But I can still see them."

Which was strange, since Marie had told me that high AGI would make people immensely fast.

"Oh, that's because the flow of time is set to slow down inside the barrier," she said. "From the fighters' perspective, they're moving at their actual battle speed, while we in the audience see it in a speed that allows us to properly observe what's going on. There's a limit to this, though."

"Well, that's convenient," I said.

"Truly," she agreed. "That's how it works from a player's perspective. But according to the setting, this is lost technology from an old civilization."

*So the arena itself is the same kind of thing as Silver, huh?* I thought.

"I'd say it's necessary, though," she added. "If they fought at their normal speed, not even a tenth of the spectators could see what's going on."

*Well, that sure says a lot about just how fast they're fighting.*

"They're Juliet the 'Black Raven' and Chelsea the 'Vagrant Golden Sea.' Both are highly experienced Masters with sixth form

Embryos. They're also on Altar's duel rankings. The former is fourth, while the latter is eighth."

That made sense, considering how well they were fighting.

"I think I saw the one in the pirate hat when we were eating sweets," said Nemesis.

*Now that you mention it, yeah, she might've been there,* I thought.

Nemesis turned to Marie. "Are 'Black Raven' and 'Vagrant Golden Sea' their nicknames?"

"Yes," she nodded. "As for jobs, well, the former is a Fallen Knight — a Superior Job derived from the dark knight subgroup of the knight grouping — while the latter is a Great Pirate — a high-rank job from the pirate grouping."

*Oh, Black Raven is in the knight grouping?* I thought. *I'm not sure whether it makes me feel any affinity for her. I mean, her equipment is a bit scary-looking...*

"I sincerely doubt the girl would like to hear that from you, of all people," commented Nemesis.

*What's that supposed to mean?*

"By the way, are Superior Jobs common?" I asked.

"Not when you look at the whole picture," Marie answered. "Still, there are far more of them than Superiors, Masters with Superior Embryos. If I had to guess, I'd say that people with Superior Jobs are in the quadruple digits. Even tians can get those jobs, after all."

That was a greater number than I'd expected.

"Strong Masters stuck with high-rank Embryos often go for those jobs," she added.

"But despite being strong, this 'Vagrant Golden Sea' lady doesn't have a Superior Job, right?" asked Rook.

"Oh, Chelsea is one of those who've yet to discover a Superior Job she could take," said Marie. "There are tons of jobs with unknown conditions, after all."

*Well, her status makes sense now,* I thought.

"Having your Superior Job get occupied before you even know its conditions must be tragic," I commented.

"Oh, that happens a lot," said Marie. "Some Superior Jobs have similar conditions, after all. There are even people who have taken two of them."

"What an unfair world… Ah!"

As I listened to Marie's explanation, something big began happening in the match. The wings of the Fallen Knight, Juliet, disappeared, and a moment later, countless black feathers gathered around her hands. Soon, they all began whirling around her arms, accelerating to speeds so great it became hard to differentiate them.

The Great Pirate, Chelsea, swung her ax and made its wide middle part face her opponent. Then the golden ax part vanished, leaving behind a hole which released a powerful flow of golden seawater.

Using all their magic and technique, the two reached the limits of their power and unleashed their ultimate attacks.

"Corpse-Eating Bird — Hræsvelgr!"

"Golden Bull Tsunami — Poseidon!"

The stage became overwhelmed by the clash between a dark whirlwind and a golden tsunami.

Even with all the layers of barriers separating us, the visual pressure and the sound waves reaching us were still overwhelming.

The struggle between a tornado and a tidal wave — likely the results of their trump cards — made for a sight that felt completely otherworldly.

Their Embryos were in their sixth forms, making them four tiers above Nemesis. Naturally, their destructive power was immense. It wouldn't have surprised me if both of those attacks were doing enough damage to instantly pulverize Gardranda.

However, there was more than just power to them. The entire battle that had led to this moment was a show of just how skilled they really were.

"So, is it safe to assume that these attacks are the 'ultimate skills' you told us about, and that their Embryo names are Hræsvelgr and Poseidon?" asked Nemesis.

"Yes," she said. "These attacks are their Embryos' ultimate skills, each named after the Embryo itself. They express the Embryo's dominant characteristics, which is why Hræsvelgr is a dark-wind mixed-element magic attack, while Poseidon is a liquid-summoning skill."

"Is there a difference between liquid-summoning and the water element?" I asked.

"In the simplest of terms, liquid-summoning is physical, while elements, including water, are magic. By the way, the liquid from Poseidon's ultimate skill is basically standard-temperature molten gold, and is far heavier than normal water. It can easily flatten fortresses."

"How luxurious," I said. "Damn freaky, too."

"Well, it all disappears after the attack is over."

That made sense. A person that could constantly spawn gold wouldn't be good for the game's market price.

"But man, I've gotta say, you're pretty knowledgeable about them, aren't you?" I asked.

"They're frequent duelists, after all," she replied. "There's lots of info about them."

That was the thing about duels. Masters who participated in Gideon's duels would receive rewards regardless of whether they won or lost — though, naturally, the victor got more. For those who fought in this arena's main events, the reward could easily reach 5,000,000 lir. With today's event being so special, that number was multiplied tenfold. Naturally, those are some high returns, but they came at a high risk of giving information about yourself to the spectators — other players included.

Marie had demonstrated this cost quite well. Being part of DIN, she knew everything from the two girls' jobs to the details of their Embryos' ultimate skills.

"Still, there are frequent duelists about whom we know absolutely nothing," she added.

I was silent.

"That's why I'm very excited about the next match."

The battle on the stage reached its end, and Juliet the Black Raven proclaimed her victory.

With that, it was time for the main event.

It was a match which would involve Gideon's ultimate king of duels, number one on the Kingdom of Altar's duel rankings: Over Gladiator, Figaro. His opponent was number two on the Huang He Empire's duel rankings: Master Jiangshi, Xunyu.

The curtains were about to rise for the Clash of the Superiors.

◇

The Kingdom of Altar had four Masters with Superior Embryos.

I'd seen them battle — no, completely annihilate — the PK clans surrounding the capital, so I was more than aware that their power was stupidly immense.

According to Marie, low-rank, high-rank, and Superior Embryos were all on completely different levels.

"To compare, low-rank are like dogs, high-rank are like tigers, and Superior-rank are like dragons," she said.

Naturally, this made for a difference so great, it left no room for hope for the lower creature. No normal players could match Superiors and their absolute power, so it was inevitable that they researched and gathered as much info on them as they could.

Therefore, because both dueling Masters were Superiors, most of these curious folks were focusing on their Superior Embryos.

There was so little info on the Kingdom of Altar's Superior Embryos that not even DIN knew much about them. Even the names of three of them were a complete mystery, while their abilities didn't even leave the realm of speculation.

The one Embryo that was known was High Priestess Tsukuyo Fuso's, but that certainly couldn't be said about the other three. Previously, Marie had suggested that the King of Destruction's Embryo was a battleship, but again, that was nothing but speculation. People merely assumed that based on the glimpses of a large shape lingering around the complete and utter destruction he left in his wake.

Due to this desperate lack of info, players were still eagerly searching for hints about their abilities. And, of course, a match involving Figaro was nothing short of a perfect opportunity.

"So that's what's been keeping you busy, huh?" I asked Marie.

"Yeah."

After the semi-event was done, there was a thirty minute interval until the main event began. It was used for maintenance of the stage and the barrier. Marie spent a lot of this time taking out various equipment from her inventory and setting it up. She was going to record the fight for her Journalist work.

Rook and Babi, seemingly tired from something they'd done in the afternoon, were spread out on their chairs and sleeping.

*Better wake them up when the match begins,* I thought.

Nemesis, as was standard with her, was emptying food she'd bought at one of the stands here.

After watching my party members, I began looking around the arena, when…

"…Huh?" I said.

"Hm?" she added.

Nemesis and I noticed something.

We saw a black shape disappear into the hallway below, and it was highly reminiscent of the black bear suit that my brother wore.

"What do you think?" asked Nemesis.

"Shu isn't the only one in this world to wear a suit, but it looked very similar to his."

However, assuming it *was* him, I could only wonder why he was there and not here in our box.

"I'll go check," I said and stood up.

"I'll come with you," said Nemesis.

After telling Marie that I'd be back before the event started, I went to search for my brother.

The arena's inner hallways were stony and had a design similar to the one used in real life sports stadiums.

Sure, there weren't any vending machines, but there were people selling light food and drinks. With the main event getting closer, many people were rushing to stock up on snacks or to answer mother nature's call, causing the hallways to be pretty crowded.

Though it didn't matter to the players — who logged out and did their business in reality — this world had flushable toilets. They were based on magic and were quite common in middle and upper class households.

Baths existed here, as well. However, they weren't too common in commoner residences, so most people opted for public bathhouses. I was even told that one of the twelve districts here in Gideon was known as the bath district.

*First a Colosseum, then bathhouses… this city is strangely similar to ancient Rome,* I thought.

"I don't see Brother Bear anywhere," said Nemesis.

"Strange, considering how much he stands out," I commented.

I didn't know for sure whether it had been him or not, but I had little doubt that I'd seen a bear suit…

"Hm? Doesn't this look suspicious to you?" she asked, pausing outside a corridor.

"It says 'Staff Only,' though," I said.

"We can just pretend that we got lost. I can even act out a good lost child."

"…Might I ask how?"

"Meow meow mew meow, meow meow mew meow."

"That's just the mewing kitten from that children's song!"

"I really don't like how it ends with the kitten still being lost."

*Well, it asked a crow and a sparrow for directions, so it's to be expected that it didn't find its way.*

Now, back to the matter at hand…

Nemesis and I entered the staff-only hallway. I expected to get confronted instantly, but it seemed that the arena staff were too busy preparing for the event in other places, leaving the hallway empty.

After going a bit further, I heard a familiar voice from behind the corner. Stealthily, I took a peek at the two speakers.

"We have two among the spectators. One's the guy from Caldina, and… Dryfe's King of Beasts, I think."

"I see. I'm sure getting some attention, aren't I?"

"Well, it's the first time you've been in an arena battle against another Superior. They're probably thinking that they can finally get info on you."

"I'm not really hiding it or anything, though."

"Yeah, it's just that your Embryo's effects are simple and not flashy at all."

"You might be right."

"Also… overall, the city's enthusiastic, but I'm smelling something really fishy. I saw some shady-looking kingdom people. They might be planning something, so you should be on your guard. I'm warning you because you're usually dense about stuff like this."

"All right… Am I really that dense, though?"

"You're a calm yet hot-blooded idiot, Figgy my boy."

"Really? I'm not sure if I agree."

"What do you do if you see a weird silhouette in the dungeon?"

"Launch a Crimson Dead Keeper from mid-range."

"What do you do if a PK group occupies an area?"

"Kill all the members, face the leader, and demand that they leave."

"What do you do if there's a horde of monsters and all you have is a club?"

"Charge at them."

"Yeah, you're hot-blooded."

"...You might be right."

Behind the corner, a black bear suit was talking to a golden lion suit.

"Why are you so stiff? What did you s—PFFT...?!" The sight made Nemesis burst into laughter, which attracted the two's attention.

"Ayy, haven't seen you fur... however long has passed since teatime," said the black bear. As expected, he was my brother.

"Well, if it isn't Ray and Nemesis," added the golden lion. "I see you made it to this city."

The golden lion talked to me in Figaro's voice. In fact, it *was* Figaro.

"Umm..."

*All right, Figaro's pretty weird, too,* I thought. *That makes three, so it's safe to conclude that suits are a sign of a weirdo.*

The four of us moved from the hallway to Figaro's waiting room.

"So, why are you in a lion suit?" I asked.

"I'm quite famous in this city," he said. "Walking around like normal can get pretty troublesome."

*Oh, so it's like the hat and sunglasses combo that celebrities use.*

"It's just a piece of joke equipment I bought at the bazaar, though," he added. "I wouldn't mind having a UBM special reward suit like Shu's, but MVPs only get what they really need."

True. My Miasmaflame Bracers and Grudge-soaked Greaves had been exactly what I'd needed.

"I've defeated many UBMs, and I've yet to get a single suit," he said and faced my brother. "How do you even get them, Shu?"

"Listen, Figgy boy, you wouldn't like it if all the UBM rewards you got except for one were suits, now, would you?" said Shu. "You can't equip more than one of them, after all."

*I'm really curious about that exception.* I thought. *What could he have a gotten that's not a suit? A portable signboard?*

"Unlike me, getting special reward equipment doesn't mean all that much to you," said Figaro. "The system probably thinks that it's best to just give you another suit."

"Damn you, Humpty... You're unbearable!" Shu complained.

"Are control AIs actually responsible for that?" Figaro asked.

"I care not!" snapped Shu.

*There's this and the thing with his first login... Is Shu actually hated by the control AIs?* I thought.

"I must say, you two sure get along well," said Nemesis. "Brother Bear already told us that you're friends, but still."

"Friends... well, yes we are," said Figaro in response. "You probably know this by now, but Shu and I are this country's Su—"

"'Super Splendid and Merry Suit Club' members!" Shu broke in. "There are only two people in it fur now."

*...Just you two? Also, it's pretty blatant that only Figaro got dragged into it.*

"U-Umm..." Figaro hesitantly spoke up. "Oh, speaking of special rewards, your bracers and boots seem like fine pieces of equipment."

"Oh, yes," I responded. "I've defeated two UBMs so far."

"Oho… Hmm… 'Miasmaflame Bracers, Gardranda' and 'Grudge-soaked Greaves, Gouz-Maise.' Oh, so you were the one who defeated the gang that everyone was talking about."

"Yes," I said.

In all honesty, I wished to have a word with him. If Figaro had done something about the Gouz-Maise Gang, they would've been defeated much earlier and there would've been far fewer victims.

However, I was aware that there was no use in saying it at this point. Figaro had probably had his own reasons for not going. Also, the idea of demanding that a person should do something simply because they were capable of doing it seemed pretty unreasonable.

"After all, you yourself are the type to attempt something regardless of whether you actually have the power to do it," said Nemesis.

*You might be right,* I thought.

The various things that had happened during that quest were now a part of me. Considering what could've been if someone else had gone instead of me was a mistake.

"Both of them have good skills… and your own feelings," said Figaro. "Make sure to treasure them."

"I will," I nodded. *But man, he just identified my equipment as if it's no big deal.*

"When identifying people's equipment, the information you get is often beary limited, but Figgy's Identification skill is almost maxed, so the details aren't hidden to him," said Shu. "Still, it doesn't work on stuff like special rewards with a concealment effect on them."

"Like this thing," said Figaro as he pointed at Shu's suit.

It dawned on me for the first time that my brother's suit, being Ancient Legendary, was a far bigger deal than I'd thought it was.

No one could really fault me for that, though. It looked like a mere piece of joke equipment. But now, I knew that it was a piece of joke equipment with ridiculously good stats.

"By the way, why were you in a staff-only hallway?" asked Shu.

I explained that I'd seen him from the box and had come to look for him.

"Why didn't you come to the box?" I asked. "You have a ticket, don't you?"

"Oh, I just had some beary unimportant business to attend to. Been walking around here and there."

"I see," I nodded. "Still, I'd like it if you got there before the match. I want to introduce you to my party."

"Yeah, I'll be there in a minute. Oh, right, I forgot to give this to you during our teatime." Shu dug through his inventory and took out something resembling ear cuffs.

"What's this?" I asked.

"Telepathy Cuffs," he answered. "It bears a power that allows you to telepathically talk to friends who also have this equipped."

"For real?" I took it from him and put it on my ear, filling up one of my accessory slots.

[Can you hear me?] Shu's voice rang out in my head.

I was used to telepathy with Nemesis, but the way I heard this was different.

[Yeah, I can,] I answered.

[Then the test went fine.]

*Damn fine, actually,* I thought.

From what I could see, his bear ears didn't have any Cuffs on them. *Well, obviously they wouldn't work unless he had them on his actual ears. He's probably wearing them inside the suit.*

“This item’s pretty useful,” I said.

“Beary useful, yes, but there’s a range limit. It should cover all of Gideon and its surroundings, though,” explained Shu. “I was actually planning on giving this to you when we split up in the capital.”

“I see. I’d say that now is the better time, though. If you’d given me this when I started, I feel like I would’ve relied on you more than I should’ve.”

“Nice to see such enthusiasm for self-reliance. Still, do call me when you’re sure you can’t handle something by yourself.”

“Yeah. Help me out when I really need it.”

“I will,” he said as he puffed out his chest. There was pride in that action, but his appearance made it seem somewhat humorous, as well.

“Oh, it’s almost time,” said Figaro.

I looked at the clock and, sure enough, the main event was a mere 15 minutes away. Figaro probably had some preparations to make, so it was time for us to leave.

“Figaro, do your best in the duel,” I said.

“We’re acquaintances at this point, so we’re cheering for you!” added Nemesis.

“Thank you,” he responded. “Oh, by the way, the reception should still be open, so you could go there and bet on me.”

Figaro used some skill or something to instantly switch from his lion suit to the equipment he’d worn when I’d met him in the Tomb Labyrinth. Then, he put on a gentle, yet strong, smile.

“I’ll win, so you will surely make a profit.”

He said that as if it were already a fact.

I felt as though those words carried the pride of an unmatched king and the weight of the entire history that led him to becoming the duel city's strongest.

"All right," I said.

*If he says it with such confidence, I have no reason to not do it,* I thought.

"I'll come after talking to Figgy a bit more," my brother said. "Wait fur me in the box."

"Well, okay," I said.

With that, Nemesis and I left the waiting room.

"By the way, what is this 'Splendid and Merry Suit Club,' Shu?" Figaro asked.

"That was the only thing that came to mind at that point."

"Have you actually not told him who you are yet?"

"Leave that aside fur now," said Shu. "What's important right now is the upcoming event."

"True."

"You pretty much just said that you're certain you'll win, but the opponent isn't that easy, right? If you ask me, your chances are 50%, if not lower."

"That's about how I see it, too. I'm facing one of the Huang He Si Ling — the country's four strongest."

"And you're the Kingdom of Altar's toughest solo player — Figaro the Endless Chain."

"I probably shouldn't say this myself, but both sides sure are something," Figaro said. "I wouldn't mind watching this fight."

"Okay, now wait just a second here."

"Don't worry. Battles such as these, ones that set my life ablaze, are the very reason why I'm here in *Infinite Dendrogram*. That's why… I'll win with all that I am."

The arena's reception counter was split into two — one for battle entries and one for gambling. The window for entries was already closed for the day. Also, with most people already having placed their bets and the match starting in but a few minutes, the hallway was almost completely empty.

The board above the counters — which looked much like an electric one due to the magic it used — displayed the odds for the main event. It said "1.2x" next to Figaro and "5.6x" next to his opponent. The difference was considerably great, but that was a testament to just how much people trusted Figaro's power.

I spoke to the receptionist and went through the betting process.

"How much are you betting?" asked Nemesis.

"Well, it's just 1.2x, so I won't win all that much if I don't put lots of money into it," I said. "So let's go with this."

I bet 60,000,000 lir on Figaro.

"YOU IMBECILE!" howled Nemesis as she hit me with a dropkick and launched me across the hallway.

"Wh-What are you doing?!" I exclaimed.

"No, what are *you* doing?! Why are you throwing all the riches you've been blessed with into a gamble?!"

"Because I believe what Figaro told me."

"Be honest," she snarled.

"...I wanted to have an authentic gambling manga experience."

"All right, sit down right there. I'll thoroughly teach you about the importance of money!" Nemesis then commenced to scold me right in front of the reception...

"Too bAd, guy. All of that's going down the dRain."

I heard a strange mutter and felt someone grab my shoulder. I gasped and hastily turned around, but I didn't see anyone before me.

Actually, I did, but the person was standing ten meters ahead. It was impossible to grab anyone's shoulder from such a distance, and indeed, nothing was touching mine anymore.

For a moment, I thought that I only imagined someone touching my shoulder because I heard the voice, but concluded that it couldn't be true, for the sensation was still there.

The touch was colder than ice, making me feel as though it had grabbed not just my shoulder, but my very heart under my ribcage.

"So Figaro's just 1.2x, eH?" the creature spoke. "I know I'm the 'away' fighter hEre and all, but damn, thEy're seriously underestimaTing me."

Even when filtered through *Infinite Dendrogram's* excellent translation function, the words still came with a strange intonation.

The creature walked while releasing an abnormal aura. As it approached, the people that were still in the hallway backed away or outright ran for it.

The receptionist lady, too, fell out of her chair and sank to the floor, looking like she was about to cry. No one could really fault her.

I had no idea what made the creature seem so unamused, so full of ire, but it was emitting immense amounts of bloodlust all around it.

I silently watched the creature. At the core, we humans were nothing but animals, and my base instincts were warning me that I was facing death itself. However, I kept looking at it regardless. And as I did, I realized that the creature's very form was as abnormal as its aura.

Also, it *was* more than ten meters away from me. The reason why I'd thought it was closer was its unnatural height, which seemed to surpass four meters.

Though the hallway had been built with tall Demi-Humans in mind, it was still just barely large enough for it.

The creature was wearing a hat with a talisman hanging at the front, making it reminiscent of jiangshi from Chinese movies. Its body was covered in loose clothing that seemed too big for it, only giving slight peeks of its limbs. However, the very fact that those limbs *could* peek from under those two meter-long sleeves was more than daunting.

Its legs and arms were ridiculously long. The nails were metallic, sharp, and intimidating enough to make me absolutely certain that they had been used to kill thousands.

Naturally, the creature was frightening.

"Gh...!" Becoming aware of my fear made my legs shiver.

The Demi-Dragon Worm, Gardranda, Gouz-Maise... not a single one of the mighty creatures I'd faced had ever made me lose my fighting spirit, but the thing before me almost made it shatter. My instincts were telling me that this tall creature was on an entirely different level than anything I'd fought and that my only real option was to run away.

However, before I could do that, I noticed that it was holding a woman as if she was piece of baggage.

"Ah!"

The pained expression on her face rendered me incapable of ignoring them and running away.

"Nemesis!" I shouted.

"Got it!" she replied and instantly merged with me, taking her greatsword form.

Feeling my partner's palpitations in my right hand instantly revived my will to fight.

"WhAt? You wanNa go?" the creature responded as I pointed my greatsword at it.

The creature raised its right hand in a bored manner while still holding the girl in its left.

The motion was followed by an unamused sigh, after which the right hand bent in a bizarre manner, taking a sickle-like shape.

At the same time, the bloodlust it was releasing into the surroundings was suddenly focused on me, which was a sign of an attack.

"Coun—"

"Too slOw."

I momentarily envisioned Nemesis breaking and my head soaring through the air.

"STOOOOP! PAWS THIS!" a voice shouted.

However, that future didn't come. "HuH?" The creature's bloodlust disappeared as if it had never been there. No — it didn't disappear — it was simply directed at someone else instead. That someone was the one who'd shouted and intervened.

"The hell are yOu?" the creature asked.

"Just a bear passing by!" answered the new target of its hostility — my brother, Shu.

No longer being the creature's target made me heave a sigh of relief. It was all but certain that, if Shu hadn't come, I would've been given my second death penalty.

"A beaR? Hmm, you seem pRetty tough," said the creature.

"Oh no, I'm just someone who's beary enthusiastic about suits."

"HahAh, now ain't that somEthing."

Less than a moment after the creature laughed, a plosive sound, a metallic scraping sound, a crashing sound, and a crushing sound reached my ears, all at the same time. It was bewildering beyond words. I'd heard the sounds, but I couldn't see what had caused them.

Before I'd realized it, Shu's right arm was positioned in a way that made it seem like it had deflected something, while the creature's right hand was aimed at him. One of the nearby pillars had been shattered, and my brother's suit's right arm had released white smoke — a sign of recent friction.

I hadn't seen a thing, but it was obvious that they'd just gone through an exchange of blows. It had simply been too fast for me to see with my naked eye.

Remembering what Marie had told me, I realized that I'd just born witness to supernatural movements caused by ridiculously broken stats — a fight that had happened beyond the sound barrier.

"Kh, he, hahAhah! You sure are somEthing, bear! Is it you, tHen? Are yoU Figaro?" the jiangshi asked.

"Bearily not!" my brother declared.

"Yeah, fiGured! You're not whAt I saw on the phOto, and I doubt the kingdom's king of dUels would waLk around looking so wEird!"

*...He did, though,* I thought.

"SeriouSly, you're somEthing! You deflected my attacks dEspite being way slOwer than me!"

*He did?*

"Altar's dying and all, so I unDerestimated it, but it loOks like coming here wAs worth it, after all! Even if the Figaro guY's no good, I think it'd be fuN to fight you, iNstead!"

"Yeah. I won't say no to a brawl with you if Figaro loses," said Shu. "But that won't be happening. I mean, he's gonna beat you."

"Heh, hehEheheHe! Guy must bE a big deaL to have *you* beliEve in him so much! Guess I now hAve two maiN dishes in sTore for me!" With those words as its last, the lanky creature passed us by and went further into the hallway.

"...Wait!" I shouted before it left.

"HuUh?" the creature turned to me and tilted its head, clearly bothered out of its mind. The murderous intent aimed at me filled me with fear again, but I couldn't back down.

"What do you intend to do with her?" I asked.

At this point, I was more than aware that I had no chance against this creature. But I couldn't turn a blind eye to what was happening. It would've left a bad taste in my mouth.

"'Her'? Oh, you meAn this?" said the creature and put the woman it was holding on the ground.

She groaned in pain.

"She's witH me. The waY we got here wAs a bit rough, so she becAme a bit nauseOus and groggy," said the creature and heaved a heavy sigh.

"Eh?" I asked in confusion.

*They're together? Seriously?* I thought. *Oh.... now that I look at her, she seems a bit pale and her expression isn't too good, but there's not a single injury on her.*

"HmM? Wait, did yoU actually staNd up to me bEcause you thought I was a kidNapper or something?" the creature demanded.

"...Sorry."

*Seriously, I apologize. I jumped to conclusions.*

I probably just hadn't been rational in the face of all that pressure, but that didn't change the fact that it would've been a really stupid death if Shu hadn't intervened.

*Damn, is this embarrassing.*

"Kh, heH, khaHahahahAhahahah!" My response made the creature burst out laughing. "You're quite somEthing, too, aren't yOu? You actuAlly tried to fight me whEn I was releasing bloodlust all aroUnd me! First thE bear, now you — therE sure are a lot of fUnny guys among this cOuntry's Masters!" it said and placed its long, metallic claws on my head.

Before I could even see it move, it brought its talisman-hidden face to my ear…

"I like you, sweetcheeks. Let's play together sometime."

…and said that with a voice that wasn't filtered by the talisman's magic.

*…Eh? Wait, that voice is…*

"HahahAh! See ya laTer!" said the creature before turning around and dragging the woman on the floor to the other end of the hallway.

As it distanced itself from us, I could still hear it say, "Hey, ambasSador, wake up alreAdy. You have woRk to do."

To that, the woman groaned and weakly said, "Please, no more supersonic air travel…"

After they left, the mood around us instantly cooled down.

"Yo, that was damn close, wasn't it?" said Shu.

"…Thanks, bro." I probably would've died if he hadn't helped me out. The creature had had both the power and the killing intent to do it.

"It's pretty cool to be able to brandish your sword against a thing like *that*, but you should bear in mind to use your courage where it actually counts," he added. "It's too early for you to be battling Superiors."

"Superiors… So that's…"

"Yeah, that's Figaro's opponent. One of the four greatest that the land of hermits has to offer — a part of the Huang He Si Ling."

*Xunyu the Yinglong.* I shivered.

"We're back," I said.

"Pawrdon the intrusion," my brother added.

By the time Nemesis, Shu, and I returned to the box, Marie had finished setting up her equipment. Rook and Babi were awake, and they all stared at my brother, visibly confused.

*Well, the sudden appearance of an unfamiliar guy in a bear suit makes for a very strange scenario,* I thought. *Wait… Is it just me, or is Marie more shocked than confused?*

"Umm… R-Ray? Wh-Who is this… bear… man…?" she asked with a stiff expression on her face.

*I guess the suit's freaking her out.*

"This is my brother," I answered. "We happened to be in the same box."

"Well, that's quite an interesting coincidence," commented Rook. "Oh? What's wrong, Marie?"

"I-It's not… It's nothing, really."

Though she said that, it certainly didn't seem like nothing. Her facial expression was visibly constrained. Also, she was muttering something along the lines of "They're so, so alike… It's a suit, not fur, but the texture is the same… The voice is similar, too… And it's a bear…"

"Marie," I spoke up. "You're…"

"Eh?!" she exclaimed. "I-I'm what?"

The agitation in her voice made me absolutely certain that Marie was…

"You're afraid of bears, aren't you?" I asked.

For a moment, my question left her completely dumbfounded. Then, she nodded in a slightly exaggerated manner.

"Y-Y-Y-Y-Yes! Th-That's exactly it! I'm just not good with bears! Yes, it's definitely not that I'm afraid of the Kin— I-I mean, your brother!"

For some reason, she wasn't nearly as articulate as usual.

*I guess bears scare her more than I thought.*

"I guess I shouldn't look like this, then," said Shu. "Bear with me for a second." Suddenly, the bear disappeared and — for some reason — was replaced by a bipedal whale.

*But then, it's a question whether a bipedal whale is actually a whale,* I thought.

"If you can't handle bears, then perhaps this is fine? Whale?" asked Shu.

"Did you just replace 'well' with 'whale'? Holy crap, what a stretch!" I said.

"Whale, you got any better whale puns for me, wise guy?!"

"No, I don't!"

*Seriously, I don't recall ever seeing a whale character that emphasizes his whaleness with whale puns,* I thought.

"U-Umm," Marie spoke up. "It's fine. I've calmed down. You can return to being a bear."

"Really? Very whale, then," said my brother before getting engulfed in light and becoming a bear again.

*Man, now that I have something to compare it to, his bear appearance seems so calming.* I thought. *Really, there's a certain sense of security about it.*

Of course, there was the big question of whether it was really a good idea to feel safe around a guy in his late twenties wearing a bear suit and talking with bear puns, but I felt it would be best to leave that for later.

"All right," I said. "Let me introduce you again. The person inside this suit is my big brother."

"Bearliest of greetings to you all. I'm Ray's brother IRL, Shu."

*What kind of greetings are "bearly," anyway?* I thought. *Oh, whatever.*

"And these are my party members..."

"I'm Rook, and this is my Embryo, Babi."

"Heyyy, I'm Babi!"

"I-I'm Marie Adler. Pleased to meet you."

"Marie Adler?" Shu repeated her name and tilted his head to the side.

That movement made Marie shake a bit.

*Are you sure you're not afraid of the bear suit?* I thought.

"Is your job 'Journalist'?" my brother asked.

"Y-Yes it is," she answered.

*How did he get her job right just by hearing her name? Is it because of all the equipment here?*

"I've read that manga, too," he said.

"Which manga?" I asked.

"*Into The Shadow.* 'Marie Adler' is the name of its protagonist, and she works as a journalist."

"I see," I said. "You like that manga, Marie?"

"Yes, I do," she admitted. "It's the reason why I chose this name and job."

Well, it certainly wasn't uncommon for MMO players to take the names and appearances of characters they liked.

"Is it also the reason for the way you talk?" asked Shu.

"Of course. It's just roleplay," she answered. "None of my peers talk this casually when they're over twenty."

*She's sure dedicated,* I thought. Also, this was the first time I'd learned that she was older than me.

"*Into The Shadow,* was it?" I said. "Maybe I should read it, too."

"Just so you know, it was discontinued by its magazine," said my brother. "The first part of its story finished and its serialization stopped, just like that."

*Well, damn...*

"It was pretty popular, though," he added. "I liked it a lot, too, and I'd love it if it restarted sometime."

"Thank you. I appreciate that," said Marie. It seemed she was a big fan.

*I should really buy it when I get the chance,* I decided. *If they think it's a good read, I might enjoy it, too.*

"Ladies and gentlemen! The wait is over! Today's main event — The Clash of the Superiors — is about to begin!" a voice called, announcing the start of the match. It rang out throughout the arena, accompanied by music.

I'd been told that, just like the toilets in this world, announcements were done by magic.

"Oh, the fight's about to begin," said Shu. "Best get mentally prepared fur it."

"True," agreed Marie. "I have to record it, too."

We all sat down and began preparing for the event.

*Man, now that I think about it, an event called the "Clash of the Superiors" is exactly what it says on the tin,* I thought. Figaro and Xunyu — two Superiors bearing Superior Jobs — were about to clash.

This would likely be a battle unlike any I'd seen so far. After all, the ones fighting were some of the most high-end, top class beings in *Infinite Dendrogram*.

"First, the eastern gate! The entrance of our venerable guest!" the announcer called.

A spotlight focused on one of the entrances.

"A Superior hailing from the land of Huang He! The great martial artist bearing the nickname of 'Yinglong'! The beast from the east! The Master Jiangshi! XUN… YUUUUUUUUUU!"

There was a boom, a crescendo of music, and even a release of smoke. A moment later, the creature broke the thick veil and showed itself.

Its frame surpassed four meters in length, causing many spectators to scream from shock. A single glance at its abnormally long limbs was enough to send chills down the spine.

To the eyes of those living in this country, which had a Western setting, even the creature's clothes seemed like they belonged in the realm of madness.

Spreading fear and shock with every step, the Master Jiangshi, Xunyu, entered the stage. The creature raised its arms and released a war cry, which was followed by explosions on both sides of the entrance.

That performance caused the audience to either cheer or scream.

"They really know how entertainment works," I said.

"Gideon is beary much a showbiz city," Shu explained. "Also, Masters gave the tians advice on how to set up these presentations."

Just as I thought. It looked exactly like something from a fighting event on TV.

However, I felt that the announcers on TV were better. The one in this arena didn't seem too used to it.

"By the way, Xunyu's number two in Huang He's duel rankings," Shu added. "You get used to this if you duel that much."

*Number two? So there's someone else at the top, huh?*

"By the way, what kind of job is 'Master Jiangshi,' anyway?" asked Rook.

"Huang He has a job called 'Daoshi,' and I hear it's a Superior Job from that grouping," answered Marie. "Its counterpart in this part of the world would be… Mage, surely."

"The main characteristic of Daoshi is that they produce and use certain consumable items — talismans known as 'Fu,'" added Shu. "Their main advantage is that they allow quick and consecutive spellcasting, while the demerit is the production cost."

"And don't forget that greater skills require you to spend time positioning the Fus," added Marie.

Shu nodded. "I've also heard that, while being in the daoshi grouping, Master Jiangshi is a direct upgrade to the job known as 'Jiangshi,' which is focused on endurance. With that in mind, it's safe to expect that Xunyu's fighting style is not purely magical, but involves melee, as well."

"Oh, that's true. After all, the daoshi grouping is the type that unlocks different Superior Jobs depending on which jobs you combine it with. In fact, it might be more correct to consider Master Jiangshi to be a Superior Job from the jiangshi grouping."

It seemed we had *two* people doing the explaining. And with Rook being the one listening to them, I basically became part of the background. Not that I minded it.

"Wait, the job is also called 'Shi Jie Xian,' right?" I asked. "That doesn't really mean 'jiangshi,' does it? So why do we read it as 'Master Jiangshi'?"

"Well, not every job translates as neatly as 'King of Destruction,' fur example," answered Shu.

"Superior Job names can be really something," added Marie. "Imagine meeting the 'Death Shadow.'"

*I guess their uniqueness comes with unique naming senses,* I thought.

"Then how does this player actually fight?" asked Rook.

I was curious about that, as well. I'd had a confrontation with Xunyu at the reception and seen the jiangshi fight Shu, but I hadn't been able to understand a bit of what was going on back there.

"The nickname 'Yinglong' might make you think otherwise, but that's not the name of Xunyu's Embryo," said Marie. "Also, Xunyu sometimes gets called the 'Landmine' or 'Divine Speed,' too."

Those two nicknames gave off completely different impressions. The former was about waiting in place, while the latter was about moving around a lot. Naturally, it made me curious about which one of these applied to this mysterious fighter.

"And in the western gate! We have the pride of Gideon! The unwavering champion of our city!" the announcer called.

The music changed and the spotlight was redirected to the gate at the opposite side.

"The king! The lone explorer! The one bearing the nickname 'Endless Chain' and the title of 'Over Gladiator'! The strongest man of all! FIIIIIIGAAAAAROOOOOOOOOOOOO!"

As introduced, the one that walked out of the western gate was none other than Figaro. While he had a gentle smile on his face, his eyes seemed to emit immeasurable pressure, and they didn't give away a single hint about what was going on in his mind.

Naturally, he wasn't wearing the lion suit. Instead, he was clad in the same curious equipment as before.

Figaro's appearance made cheers ring out throughout the arena.

"FI-GA-RO! FI-GA-RO!" the audience chanted as he slowly made his way towards the stage. Just as I'd been told, he was extremely popular around these parts.

*Well, I can see why he needs to wear that suit,* I thought.

"All right! Let's prepare for the fight of the century!" the announcer called.

Now that the participants were both on the stage, they opened up a settings window. I'd seen one of those at the semi-event, too. The windows were used to configure the barrier. Like in the semi-event, both sides looked through the rules displayed and confirmed if they were okay with them before starting the match.

Most duels here in Gideon were 1v1 and didn't have many rules. All attacks and tactics were allowed. What *wasn't* allowed were accessories that prevented instant death damage — such as the Lifesaving Brooch and the Dragonscale Ward I was familiar with — and consumable healing items. Healing from equipment skills was perfectly fine, and I was still too much of a noob to see any reasons why they were treated differently.

"Figgy would've had a serious advantage if they were allowed to use accessories like that," said Shu.

"Eh? But the rules are the same for both fighters, so would it really make that much of a difference?" I asked.

"Trust me. With Figgy, it would."

*So Figaro has something that greatly benefits from those accessories?* I thought.

"Both duelists are done checking the rules! Now, let's activate the barrier and… oh?" The announcer was about to signal the start of the battle, but stopped when he saw Xunyu raise one of those long arms.

*Were the rules unsatisfactory or something?*

"One one, teSting. You people heAr me?" said Xunyu, the voice resounding throughout the arena.

"So yeah, I'm about to duEl this Figaro gUy, but let me juSt say something to make the fight mOre interesting."

Well, that definitely sounded intriguing. I readied myself for the words…

"I won't move a siNgle step until Figaro falls to his knEes."

Xunyu's words were something that no amount of readiness could've prepared me for.

For a moment, everyone in the arena was completely dumbfounded. It seemed as though every single member of the audience became of one mind, thinking nothing but *What did I just hear?*

"Did any of yoU even hear me? I'm saying that I won't move a siNgle step, *and* I'll make this Figaro gUy fall to his kneEs."

After another moment of silence, the spectators realized that Xunyu's words were a provocative insult towards Figaro — and the duel city of Gideon, which hailed him as their champion. Suddenly, the whole arena was drowned out in anger and booing.

However, it only made Xunyu laugh. "Great! Now I'm a pRoper bAdDie! Oh, the laUghs I'll have WheN I beat you in tHis situation!"

Instead of responding, Figaro just silently looked at his opponent. I couldn't tell whether his silence came from confidence or due to some other reason.

However, I was almost completely certain that the scenario Xunyu described wasn't impossible. At the very least, if I were in Figaro's position, I'd definitely get killed before the jiangshi moved even a single step. That exact situation had almost happened a few minutes ago. Still, I had a feeling that Xunyu's words weren't just a provocation.

"Those certainly are some abrasive words," said Nemesis. "Do you think there's any meaning to them?"

"If you're asking whether I think that was just a meaningless provocation or a meaningful preparation for something… it's definitely the latter," I answered.

Facing Xunyu once was enough for me to know just how murderous and relentless the jiangshi was. That certainly wasn't all, though. There was more to this Superior than met the eye.

From the incident at the reception and entrance and the words just now, I could easily tell that Xunyu was clever enough to calculate and manipulate people's impressions. The jiangshi's battle tactics and preparation covered even the very mood of the surroundings.

"We will now turn on the barrier!" said the announcer.

The booing towards Xunyu subsided and the barrier became active, setting the stage for the match.

"And so! Let the main event, The Clash of the Superiors… COMMENCE!"

A split-second later, a booming sound rang out as something golden flashed across the stage. It was merely a moment. However, it was a moment during which way too many things had happened.

At least, I assumed it to be so. After all, I could only see the results.

Before I knew it, Figaro was wielding two swords and had deployed four chains, three of which were already broken.

He was swinging his dual blades at an immense speed, using them to deflect "something." The "something" seemed to cover the whole stage at this point.

When it became spread out like that, I could finally see it with my eyes.

It was extremely long and moved at a speed so great, it was reduced to nothing but a blur. I probably couldn't have even known it was there if it weren't for its length. The very tip of the "something" was completely invisible to me. By following its long trails, however, I realized that it was connected to Xunyu's sleeves.

At first, I thought that the "something" were chains, like the ones Figaro used. It only took a moment to realize I was wrong. Xunyu's sleeves didn't hide any hands that could hold such things.

There was only one "something" attached to those sleeves — Xunyu's arms.

Reaching speeds my eyes couldn't follow, the arms reached for and attacked Figaro like a duo of serpentine dragons.

"It's too fast," I muttered.

"They put the wrong setting on the barrier," Nemesis spoke to me telepathically. "The time inside is slowed down, but their speed is so great that it means nothing."

She'd said exactly what I was thinking. I looked at my brother sitting next to me, and wondered if *he* could see it.

Suddenly, the last of Figaro's chains flew straight towards Xunyu. Its speed was immense, but before it could even reach its target, it was sliced into five pieces in less than a blink of an eye.

The chains that had almost killed me back in the Tomb Labyrinth were just too slow in comparison to Xunyu's arms.

"Supersonic, extension-based attacks... They're faster than..."

Those were probably Marie's words, but I wasn't certain.

A bit belatedly, I finally realized that the booming sound that had rung out at the beginning of the battle was an actual sonic boom. Also, I came to see that, despite the ludicrous speed, the jiangshi's arms were properly controlled.

While realizing just how well-deserved Xunyu's title of "Divine Speed" was, I couldn't help but notice that the extending arms were much like the snake-like dragons from Chinese myth.

It made me more than certain that, if our fight in the reception had continued, I'd have been killed before I could even use Counter Absorption. Even in the off chance scenario of my being successful, Xunyu would've probably killed me by moving one of those arms around the barrier and simply lopping my head off.

While I could make out the trails of the extended arms, their very ends — the hands — were completely invisible to me. The fact that this was their speed after they were *slowed down* by the barrier made chills go down my spine.

However, Figaro was impressive, as well. Though he was exposed to a barrage of those supersonic attacks, it didn't look like a single one of them had landed on him yet. He saw, dodged, and deflected them all.

Also, little by little, it became harder and harder for me to see his movements, too.

"A certain old manga had a term for how I'm feeling right now," I muttered. *I think it was called "Yamcha Vision,"* I thought.

Nemesis, Rook, and Babi seemed to be in the same state as me. But that didn't seem to be the case with Shu and Marie. From his demeanor and from the movements of her eyes, I could tell that they could see and follow Xunyu's arms.

"You two can actually see them?" I asked to confirm.

"To an extent," answered Shu. "I'm not an AGI build, so sometimes I can, sometimes I can't."

*High AGI allows you to see this stuff?* I thought.

From the battle at the reception and the fact that he was on the rankings, I was pretty certain by now that Shu's level was pretty high. However, it didn't make sense that Marie could see it, too.

"I can follow the movements because we Journalists have a passive skill that improves our sight," she answered my question before I could even ask it.

*I see. So there are non-battle jobs with such skills, huh?*

"This is barely visible at all to me," I said. It was my first exposure to a battle between two top players, and my first glimpse into the speeds they could reach. I wasn't even sure I could really say that, in fact, considering that they were slowed down by the barrier.

"We will now slow down the battle speed inside the barrier even further!" said the announcer, and — sure enough — the two fighters' movements lost a lot of speed.

*And yet, they're still faster than the semi-event fighters,* I thought.

"So they set the slowdown to max, huh?" said Shu. "Well, way too many spectators couldn't have seen what was going on if they didn't."

"Yeah. I'm one of them, to be honest," I said.

Now, I could somehow see the details of the battle. A golden right hand was going for Figaro's head from his left side. He evaded it by bending backwards.

The hand that passed him made a U-turn and attacked his head yet again. This time, Figaro deflected the attack with the sword in his right hand.

The battle that had been completely invisible was now sufficiently slowed for my inexperienced eyes, and yet it still made me feel like I was watching a video on fast-forward.

*Seriously, just how fast are these two fighting?*

"You can't even land a hit if you can't keep up with this speed, huh?" I asked.

"Well, you could try surprise attacks while they're not in battle-mode," said Marie. "That's impossible in duels, though."

Of course. Duels began when both sides agreed to a set of rules and were ready to fight. There was no room for surprise attacks. They were 1v1s where both sides fought with everything they had until the stronger one emerged victorious.

Figaro was the one sitting at the apex of Gideon, the city of duels. That meant that he was the greatest 1v1 fighter the kingdom had to offer. And yet, Xunyu was fast enough to force him onto the defensive.

I was about to assume that Master Jiangshi was a Superior Job focused on AGI, but then I remembered what Marie had said about it: *Its counterpart in this part of the world would be... Mage, surely.*

"Wait, magic!" I burst out. "Xunyu still isn't going all out!"

A moment later, the stage was overwhelmed by thunderous roars and a crimson light that dominated the entire area behind the barrier.

I looked and saw that the extended arms were releasing countless crimson heat rays. They were boisterously dancing as they burned the air and scorched the stony floor of the stage.

The origin of the heat rays were the *pieces of paper* covering Xunyu's arms whole.

"Are those...?"

"Daoshi's Fu," said Shu.

"Xunyu covered the arms in Fu enchanted with offensive magic and is now using them to cover the stage in heat rays," explained Marie.

"That's nuts," I muttered.

Naturally, with there being so many heat rays, some of them hit Xunyu's long arms. But the arms seemed to be extremely tough, not taking any damage whatsoever. The rays did make some of the Fus get detached and slowly drop down to the stage, but the arms continued their relentless attack.

*Just how tough are they?* I wondered.

"If they weren't tough, our slit-eyed friend would've severed them by now," said Nemesis.

Arms that were unaffected by heat rays and possessed a hardness that even Figaro had trouble breaking through. From the fact that Xunyu could fight at supersonic speeds while being the Master Jiangshi, a primarily magic-oriented job, I could only assume that...

"...those arms are Xunyu's Superior Embryo," I said.

Prosthetic limbs that emitted a golden gleam and attacked the opponents at speeds that broke the sound barrier. This Embryo's characteristic abilities could be described as "strong arms that reach far at great velocity." Though that sounded basic, seeing it in action in the display before me awed and scared me.

Strength, speed, range — it had the whole package. It was simple, but that was exactly what made it nigh impossible to counter.

"If there's any power that *can* counter it, though…"

"…it must be something simple, as well," Nemesis finished for me.

As Nemesis' words entered my ears, something else entered my vision.

Crimson light and countless freed Fus danced all around as Figaro broke through the hell of supersonic destruction and came out of it completely unscathed.

He didn't do anything special. Figaro simply dodged, deflected, and dashed.

Avoiding the heat rays and parrying the arms, he gradually closed the distance between him and his opponent.

The battle itself was simple, but the level at which it was happening made it seem beyond abnormal.

"Amazing," I said, lacking any better words to describe the battle I was seeing.

At first, I thought that Figaro was completely on the defensive, but I was wrong. He was closing in on Xunyu, growing faster with every passing moment, and dodging every single one of the jiangshi's attacks.

It was only a matter of time until Xunyu would be within his attack range. That made it pretty obvious that the odds were right, and that Figaro was going to win.

However, I suddenly noticed something. Not about the two fighters, but about two of the people sitting next to me — Shu and Marie.

The aura about them was different.

It wasn't the first time I'd been exposed to such an aura. I'd felt it when I'd fought the Demi-Dragon Worm, gotten killed by the Superior Killer, and faced Gardranda and Gouz-Maise. Looking at them made me feel as tense as I'd been during those deathly encounters.

Soon, I realized that both their gazes were directed at the same thing.

It wasn't anything on the stage, but one of the monitors installed in our box — specifically, the one showing a close-up of Xunyu's face.

The visage was still hidden by a jiangshi-like talisman. However, there was an instant in which it was raised by the battle winds, revealing an indomitable grin.

"Call — Baolei!"

Right after the jiangshi spoke that word — meaning "raging lightning" — there was a new development. The back of Xunyu's hand suddenly burst open, revealing a Jewel used to store monsters. From it came a creature that seemed to be wrought of lightning.

Released at nearly point-blank distance from Figaro, it instantly bared its electric fangs at him.

"An elemental," said Shu. "A rare kind, too."

"Seems like a type of Lightning Elemental that's focused on speed and offensive ability," added Marie. "It's just a fancy distraction, though."

Before I could even ask what she meant by that, Figaro swung the swords in his hands in the shape of a cross and sliced the monster apart.

It happened in but an instant. Just as Marie said, the elemental ended being nothing but a momentary distraction. However, that moment was enough for Xunyu to safely retract one of those golden arms.

It returned to its original size, and between its index and middle fingers, there was a single Fu. It was detailed and elaborate, making it reminiscent of a painting, but rather than finding it beautiful, I felt mostly fear.

Then, the hundreds... no, thousands... of Fus that had fallen on the stage during the fight began emitting a crimson light.

*The main characteristic of Daoshi is that they produce and use certain consumable items — talismans known as "Fu,"* I thought, remembering what Shu and Marie had said. *And don't forget that greater skills require you to spend time positioning the Fus.*

"Zhenhuo Zhendeng — Baolongba!" Xunyu called.

Those words — meaning "True Flame True Light, Explosive Dragon Dominance" — caused most of the duel field to be engulfed in a pillar of fire.

The scene made me remember one of the jiangshi's other nicknames: "Landmine."

The pillar of fire had no trouble breaking through the upper part of the barrier separating the fighters and the spectators.

In fact, it went high enough to make it seem as though it would scorch the very heavens themselves. Though not great enough to cause damage, the pillar's heat reached us and just about everyone else in the audience, causing many to scream in fear.

The panic might've made it seem otherwise, but no harm came to any of them. If anyone was hurt by it, it would be the two fighters on the stage.

But the pillar didn't extend to its caster, Xunyu. Before I'd even realized it, the jiangshi's right arm was retracted back to its original length, just like the left one, sparing it from the flame.

The same couldn't be said for Figaro. Dealing with the elemental had rendered him unable to evade the attack, and it obviously wasn't something that could be deflected with mere swords.

Just about everyone in the audience held their breaths as the pillar of fire faded and allowed them to see what was happening on the burning stage.

What we saw was Figaro, completely surrounded by a searing hot heat haze and a spherical barrier that shielded him from all harm.

"He survived it completely unharmed?!" Marie voiced her shock, and I couldn't agree more.

"Is that one of Figaro's Embryo's skills?" I asked. "Or is it an Over Gladiator ability?"

"Neither," answered Shu. "It's an item skill. That longcoat he's wearing is a special reward. Its active skill allows him to prevent all and any outside influence for a short time."

*So it's a special reward skill. Like the ones on my Miasmaflame Bracers and Grudge-Soaked Greaves,* I thought.

"Oh, but it has a cooldown of 10 minutes," Shu added. "Meaning that the attack cost him his ultimate means of defense."

"I think that Xunyu is also out of viable moves, though," Marie said. "The elemental can't fight anymore, and I don't believe it's easy to recast a spell that costs so many Fus, which means that the same trick can't be repeated, and that..."

"...Figaro will win!" I cried with certainty.

"All that's left is to figure out the effects of the last skill that Xunyu used," Rook said.

Nemesis and I, and even Babi, didn't understand what he was talking about.

Shu — clearly noticing something — was looking at Xunyu. A bit belatedly, Marie joined him in that.

"What do you mean by 'last skill,' Rook?" asked Babi.

"Xunyu used a skill besides the one that created the flame pillar, no?" Rook asked.

"Well, I... Really?" I asked. I hadn't seen that happen.

"Figaro's defensive skill's about to end," said Shu, and sure enough, the shield protecting Figaro from outside influence disappeared.

I fully expected the duelists to start clashing at supersonic speeds again, but what actually happened was the complete opposite of that.

Neither Xunyu — the one used the fearsome skill — nor Figaro — the one who negated it — were moving a muscle.

Naturally, that was strange, for it was clearly time for the former to get into a proper stance and for the latter to charge. Despite it all, however, Xunyu was still grinning.

"'Arms and Legs Reach for the Horizon — Tenaga Ashinaga,'" Rook broke the silence.

"Rook?" I asked.

"That's what Xunyu said right after creating those flames," he said.

*I didn't hear anything like that,* I thought. The soundscape had been dominated by the fiery roaring, and Xunyu didn't have a mic or anything of the sort.

"How do you know that?" I asked.

"I saw his lips move," he answered. "The mouth movement for proper nouns here is the same as it is in reality."

*He was lip reading? When did he get this skill? Or wait, is it like Marie's drawing? Did he bring it over from reality? More importantly, is "Tenaga Ashinaga" the name of Xunyu's Superior Embryo?*

The name referred to a certain type of yokai from Japanese myth — one that would be a perfect fit for the jiangshi's abnormal frame.

A skill bearing such a name could only mean that...

"...Xunyu used the Embryo's ultimate skill — the one named after the Embryo itself!" I cried.

Suddenly, the jiangshi raised the right leg, which was hidden by cloth. The one which hadn't moved an inch since the battle had started.

Just like the arms, the leg was a golden, prosthetic limb — a Superior Embryo.

Its toes were as sharp as the fingers on the arms, and there was something between them. Unlike the Fu from before, its shape was indistinct.

The same could be said for its color. It looked white, pink, and red at the same time, which — combined with its apparent softness — made it look much like *a human organ.*

"I missEd your heaRt," said Xunyu. "This iS a damn luNg."

A moment later, blood splattered from Figaro's mouth as he dropped to his knees.

*Paladin, Ray Starling*

"Arms, Guardian, Chariot, Castle, Territory. Those are the five base categories in Embryo evolution. Which, do you think, is the most common?" asked Shu.

It had happened on my first night in *Infinite Dendrogram* — specifically, at the welcoming party. I'd forgotten most of what we'd talked about after he'd told me about the war, but this part had stuck with me.

"Arms, I think?" I answered his question, not having much basis for it.

Nemesis was both a Maiden and an Arms type, while my brother's Baldr was a gatling gun. I didn't know any Masters besides myself and him, so my answer was just a guess based entirely on the fact that both our Embryos were Arms.

"That's right," Shu nodded. "Arms is the most common category in *Infinite Dendrogram.*"

And my guess ended up being correct.

"It's also the most varied one," he added.

"What do you mean?"

"The Arms category covers all sorts of Embryos. It's not just weaponry like your greatsword or my gun — there are utensils like pots or lamps, and even artificial eyes and limbs that replace parts of the body."

"So there's lots of strangeness in this category, huh?" I asked.

"Yeah, there certainly is." He momentarily turned silent, then seemed to remember something. "Still, I don't think that any Arms is stranger than *his*."

Back then, I'd had no means of knowing what he was referring to.

Gideon's central arena was shrouded in silence.

Not a single member of the audience seemed to understand what had happened.

The only people who did were probably the ones on the stage, Figaro and Xunyu.

"So this is the result of all of Xunyu's groundwork," Shu said.

No — my brother seemed to understand it, too.

"First, there was the 'I won't move a single step' declaration," he said. "It was actually meant only to make it not seem weird that Xunyu wasn't using the legs."

One of those legs was now grasping one of Figaro's lungs.

"Then, there was the long-ranged barrage of supersonic attacks. It was meant to make it seem like the declaration was based entirely on confidence, nothing else. Figgy probably knew that it was just a bluff, though."

However, he still hadn't been able to avoid it.

"The Fu magic attacks were just used to position the Fus needed for the great spell that followed. That 'Baolei' elemental was just a momentary distraction. As for the great spell itself..."

The skill that had used the hundreds of Fus littered all over the stage and created a pillar of fire strong enough to break the barrier.

"'Zhenhuo Zhendeng Baolongba,' was it?" Shu continued. "From its power, it's pretty clear that it's among the strongest Master Jiangshi skills — probably the ultimate one. However, Xunyu used it to do nothing more but keep Figaro in place."

"What do you mean?" I asked.

"The spell had both immense power and range. It would've damaged Figgy a lot, but he couldn't escape to safety due to the presence of Xunyu's arms. The rules prevent them from using accessories that negate instadeath damage, and that's why he had to use an omni-directional defensive skill."

*So it would've been over for him if he hadn't used the special reward's skill,* I thought.

"However, that was exactly what Xunyu wanted him to do," said Shu.

"What?" I asked.

"Most powerful omni-directional defensive skills prevent the users from moving or using any other skills. That leaves them stiff and open to attacks, and Xunyu simply took advantage of that... just like planned."

*So the jiangshi was waiting for that moment from before the fight even began... I can see where the nickname "Landmine" comes from.*

"But wait," interjected Marie. "If the special reward's skill's effects are like you described, no attacks should've reached him, right?"

I could see her point. After all, it was supposedly a barrier that protected from every direction.

"Yeah," Shu replied to Marie. "Attacks from *the outside*, at least."

Apparently, that was enough for Marie to understand everything.

"So you've already figured what that ultimate skill does?" Rook asked my brother.

"Yeah," nodded Shu. "You seem to have guessed, too, Rook."

"It's based on circumstantial evidence, though," Rook said.

Apparently, I was the only player here who was still lost about this.

"Brother Bear, might you tell us what kind of attack could've given Figaro such a grave injury?" asked Nemesis, clearly as confused as I was.

"It's pretty simple when you observe," said Shu. "Look. Figgy lost an organ and is hurt enough to spit blood, but there's not a single scratch on his skin."

Though covered in blood that had escaped his mouth, Figaro's equipment was completely intact, too.

An attack that gouged out a lung would normally leave a hole in both apparel and the flesh.

"Also, an ultimate skill is the culmination of an Embryo's main trait," he added. "You can figure it out from here, right?"

"Oh, I see!" I cried.

Ultimate skills were the greatest show of an Embryo's dominant characteristic. It was safe to call them the crystallization of an Embryo's and its Master's power. Due to that, they were extremely varied, causing them to include oddities such as tornadoes of darkness and tsunamis of gold.

With that in mind, I had to figure out what the culmination of Xunyu's Embryo would be, an Embryo that had speed and range as its main traits.

Its velocity had already broken the sound barrier, so it might've been safe to assume that the ultimate skill approached or surpassed the speed of light. However, superluminal velocity was an insurmountable barrier for anything that had the least bit amount of mass, so there was a limit to how great the speed could grow. But if such limits meant nothing for the Embryo, the culmination of speed and range would be something that was found in science fiction.

"Warping," said Shu.

That was the only answer — a superluminal, super long-distance, ultradimensional movement ability.

"Xunyu warped the right leg directly into Figaro's body and tore out the lung," he explained.

Figaro's equipment had prevented all outside influence from every direction. However, it had been able to do nothing against Xunyu's ultimate skill. It was like a scenario in which a piece of paper had two points on it — A and B. Even if there was a circular barrier around A that prevented B from getting to it, one could simply bend the paper to make B touch A directly. Walls and barriers meant absolutely nothing.

"If that's how it is, wouldn't it have been more effective to place a Fu in the body and blow it up?" asked Rook. "Also, instead of taking just one, couldn't Xunyu have torn *all* the organs apart?"

*You have some freaky ideas, man,* I thought.

"The skill probably has limits that prevent such things," said Shu. "Maybe it can only warp the Superior Embryo itself? Or perhaps the time during which it's connected to the other side is very severe?"

"I see," nodded Rook.

One of the duelists on stage, Figaro, finally began to talk.

"A forced teleportation attack that goes straight *into* the body, eh? A true ultimate skill if I ever saw one." The words leaving his bloody mouth made it obvious that he, too, understood the nature of Xunyu's attack.

"I've been waitiNg for you to stop in plAce," said the jiangshi. "Though, hOnestly, it would've been better if you'd just leT my insult go to your hEad and chosen not to move. I've actUally fought some iDiots who lost like that! GheaHahAhah!" Xunyu's laugh echoed throughout the silent arena.

"It's normally a super long-distance skill, isn't it?" asked Figaro. "You sure went through a lot of trouble to make it viable in a duel."

"Well, tHat's just how I rOll." Just as Shu had said, Xunyu had been waiting for the right moment to use the ultimate skill.

However, I was pretty certain that the jiangshi had intended to kill Figaro with every move that'd come before it. The supersonic nail attacks, Fu magic, Baolei, Baolongba — each and every single one of those would've instantly killed most lesser creatures.

The ultimate skill was but a trump card Xunyu kept for anyone who was capable of withstanding it all. And its effects were obvious. Figaro — though still alive — was greatly hurt.

"Can he heal that injury?" asked Nemesis.

"This isn't just an external wound or a broken bone — he lost an entire organ," answered Marie. "That lowers a person's maximum HP, limits their movements, and continuously damages them… Not even magic would have an easy time healing that."

"I know that duels don't allow them, but would an Elixir work?" I asked.

"Elixirs don't do much about injury-based status effects. To fix organ loss quickly, you would need a healing skill from a Superior Job. However, if normal healing is your only option, fixing it would take a long while. You might as well get the death penalty. Mind you, they're fighting in the barrier, so that won't be necessary."

From Marie's words, it was safe to assume that Figaro wouldn't be healed for the duration of the battle.

"Wait. Why are they still not moving?" asked Rook, bringing that fact to my attention.

Figaro's lack of movement was likely caused by the injury, but I didn't see a reason for Xunyu to become immobile, as well.

"Is it a side-effect of the skill?" asked Nemesis.

"No," answered Shu. "Xunyu's just being cautious."

"But why?" I asked.

*Figaro is completely cornered and... Oh, I see,* I thought.

"Xunyu's being careful about the thing that Figaro has never yet shown in any of his many matches — his Superior Embryo," said Marie. "He's yet to use it in this duel, too."

Hearing those words, I nodded. Figaro still hadn't used his Embryo, and if he did, he'd probably have a chance at victory.

"But Figaro *is* using his Embryo," said Shu.

"Huh?" Nemesis, Marie, and I simultaneously expressed our confusion.

"He is? Since when?" I asked.

"Ever since the duel started," Shu answered. "Hell, he probably used it in all his other matches, too. Guy's not one to hold back all that much."

That was probably a fact that no one in the audience was aware of. Figaro's Superior Embryo's name and details were a complete mystery to everyone. And yet, he was *always* using it.

"So, is he wearing it?" I asked.

"That can't be," said Marie. "I'm constantly checking him with Identification, and I can assure you that everything he's wearing and wielding is an item."

That made sense. Identification skills had no effect on Embryos, after all. If there was something that couldn't be Identified, it would obviously be that, but Marie had said that there was no such item on him. Thus, it was safe to conclude that his Embryo wasn't a piece of equipment. But in that case...

"Then what *is* his Embry—"

Before I could finish my question, the audience became astir.

I hastily looked to the stage and noticed that something strange was happening with Figaro.

He was still on his knees, but his apparel was changing.

First, his coat was engulfed in light and vanished. Next was his light armor and the shirt underneath. Then disappeared the ten rings on all his fingers and even the hat that stayed on his head even as he fought at supersonic speed.

All that was left were the leg armor reminiscent of a hakama, his greaves, and the swords in each of his hands.

For a second, I thought that Xunyu was responsible for this, but the jiangshi seemed as puzzled as everyone else.

*Wait a second, isn't that the same light that covered him when he changed in his waiting room?* I asked myself.

"Instant Wear," said Marie. "It's a skill that does exactly what it says — allows instant switching of armor."

I remembered the skill I had, but hadn't used yet: Instant Equip. It allowed the user to instantly equip weaponry from the inventory, and I could only assume that Instant Wear worked the same way.

"But..." I said.

Figaro had used it to simply take the items off, instead of switching them for something else. Switching to better equipment would've made sense, but as things were, it looked like he'd only made it worse for himself.

As just about everyone in the arena became confused, Figaro stood up. With his upper clothing gone, his toned chest was completely exposed. His skin and pectoral muscles did little to hide the fact that he'd lost his lung. The area had become unnaturally dark due to all the internal bleeding.

"Was it *tHat* hard to bReathe?" Xunyu asked — not mockingly, but with genuine curiosity.

Instead of responding, however, Figaro merely grinned.

"GuesS this duel's over, tHen," Xunyu muttered before launching the supersonic arms again.

However, again, Figaro deflected it with one of the swords in his hands.

It was just like the start of a battle before Xunyu had used his ultimate skill. Yet again, Figaro was on the defensive.

"Hm...?" I murmured.

The sight made me puzzled. After all, it barely made any sense. The result of Xunyu's attacks simply *couldn't* be the same.

Figaro had lost a lung.

Sure enough, his movements were a bit duller, causing him to get a few scratches here and there.

But in what world did it make sense for a person who'd lost a lung to *just* become a bit slower? It needn't be said that it was a fatal injury. Though Masters were superhuman and could survive through it, it should've taken a *huge* toll on his mobility.

Thus, I could only question why the injury had such a light effect on Figaro.

"ShgHh!" Xunyu attacked with both arms at once while increasing their speed, causing them to become a blur, even with the barrier acting at its maximum.

"■■!" Figaro released an inhuman sound as I noticed that his expression changed.

He was now making the same berserker-like expression I'd seen him make in the crystal.

"Physical Berserk," said Marie. "That skill gives an immense bonus to physical stats while rendering the body uncontrollable and preventing the use of any other active skills. Is this really a good situation to use it?"

"He nullifies the uncontrollability with another passive skill," answered Shu. "The mad expression and the bloodlust might make you think otherwise, but he controls himself just fine. Also, he simply chose to focus on increasing his stats rather than using some tricks."

Indeed, Figaro was even faster than before.

"Not a baD face you're mAking, Figaro!" shouted Xunyu while launching those golden arms behind the Over Gladiator.

Figaro momentarily looked behind him, then dodged one of the arms and charged at the other one. He didn't deflect it this time — he actually hit it head-on.

As a result, both Figaro's sword *and* one of the Superior Embryo's golden nails shattered into many pieces.

As Xunyu became overcome with shock, Figaro used Instant Equip to take out another sword. What followed was another clash, and the result was the same as before.

No — this time, both of Xunyu's arms lost a metallic nail each.

"WhaT did you dO?"

I couldn't help but relate to Xunyu's confusion. It was very clear that the question wasn't directed at the results of the Physical Berserk skill.

What puzzled the jiangshi and me was the fact that, despite being weakened by the loss of a lung, Figaro had been able to damage Xunyu's Superior Embryo, which he'd only been able to dodge and deflect before.

I didn't know how strong the skill was, but I couldn't believe that a single power-up skill could turn the tides like this. Also, even before using the skill, he hadn't really seemed to be behaving like he was severely injured. Which was made even stranger by the fact that he'd been weakened due to removing most of his equipment.

*Was he really weakened, though?* I thought. "Hmm."

*Does he have a skill that strengthens him when he unequips his items? No, he would've done it at the start, then. Still, it should be something that relates to the act of equipping stuff and...*

"Is something wrong, Ray?" asked Nemesis.

"Hey, Nemesis," I said. "Remind me how many equipment slots there are in *Infinite Dendrogram*."

"Equipment slots? Well, there's headwear, upper and lower armor, innerwear... no, it doesn't count. Then there's the cloak, armwear, boots, five accessories, and weapons for each hand... That makes 13. No, special equipment like Silver makes it 14."

"What about Figaro?" I asked.

"Our slit-eyed friend has skills that give him more slots. He had accessories on every finger and can clearly equip six weapons at once. There might be more, but I'd assume it's somewhere around 25."

At this moment, however, he only had his lower armor, greaves, and a weapon in each hand, making for a total of 4.

"Bro," I said.

"Do you address me bearing questions?" he replied.

"What are the effects of the hakama and the greaves Figaro's wearing?"

"The hakama is called 'War Might Cloth (lower),' and it gives a bonus to STR, AGI, and DEX, while the greaves are a special reward called 'Unbound Sabatons, Unchain' and they give a large bonus to AGI and a resistance to movement limitations."

Equipment that strengthened him. A reduced amount of equipment. Increased fighting ability. An Embryo he'd been using from the start.

And the thing Shu and Figaro had been talking about in the hallway. When all of that was considered...

"...Oh, so that's how it is," I muttered. If I was wrong about this, him taking off his clothes would've been completely meaningless.

"Bro."

"I'm listening."

I voiced my guess. "Figaro's Embryo's trait is 'strengthening equipment worn inversely proportional to the number of items equipped,' right?"

My words made everyone except Shu look at me in surprise.

"Why do you think that?" he asked.

"Normally, you're stronger the more items you have equipped, so if someone becomes stronger *after* taking them off, I can only assume that it's a skill like that."

That said, the fact that he hadn't taken them off right at start was proof that it wasn't just a skill that made him stronger the less he wore. I assumed it was a skill that split a 100% total bonus among all the items he had equipped. When using 25 items, that bonus would be 4% on each, while equipping just 4 items would make it 25%.

He'd taken off the unnecessary equipment to make his power more focused.

"Is that all the proof you have?" asked Shu.

"No, there's more," I said. "Figaro goes through the Tomb Labyrinth solo, but that's not exactly doable, is it?"

"You're saying you don't think it's pawssible for *anyone* with Superior Embryos?" my brother asked.

"If it were, other Superiors would do it, too. But Figaro is the only one who's famed for being a solo explorer. That has to be because he has something others don't."

"Which is?"

"Utility and countermeasures."

"Hoh."

The equipment Figaro usually had on him was probably a utility-focused combination that strengthened his body, increased defense, gave resistances to status effects, and helped him with healing. However, no matter how strong Figaro was, such equipment made him nothing more but a jack of all trades, yet master of none.

It might work fine against normal monsters, but it was clear that it would be difficult for him to fight bosses that way. That went doubly for UBMs, like the ones I'd beaten, which often had highly specific, unique abilities.

When fighting Gardranda and Gouz-Maise, I'd miraculously emerged victorious because I'd had powers that fit the situation. Though I'd gotten into those fights by chance, I'd been equipped with the right countermeasures.

That was the keyword here — countermeasures.

This was merely an assumption, but I believed that Figaro fought and beat his enemies by adjusting and improving his equipment based on his opponent. For example, when facing an ice monster that was weak against fire, he'd use only a fire-based weapon and equipment that increased his frost resistance.

That was exactly what he had done to that player killer in Sauda Mountain Pass. He'd reduced the number of chains he used to strengthen the "resistance to movement limitations" effect on his greaves, allowing him to break free of the binding and emerge victorious.

And now, he'd concluded that defense and resistance to debuffs were useless against Xunyu, leading him to focus exclusively on equipment that increased his speed and damage.

He fought in full gear to safely see what kind of enemy he was dealing with, then switched to wearing only the equipment he really needed. That was Figaro's battle style.

"You're half right," said Shu.

*So there's more to this, huh?* I thought.

"Just so you know, when he's fully geared, all his equipment's starting numbers are multiplied by two."

"Multiplied by... *BY TWO?!*"

That meant that now, when he was wearing less than a fifth of his total equipment, that number ought to surpassed ten. Clearly, that was more than enough to cover for the loss of a lung.

*Wait... 'starting numbers?'* I thought.

"...Bro."

"What?"

"You said I was half right because...?"

"You know how you were talking about the total bonus?" Shu said and then went silent for a moment before continuing. "*It increases in proportion to battle time.*"

Cheers echoed throughout the arena. Figaro's slash had broken another one of Xunyu's metallic nails. This time, however, his sword didn't break.

"He becAme even stRonger!" panicked Xunyu.

If we were to assume that the equipment strengthening increased by 1% every second, the difference that would cause when in full gear would be negligible. But, as Figaro was demonstrating, the same couldn't be said for when he was using only a few items.

Figaro grew stronger with every passing second and with each exchange of blows. He had already surpassed Xunyu's supersonic speed and dealt enough damage to break Superior Embryos.

The constant growth in his power became all the more obvious now that I knew how it worked.

Strengthening proportional to battle time.

Strengthening inversely proportional to the number of equipped items.

Those two were the main traits of Figaro's Superior Embryo.

They were qualities that could only shine in a long battle. Thus, now that the battle had gone on for quite some time, Figaro was in top shape even after having lost one of his lungs.

A man who grew endlessly stronger the more he fought — Figaro the Endless Chain.

"That's nuts," was all I could really say about it.

Nemesis, sitting next to me as she'd read my mind, nodded in agreement.

*So that nickname wasn't actually referring to the chains, huh?* I thought.

From the fact that it also covered the true nature of Figaro's Superior Embryo, I could only assume that Shu, who'd known the truth about it, was the one who'd thought of the nickname and made it popular.

"Still..." I murmured.

There was something I found strange. Even though I'd had hints from my brother, I'd been able to figure out the nature of Figaro's Superior Embryo just by watching him fight once. And yet, all this time, it'd been considered to be a great mystery.

It didn't take too much thought to figure out why. Figaro — being exclusively a solo player — did all his explorations by himself. He was alone in his boss battles, and most of them happened in the Tomb Labyrinth. Obviously, no one ever saw him fight after removing his equipment.

As for duels... Well, the large audiences had never noticed his abilities because each and every single one of his opponents so far simply hadn't been strong enough to force him into focusing his gear.

Perhaps he *had* powered up by removing one or a few of his accessories, but he'd never had to take off so much of his equipment that the spectators would've found it weird. Today was the first time that had ever happened in a duel. Figaro had had to go all out because his opponent was the strongest he'd ever faced in a duel.

Xunyu *was* truly strong.

"Hah! You surE are somethiNg, Figaro!" shouted the jiangshi as his left arm was completely severed.

If that wasn't a show of just how strong Figaro had become, nothing was. Even with a critical injury, he surpassed Xunyu at just about every front.

The tables had turned.

Figaro evaded the nails with little effort as the jiangshi's legs distanced the body from him. Xunyu attacked even while backing away, but none of it seemed to work.

Though both were fighting at supersonic speeds, there was now a clear difference in velocity between them.

And, of course, that difference only kept growing.

"Damn, I mesSed up!" said Xunyu. "I shouLd've aimed for thE head, even if the riSk of you dodgiNg would've been biGger!"

Though cornered, Xunyu showed no signs of using the ultimate skill again. It probably had a cooldown or a limited number of uses.

Xunyu was strong and had certainly had a chance at victory. However, that chance had disappeared the moment the jiangshi had failed to grab hold of Figaro's heart.

"■■" Figaro voiced another inhuman sound as I noticed that he now held only one weapon instead of two.

It would probably be categorized as a broadsword. But it was definitely not *just* a sword.

It was hard for me to say what made it so different from the other weapons he'd used. Its presence was simply unmatched. I felt as though merely looking at it for too long would reduce me to nothing.

"That sword... Figaro's going for the finishing blow!" said Shu.

"You know what that weapon is?" asked Marie.

"You can't Identify it?"

"I can't. Using Identification doesn't even give me its name."

*I understand not being able to Identify stats, but not even seeing the name?* I thought.

"The Zenith Dragon's Brilliant Fang, Gloria α."

"Ah?! So that's…?!" Marie became shocked, and yet I didn't know why.

The intimidating air about it made it obvious that it was a special reward. However…

"It's on a completely different level," said Nemesis, and I couldn't help but nod.

It was above any and all equipment I'd seen so far. I wouldn't have been surprised if it was a greater weapon than Xunyu's Superior Embryo.

"That's a cooL toy you hAve, Figaro! GheAhahaHahahahhah!"

And yet, the jiangshi was still laughing. Despite it all — despite being the very target of that menacing blade, Xunyu was still laughing.

The two duelists were no longer fighting, allowing the laugh to freely echo throughout the arena, which had turned silent with anticipation. And once the echoes subsided…

"Then I'm goNna use tHis!" Reaching into a sleeve, Xunyu took out a dagger and gripped it with the right prosthetic arm.

A second later, a menacing air came from the jiangshi. Specifically, from the dragon fang-like dagger.

"Yinglong's Fang, Suling Yi. It's just like youRs — a Superior Item. I got it wheN we dealt with the SUBM thAt attacked our Huang He."

SUBMs and Superior Items.

When I'd checked the help window, I'd learned that was the highest tier of special rewards. The two duelists were owners of Superior Jobs and Superior Embryos. And now, they wielded Superior weaponry, as well.

"Still, it's nOt like I can surpaSs you when you're so bUffed," Xunyu said.

Of course, Xunyu was aware. It was something that I'd been able to figure out. There was no way that an experienced Superior facing Figaro couldn't realize the nature of his Embryo.

"Don't worrY, though. My Yinglong's Fang deals moRe damage the more MP and SP I giVe it," Xunyu said while baring the fang at Figaro. "I'll give mY all to this one attack. Next time's goNna be the laSt."

That declaration was followed by more silence, which created a thick air of tension.

Figaro's Superior Embryo was sending more and more power into Gloria α.

Xunyu the Master Jiangshi, a Superior Job with immense MP and SP, was giving it all to Yinglong's Fang.

The air became so tense that it felt as though the very space around them would crack.

Nemesis, Shu, Marie, Rook, Babi, I, and just about everyone else in the audience looked at the menacing duelists while holding our breaths in anticipation.

Now that the tension had reached its apex, I was so immersed in the scene that I didn't even notice that I'd pushed off the glass that was on the table. Right before it shattered, I heard the high-pitched sound caused by it touching the stony floor echo within our box.

At that moment, the Over Gladiator charged, while the Master Jiangshi launched his right arm.

Both their speeds surpassed and went far above supersonic. Even though they were slowed down by the barrier running at full capacity, I still couldn't see what had happened. All that entered my vision were the results.

Figaro's left arm and Xunyu's right arm — still holding Yinglong's Fang — had been severed from their bodies and were now airborne.

Still holding Gloria α in his right, Figaro dashed to Xunyu's side, to which the jiangshi responded by instantly launching the left arm, the one with a hand that had lost its metallic nails, towards the Over Gladiator.

At that particular moment, Xunyu was faster than the opponent and quickly forced the *golden nail* into Figaro's chest.

"Got ya nOw!"

Before I'd realized it, one of the very same golden nails that had been broken and dropped to the stage was affixed to the hand once again.

Xunyu's claim about giving it all to Yinglong's Fang had been merely but a setup for this surprise attack.

The jiangshi had predicted that Figaro would focus on speed in exchange for defense and took advantage of that.

Xunyu the Yinglong was *both* the Landmine and Divine Speed.

And still, the Over Gladiator came out ahead.

I could see shock on Xunyu's partially concealed expression. It was caused by the fact that the golden nail hadn't pierced through Figaro's body.

The golden nails were supposed to break through the skin, tear the pectoral muscle, rip the heart, shatter the ribcage, and come out on the other side. However, *something* had stopped it right after it tore the pectoral muscle.

It was an object capable of withstanding an attack from a Superior Embryo.

It was...

"...a heart," I muttered.

An Embryo that no one could see, despite Figaro always using it.

An object that Xunyu had failed to grab with the ultimate skill and couldn't pierce with this surprise attack.

They were the same thing.

A heart-shaped Superior Embryo.

"Thank you," said Figaro. "You were a wonderful opponent."

He'd taken off the Physical Berserk and sent his praises to his fellow duelist...

"Fang of Gloria!"

...and then split Xunyu in two from the top of the head.

"GHH!" the jiangshi groaned, and then struggled to try to do something.

"OVERDRIVE!"

Figaro swung Gloria α back upwards while making it release a pillar-shaped burst of light that greatly surpassed Baolongba in terms of heat.

The light was blinding enough to cause a whiteout. Though we couldn't see anything, it was easy to tell that it was silently evaporating everything within the barrier. And once the light faded, all that was left was Figaro, while Xunyu had vanished without a trace.

I heard a belated announcement of Figaro's victory.

Once the audience realized what happened, the arena was engulfed in applause.

Nemesis and I and everyone else in our box were cheering, as well.

The Clash of the Superiors — a duel that would be sung for a long time to come — had ended with Figaro's victory.

## Conjunction
### The End of the Match, the Beginning of Madness

*Central Arena, audience seating*

The moment Figaro won, ovation roared throughout the building.

"What a great duel…" A certain young spectator seated in the west side couldn't hold his honest opinion about the battle he'd just witnessed. The spectators around him were standing up as they sent cheers and applause to Figaro — no, the spectacular battle itself — and he was no exception.

"Truly a wonderful fight," he said, clearly moved.

"Yeah!" agreed a middle-aged man standing next to him. "I've seen many arena battles in my life, but a duel *this* good is a first!"

"Really?"

"You'd better believe it! The best match before was the one between Figaro and Tom Cat, the previous champion, but this was above that one!"

"I suppose I am quite lucky, then. This makes the journey through the desert all the more worth it."

The middle-aged man then noticed that the youth next to him was wearing a turban and loose, skin-concealing clothing that was popular in Caldina.

"You came here all the way from Caldina?!" he exclaimed. "Wasn't it hard?"

"Oh yes, it was," nodded the youth. "But again, it was worth it. I now have a good story to tell my friends back there."

After forming a satisfied smile, he then tilted his head in confusion.

"Oh?"

Gradually, more and more people in the audience became as puzzled as he was.

"What's wrong, lad?" asked the middle-aged man.

"Umm, Mr. Figaro is..." He told the man of the oddity that he had noticed.

Eventually, the confusion spread all across the arena.

"What a joke," said a woman in the eastern part of the audience. Obviously, she wasn't as ecstatic about the battle as everyone else in the audience.

Though what she'd said were pure fighting words to all the duel enthusiasts around her, they were drowned out by the cheering and failed to reach anyone's ears.

It there was anything that could hear her voice, it would be the porcupine sitting on her lap.

The woman was deeply unsatisfied with the battle she'd just witnessed.

*A battle between two Superiors. I would be lying if I said that I wasn't expecting anything. However, both of them ended up being complete eyesores. It made me wonder if they are really Superiors. Nothing but trickery and gimmicks. How trifling. The only worthwhile thing was at the end. Are they that useless because they're based on such shoddy things as hearts and limbs? And yet you're supposed to be the same as...?*

Her expression turned stern as the woman's irritation became even denser.

Right when it was about to turn into murderous intent and be unleashed upon her surroundings…

"know your place, and shut your mouth" the porcupine on her lap suddenly said.

The woman knew exactly what it meant.

"My apologies," she said. "Pardon my abusive thoughts. I almost let them out, but I'll hold them back now."

"k"

After apologizing, the woman petted the porcupine.

Then, she looked at the stage with a bored expression on her face.

"Oh, its begun," she said. "Well, with the first princess not being here, it has nothing to do with us."

"spec"

"Very well. Let us spectate. This might be good *entertainment*."

*Paladin, Ray Starling*

Something was very off.

Figaro was stuck in the very same position he'd been in after finishing Xunyu off with that upwards swing. Also, despite the match being over, Xunyu showed no signs of reviving.

The inside of the barrier was completely still in every sense of the word.

"What's going on?" I asked. "Hey, br—"

Before I could call out to Shu, I cut my words short. That was because of what I felt when I looked at him.

Even though he was clad in a full bear suit, I could easily tell that he was extremely pissed.

The others here — Nemesis, Rook, Babi, and Marie — seemed to feel it, too, causing them to back away a bit.

That was completely understandable. After all, at that moment, Shu was actually a bit scary.

"Bro, what's up?" I asked, feeling that I had to be the one to do it.

That was enough for the air of intimidation to disperse.

"Hm," he said. "Looks like someone went and did something unnecessary."

"What do you mean?" I asked.

"Well, the reason why Figaro is immobile is because the time inside the barrier got stopped."

"The time is stopped?"

"Yeah, the barriers here have that function, but it's rarely used. There's just no reason to, unless maybe if some show monsters went a bit too crazy," he said. "During the match, the time inside the barrier was slowed down to the very limit, but time stopping is a different thing entirely. Just like with slow playback and pause on videos."

"If time is stopped, what about their consciousness?" I asked.

"I've never been through that myself, but I think they're conscious. Tian and monster thoughts would probably stop, but just like with mental status effects, the player preservation function keeps every Master's mind active. Otherwise, players couldn't log out when they really needed to. However, the light and air movement is stopped, too, so they likely don't see or feel anything. Though, honestly with the evaporation that happened, I can't even imagine the state that Xunyu's in."

*That's certainly not something I like to picture, but the two fighters are experiencing it right now,* I thought.

"This timing..." said Marie. "Was it set up to stop the very moment the duel ended?"

"Most likely," nodded Shu. "Now we just have to figure out what kind of asshole is responsible for—"

He cut his words short.

A thing had appeared on the top of the barrier, gathering everyone's attention.

"That's..." I said.

It was a single silhouette. It had the shape of a costume, and it was one I was very familiar with — an Adélie penguin costume.

"Ayy! Good evening, ladies and gents! What a great fight! Hella hype, wasn't it?" Once everyone's attention had focused on him, the penguin began speaking. As he gestured to everyone in the arena, the voice he spoke in was that of...

"...the announcer?" I asked.

It was the very same voice that had done the announcing for today's battle. It was different than the voice he'd had yesterday.

*He didn't seem used to announcing, so can I assume he infiltrated and stole that role?* I thought.

Though he clearly had no intention of answering my question, he touched something on his neck and changed his voice back to the familiar one.

"Aaall right! With the hype fight done, it's probs time for the Count and Princess to bore you with some speeches and directions," he said. "But let's skip that crap and do something fun, instead!"

The penguin followed those words with a spin. Though he was in a suit, it was easy to tell that he was laughing.

And no, it wasn't because I was used to my brother and his bear costume. Anyone who'd heard the penguin's soft voice would tell you that it was thick with wickedness and malice.

"Name yourself, you cur!" said a voice from one of the boxes.

The box was significantly larger than most — clearly meant for the guests of honor. I knew the identity of the one who'd said that. It was the person I'd seen when the event began: Count Aschbarray Gideon.

"Why are you besmirching this event?!" the count yelled.

His rage was not without reason. After all, the penguin was making a mockery of a such masterful duel and the very successful event. Even I had a thing or two to say to him.

"HA HA HA! I just said it, didn't I? I want to do something fun!" After some loud laughter, the penguin put his hands on the back of the suit's head. "But yeah, I haven't revealed who I am yet! Allow me to do so!"

Then he took off the penguin suit.

"Get a load of *this* handsome mug! Ain't I charming?"

The one inside the suit was a thin man with an Embryo crest on his left hand. He was now wearing glasses and a lab coat, but nothing else really stood out — at least not as much as the penguin suit. Sure, his face was good, but with Masters being able to customize their appearances, it wasn't anything special.

However, the only ones with such lukewarm thoughts about him were people like me and Rook. The rest of the audience seemed to be extremely shocked.

"You… YOU…!" Count Gideon knew the man, as well, and his presence seemed to rid him of words.

"Oh boy, oh boy! Look at all these people that know who I am!" Despite it being dark, the former penguin purposely put his right hand above his eyes to protect them from sunlight and looked around. He was clearly enjoying the reactions his face reveal had caused. They were a testament to just how well-known his identity was.

"Identity..." I murmured.

When I'd met him yesterday, he'd pronounced himself as "Dr. Flamingo." It had been clear back then — and now more than ever — that he was just fooling around. That wasn't his name. It was...

"Why are you here... Franklin?!" Count Gideon demanded.

"BIIINNNNGOOOOOOOOOOOO!" Franklin yelled.

Fireworks began exploding in the air not far from the arena.

Though they were a beautiful sight that made Gideon's night sky more vibrant, few in the arena could enjoy them. It wasn't just tians, either. I saw some Masters who looked like they couldn't even stomach the man's presence.

It was only obvious. No one here could feel good with Franklin nearby.

Despite being a newbie, even I knew what his name meant to this country's people.

"Yeah, it's ya boy! The same guy who fed your king and a bunch of other nobodies to monsters! The Dryfe Imperium's Superior! The forefront of robotics and monster synthesis! Better check yourselves before you wreck yourselves. Because it's me, Giga Professor Franklin!"

It was safe to call him the kingdom's greatest enemy.

To Be Continued in the Next Episode...

## Midword

**Bear:** "I bear good news: it's time for the midword!"

**Cat:** "Yaay! Something neew!"

**Bear:** "In Volume 3, the main story stops with Figgy's and Xunyu's battle."

**Cat:** "Now, it's time for some side stories that take place during Volume 2!"

**Bear:** "They're about Ray's beary merry party members — Rook and the shaded journo."

**Cat:** "These stories are told from perspectives other than Ray's."

**Cat:** "You might come to see things that you cannot see through Ray's eyes."

**Bear:** "They're also strongly linked to the events in Volume 4."

**Bear:** "Now, it pawsitively saddens me, but we must say goodbye! Until the afterword!"

## Side Story The Case of the Untamable Slime

*Pimp, Rook Holmes*

"Lucius, you've already learned the English patterns?"

"Yes! I'm also halfway done with Japanese and German, as well!"

"Amazing. Not even I could do that when I was your age."

"I'm doing my best, Father! After all, I'm your and Mother's..."

"It's morning," I muttered as I woke up at my usual time at the break of dawn, on my first day after our arrival at Gideon.

A night of sleep here in *Infinite Dendrogram* made me feel as if I'd actually slept that much, which was quite curious, since the tripled flow of time here meant that I'd only slept a third of that time in reality.

"Good morning, Marilyn," I said. She was already awake in the jewel. "Let me do something, and then we'll have breakfast."

I got dressed and began going through my daily routine.

It was lip-reading practice. Something I'd been doing for nearly ten years now, ever since I was five years old. It consisted of checking the shape of the mouth when pronouncing various sounds from various languages.

However, in *Infinite Dendrogram*, things were a bit different.

"It's quite clear by now that any words with a meaning have the exact same shape no matter which language you use... It all gets translated into *Infinite Dendrogram's* common," I said. "I haven't fully learned it yet, so it might be a while until I'm able to lip-read here."

Whether I used English and said "hand" or Japanese and said "te," the shape of the mouth was exactly the same. It seemed to me that any words were translated into *Infinite Dendrogram's* common the moment they were given meaning. However, meaningless sounds — such as "h," "a," "n," "d" — came out like they were supposed to.

In real life, I could freely lip-read conversations from several languages. Here, though, I was sent back to square one and now had to spend every day increasing the vocabulary I could read.

"Sorry for the wait, Marilyn," I said after about an hour's worth of practice. "Let's eat."

"Morning, Rook!" Babi said. "Yay! Food!"

"KIEEH..." Audrey added. ("Man, I'm hungry...")

Babi and Audrey had awoken, as well, so we all went to eat breakfast.

Once that was done, I returned Marilyn and Audrey to the Jewel and walked through Gideon's streets.

Marilyn and Audrey had been fighting ever since they woke up.

"MHOOO!" ("You uncouth red chicken!")

"KIEE! KOOO!" ("You hard-headed turtle bitch! Fuck you!")

This had been happening ever since Audrey had joined us. It might've had something to do with Marilyn being very diligent and Audrey being the delinquent kind of girl, but I'd also heard that land-dragons and avians just naturally didn't get along too well.

*We're a team, so I'd really like it if they became friends,* I thought.

"What do we do today?" asked Babi, causing me to ponder.

According to my friends list, both Ray and Marie were offline. From their vocabularies and the expressions they used, it was safe to assume that they were Japanese, and with it being nighttime over there, they were most likely asleep.

Due to that, it was best for me to take care of business that was entirely my own.

"We'll first go to the Pimps' Guild," I said. "There's someone I want to see there. After that, we'll look around the tamed monster market."

I had to meet a certain person in the Pimps' Guild and then buy one or two new monsters, which was the reason why I'd come to Gideon in the first place. However, the latter priority had dropped a lot when I'd gotten Audrey to join us.

"MHOO." ("Master, please do not get another bird.")

"KIEEE." ("Turtles either, Boss. We have one too many already.")

Hearing Marilyn and Audrey say that from inside the Jewel on my right hand, I thought about what I really needed.

"Well," I said. "We have Marilyn for land and Audrey for air, so now we need someone for water. I don't think it'll be a bird, but it might actually be a turtle."

After giving appropriately differing reactions to my words, the two suddenly looked confused. From what I could tell, they had only just realized I could understand what they were saying.

"Who are you going to meet, Rook?" asked Babi.

"A person called Catherine," I answered. "She helped me a lot back at the capital when I became a Pimp. She's the one who told me that I should do some part-time work and get the Identification skill."

"We actually met someone like that?"

"It happened when you were sleeping."

After the Catalog Ray had lent me had told me that my suitable job was Pimp, I'd had trouble finding the capital's Pimps' Guild due to it being in a relatively secretive place and me being a newbie with little knowledge of the area. Catherine, an experienced Pimp, had helped me find it.

She was also the one that'd told me that the headquarters of the Pimps' Guild was here in Gideon. Catherine regularly visited the place, so I didn't see any reason not to drop by and say hi.

After following my map to a back alley in Gideon's eighth district, I arrived at an establishment that seemed to be a mix between a bar and an inn. The sign near the entrance said "Pimps' Guild's Headquarters," so there was little doubt that I had the right building. The Adventurers' Guild doubled as a bar, too, but the fact that this one was also an inn probably meant exactly what most would assume.

"I'll go eat over there!" said Babi before going to a table.

Though she wasn't as much of a big eater as Ray's Nemesis, Babi did eat quite a lot. Of course, the amount she consumed meant little when one noted that she ate solely sweet things turned spicy.

Anyway, likely due to me being a Pimp that was clearly too young, I attracted quite a lot of attention.

"Excuse me," I spoke to the high level-looking man working behind the counter.

"Welcome, boyo," he replied. "Well, aren't you a young'un! Oh no, that won't be a problem! We don't have age restrictions here! Anyone's free to enjoy themselves at any time!"

Though he talked with a fake-looking smile, it didn't seem like he had any malice towards me. That was probably how he interacted with any average customer.

"Oh, I'm not a customer. I'm a member of the guild," I said as I showed him my card.

"Well, whaddya know, you really are," he spoke as he looked at it. "It's rare for Masters to become Pimps. We have two or three others, but you're easily the youngest among them." The fake smile was all but gone as he changed his attitude towards me.

Just as he'd said, Pimp — despite being a useful job — wasn't too popular among Masters. As far as I was aware, the most popular jobs here in the kingdom were from the knight grouping, and though watching Ray made me understand why, I still wondered why the pimp grouping was so niche in comparison.

"So, you're lookin' for someone you can offer your services to?" he asked. "Or do you need some workers?"

The first question referred to guild quests, like the model-searching one I'd taken back at the capital. The second question referred to buying tamed monsters and the like. In Gideon, just like this place, they could be bought in the fourth district.

"The latter, please," I said. "May I ask something, though?"

"What is it?"

"Is the Master known as 'Catherine' here?"

The moment I spoke that name, the guild turned completely silent. Some people dropped their glasses, some went into a fetal position and cowered, while others just quickly paid their bills and hastily walked out.

*What am I supposed to make of this reaction?* I thought.

"Do you know her?" he asked.

"Yes," I nodded. "She helped me a lot in the capital's guild."

"Well, she *is* good at taking care of pretty boys," the bartender said. "Though most of them just avoid her... Anyway, she should be here soon."

I decided to wait for her. I went and sat at the same table as Babi and let the time pass by while I drank the free tea they gave me.

During that time, I felt that Marilyn and Audrey — still in the Jewel — were fighting about something again. I heard sounds that seemed to refer to my tastes, Catherine, love rivalry, dragon anthropomorphization, and love between birds and people.

*What are they talking about?* I thought.

After nearly an hour of such waiting, the guild's door opened, and I heard a familiar, high-pitched voice.

"Heeyyy! Good morning to you allll!"

"Ah, she's here," I said.

The owner of the voice was the Catherine I was waiting for.

She came into the guild accompanied by four maids and, upon noticing my presence, walked up to our table.

"Oh my! It's really Rookie!" she said joyously. "I'd heard that the PK blockade had stopped, but I didn't think that you'd have arrived in Gideon already."

"I did, as you can see!" I responded. "I came here with Babi, my party members Ray and Marie, and these girls right here!" I introduced Babi and the two girls inside my Jewel to her.

"Rook, who is this?" asked Babi.

"She's the one I told you about — Catherine Kongou," I answered. "She's a highly skilled Pimp and a very reliable person."

"Oh come, now, Rookie, praise like that will make me blush!" Catherine cried.

A moment later, I noticed that Marilyn and Audrey seemed really shocked, for some reason. It seemed as though they were surprised by Catherine's appearance. Thinking that, I re-examined how she looked.

Long blonde hair bearing the slenderness and glamor of silk.

Eyes of a deep blue color reminiscent of a clear sea.

Custom-made clothing of a lavish design, clearly created from high-quality materials.

Nails covered in simply masterful art that she'd probably done by herself.

A voice as charming and enchanting as a mermaid's.

Over two meters in stature.

Huge biceps, about as thick as a horse's neck.

A slightly exposed chest which revealed pectoral muscles that seemed to rival steel.

A face with a boorish structure and features that clearly belonged on a dominating overlord.

Indeed, it was the exact same Catherine that I'd met back at the capital.

Her appearance was certainly unique, so it wasn't too hard to believe that she'd surprised Marilyn and Audrey.

*It's actually pretty interesting that even monsters can be surprised by what we humans wear,* I thought. *This has been on my mind for a while, but it really does seem that their thoughts are similar to those of humans.*

Catherine Kongou was a veteran Pimp. However, rather than being from the pimp grouping, her current main job was Siren — a Superior Job from the harlot grouping bearing conditions such as "Charm a total of 100,000 people or monsters."

Apparently, she was also really high on the kingdom's kill rankings. I knew how effective Charm was in large-scale battles better than most, so I could fully understand why she was up there. Still, it was pretty obvious that her battle style had more to it than just that skill.

Also, Catherine's avatar was a man made to look like a woman, making the popular term "transvestite" to be the most apt description for her. However, I couldn't tell what her gender was in real life. That was something I could normally guess after a while of talking, but the way Catherine mixed masculinity and femininity made it really difficult for me.

Due to her being like that, however, you could safely say that she had both male reliability and female attentiveness, making her fully deserving of respect.

"Did you meet the PK terrorists on your way to Gideon?" I asked Catherine while we had a chat over some tea.

"I flew over here on one of my girls," she answered. "Seems like the meanies couldn't do anything about those in the air."

The words "my girls" made me glance behind her, where I saw the four maids that accompanied her.

"You've already met Rubiella, haven't you?" Catherine asked upon noticing where I was looking.

Indeed. One of the four, the maid with red hair, had been with Catherine back when she'd helped me out in the capital.

"Yes," I nodded. "She was with you when we met."

"Well, then let me introduce you to the other girls," she said. "The blue-haired one is Sappheanne, the green-haired one is Emerada, while the one with the eyepatch is Crystella."

The maids bowed to us respectfully.

"A pleasure meeting you," I responded. "I am Rook, Catherine's junior in this trade."

"Could you be a dear and show me *your* girls, too?" Catherine asked.

"Certainly. Oh, but they might break the floor here," I said. Marilyn was a heavyweight Demi-Dragon, so she could easily break through the wooden boarding beneath us.

"Let's go somewhere else, then," she said. "Guildmaster! We're borrowing the back of the building!"

"Go ahead," said the man behind the counter. "Also, there's a job specifically for you, so do come back and take it when you're done."

*I had a hunch that the bartender was high level, and now I know why — he's the guildmaster here,* I thought.

Behind the guild, I summoned my monsters from my Jewel. "Call — Marilyn, Audrey."

"My, what a lovely pair," commented Catherine. "They'd be a match for your usual high-rank Tamer's monsters." She then made a friendly smile.

*...Why do Marilyn and Audrey look so afraid?*

"A Demi-Dragon and a Roc Bird surely take lots of space, but your Jewel looks pretty fancy, so I assume it still has room for more?" she asked.

"It does," I said. "I'd like to get one that could travel on water. Would I find any in the marketplace?"

"An aquatic monster? Finding one here might be difficult." According to her, most of the city's water came from the underground, and there weren't any lakes or rivers nearby. Due to that, not many traders here dealt in aquatic monsters. The Pimps' Guild actually didn't sell a single one of those.

"Oh, but you might get lucky and find one in the market," she added.

"I see! I'll go there right now!" I said.

"But the roads there are complicated, and the place isn't safe, even for us Masters. I'd come along, but I have a job to do… I know, let's do this."

Catherine turned to face the maids behind her and beckoned the red-haired one, Rubiella.

"Rubiella, be a dear and guide Rookie through the market."

"As you wish, milady." The maid bowed.

"Is that really okay?" I asked.

"Yes. Don't you worry," said Catherine. "Just tell her to come back to me once your business is done."

"Thank you very much, Catherine!"

Catherine gave me gentle smile and patted me on the head. That action reminded me of my dad — or mom, maybe — and made me feel somewhat happy.

*Though, I still don't get why Marilyn and Audrey become so scared whenever Catherine smiles,* I thought.

After parting ways with Catherine, Rubiella guided us to and around the market in the fourth district.

"In this market, there's a street-based bazaar and shops set up in buildings," she explained. "You might find bargains in the bazaar, but if you don't have a high enough Identification skill, you could end up purchasing counterfeit or inferior goods, so I cannot recommend it. The wares in shops are far more trustworthy when it comes to quality and authenticity, but that makes their price a bit higher."

"So, first-time shoppers like myself are better off using the shops, right?" I asked.

"Indeed," she confirmed. "Also, you can set up your own stall in the bazaar. The places you can use are managed by the fourth district's manager. For a daily payment, you can sell your products here even if you're not a merchant."

As she told me such things, we entered a small, secretive alleyway.

"Since you wish to purchase an aquatic monster, I will introduce you to a shop that Milady is well-acquainted with. If you don't find what you need there, we will look around the bazaar."

"That sounds good," I said.

As she guided us, Rubiella repeatedly did a strange hand-waving motion. I found it curious, but before I could ask what it meant, we arrived at a shop at the very end of the alleyway.

The secretive establishment had a sign saying "Monster King's Shop, Central Continent Branch."

That name was strange. After all, *Infinite Dendrogram* had only one continent, so "Central Continent Branch" didn't really make sense, since it implied that their main shop was somewhere else. The only places that came to mind were the far-east island nation of Tenchi or the maritime country, Granvaloa.

*Or perhaps... No, I still don't have enough knowledge to theorize about this,* I thought.

"Welcome!" the person behind the counter greeted us as we entered. "Oh? Well, if it isn't Rubiella."

The person was small in stature — about one head shorter than me. He was notable for the pitch-black robe and the hood hiding his face.

"It's been a while," said Rubiella. "Are you the one tending to the shop today, manager?"

"Yeah, I do it every once in a blue moon," answered the person. "Where's Catherine?"

"Milady is not here this time. She told me to help out young master Rook."

"A pleasure to meet you," I said. "I am Rook, Catherine's junior in the trade."

"Well, now that's rare," said the shopkeeper. "I assume you're here to buy monsters, then? What do you have in mind?"

"An aquatic monster, please."

"Aquatic, eh? There's little demand for those here, so we don't have anything particularly rare. We do have a corner for them, though." He left the counter and began leading us to it.

This shop seemed to deal exclusively in pre-tamed monsters. The shelves had countless Jewels on them, and I could see the monsters they held by simply looking inside.

*Oh, there are even Jewels with Tri-Horn Demi-Dragons like Marilyn inside. It's kinda hard to tell whether this is more of a pet shop or a jewelry shop,* I thought as we approached a booth lit by a bluish light.

"This is the aquatic monster corner," said the shopkeeper. "Do look around."

"...Wow," I muttered. Though the keeper had said that they didn't have anything particularly rare, I could see several jewels with aquatic Demi-Dragons. It was clear that the selection was good.

"Our varied selection of land-dragons and sky-dragons extends to Pure-Dragons, too," he said. "Not sea-dragons, though."

Still, the wares here in the Monster King's Shop were far above the ones sold at the market we'd passed. They even had tamed Pure-Dragons, which were considered to be a rarity. Despite that, the prices here weren't particularly greater than the ones in the bazaar. One would expect them to have completely sold out by now.

That reminded me that Rubiella had made some strange action before entering the shop, so this might've been one of those establishments that only allowed a select few individuals to browse. I wasn't completely certain about that.

In any case, it was quite obvious that, in this shop, I'd have no trouble finding a new teammate that matched Marilyn and Audrey.

"Since you're a friend of Catherine's, I'll allow you to pay by installments," said the shopkeeper.

"How nostalgic," commented Rubiella. "When Milady and I met here, she also paid by installments."

"Oh, that was a bit over four years ago, wasn't it?" he said. "Time sure flies..."

While the two were conversing, I examined the aquatic monsters on display, but...

"I just don't know," I muttered.

"What's wrong, Rook?" asked Babi.

"Demi-Dragons not good enough?" inquired the keeper.

"No, I wouldn't say so. It's just that..."

I had nothing against Demi-Dragon class monsters. In fact, when taking cooperation with Marilyn and Audrey into consideration, they were actually better than Pure-Dragons. However…

"They just… don't click," I said. "When I met Marilyn and Audrey, the monsters with me right now, I had some strange feeling drawing me to them. Here, however, I'm not getting it at all."

When I'd chosen Marilyn as my reward from Grantzian and when I'd faced Audrey in that battle, I'd had a sensation drawing me to them. I didn't get it when looking at any of the monsters here in the shop, and that included the Pure-Dragons, which were supposedly stronger than both Marilyn and Audrey. It was a really vague feeling that I found hard to describe.

"Oh, I see." The shopkeeper nodded as if he could understand me completely, and Rubiella seemed to share his sentiment, as well.

"'Rook,' was it?" he said. "I can see that Pimp is your vocation, but you seem to have the makings of a Tamer, as well. Not many people are equipped with intuition like yours."

"Really?" I raised an eyebrow.

"Yes. And because of that, I don't think you should limit yourself to aquatic monsters. Take a look at every Jewel in my shop and search for the one that clicks."

"All right. I'll see if I find anything," I said before walking away from the aquatic monster corner and looking at other Jewels in the shop.

"A natural, non-sense skill Beast Judgment, eh?" said the shop owner as I walked away. "With Catherine and that other person, that's a total of three now." Those words stuck with me, for some reason.

After that, I spent about two hours looking at the Jewels here, but the results weren't great. No matter how many thousands of them I examined, I didn't find a single monster that "clicked."

"Well, that's a shame," said the shopkeeper.

"Sorry for wasting your time," I apologized.

"No need for that. A business wouldn't function if we didn't allow our customers to examine our wares as long as they liked. Though, now you'll have to look around the bazaar..."

"Indeed," agreed Rubiella. "However, using Beast Judgment in the bazaar is quite..."

"Oh, right. Even a Master would be in trouble if they found out."

They were talking about something, but I didn't know what "Beast Judgment" entailed, so I couldn't really follow the conversation.

"...Huh?" I asked.

Suddenly, I noticed something.

On one end of the shop, there was a metallic pot, large enough to fit a child. The lid was off and lying at the base of the pot. For some reason, it was surrounded by a chain bearing a warning coloration, as if to say that the pot was off-limits.

*It stands out so much, so how didn't I notice it before?* I asked myself before curiosity took over. I approached the pot and pointed my left hand at it.

"Shopkeeper, this pot is..."

"Pot? Ah...?! GET AWAY FROM IT!"

His shout startled me into quickly backing away. A moment later, *something silver* passed the space where my index finger was. I looked and noticed that the warning chain was severed. The cut was so clean and flat that it almost felt as though it could be fixed if you simply put the pieces back together. My finger was slightly damaged, as well, but a bit of rubbing was enough for the cut to close and leave only a small mark. It seemed like I was cut by an extremely sharp blade moving at an immense speed.

However, that was quite far from the truth.

What had cut me wasn't a blade, but a liquid. I saw some of it hang on the edge of the pot before returning inside. The liquid was silver and had a mysterious glossiness. The sight was bizarre, and I simply couldn't look away from this *monster.*

"Sorry about that," said the shopkeeper. "This one's dangerous, so I had an isolation barrier around it. Seems like it got broken."

"I'm quite fine," I replied. "What is this, though?"

"It's a Mithril Arms Slime," answered the shop owner as he cast some spell and fixed the chain. "A rarity among the already-rare metal slimes. They have bodies made of liquid mithril and attack by quickly turning themselves into weapons."

*Mithril Arms Slime,* I repeated the monster name in my head.

"I got it in an auction, but it wasn't tamed, you see," he continued. "I was planning to ask a Tamer I was acquainted with to tame it, but before I could do that, I accidentally unsealed it, and now it's in this state."

"'This state,' as in...?" I asked.

"Constantly on alert and prepared for battle. Thing's now completely volatile, cutting any living creature that comes close. It's also more difficult to tame it now, and moving it from there is really tricky, so I couldn't really do much besides creating a barrier around it. Slimes don't even get tired, so waiting it out isn't an option, either. Sure, killing it would take care of this mess, but I don't want to see the money I've spent go down the drain."

"How much did you spend on it?" I asked.

"10,250,000 lir. These slimes aren't the strongest things, but their rarity makes them cost a pretty penny."

Hearing the price made me freeze for a moment. However...

"Shopkeeper," I said.

"Yes?"

I gathered my resolve and told him what I wanted. "I'll tame the slime, so could you sell it to me?"

My words made the shopkeeper, Rubiella, and the monsters inside my Jewel turn silent with surprise. Only Babi had her usual smile on her face.

"Though I'd like to pay by installments, if you don't mind," I added.

"I've already said that I would allow that," he said. "Are you sure, though?"

"Yes. I mean... the slime clicked with me," I responded with a smile, caused by an unwavering belief in my own intuition. "I *will* tame her."

Simply because I wanted her, I chose to tame the Mithril Arms Slime — a creature yet to be tamed by anyone.

Mithril Arms Slime.

According to the shop's owner, they were a rarity even among the already-rare metal slimes.

Not carnivorous, herbivorous, or omnivorous, their diet consisted of water and metal ores, especially mithril.

All slimes had liquid bodies, and these were no exception. However, Mithril Arms Slimes had the special ability to instantly harden and turn parts of themselves into weapons. When attacked, they either turned their bodies into mithril shields or used their slime-like liquid state to maneuver out of harm's way.

The number of these slimes that humanity had found was still in the double digits, while the amount that had been killed didn't even break twenty. And so far, not a single one of them had ever been tamed.

Again — the Mithril Arms Slime, as a species, had yet to be tamed.

I was told that some Tamers had gotten them into a tamable state, but had gotten their right hands cut off when they'd tried to form a contract.

Normally, when monsters are in a tamable state, all the person has to do is touch them and form a contract to complete the taming. I'd already gone through that with Audrey, and she hadn't resisted at all.

However, Mithril Arms Slimes were different in that regard. As long as they were in an alert state, they didn't hesitate to attack the Tamers even after they became tamable.

Due to that, they were considered to be even more difficult to tame than Pure-Dragons.

"We've had some customers who wanted to try and tame it, but they've all failed," said the shopkeeper. "There were people with maxed out high-rank tamer grouping jobs, but even they weren't successful."

Basically, it was impossible even to the best of Tamers.

Some would probably laugh at the idea of a newbie such as myself having a go at such a challenging task, but that didn't mean that I couldn't try.

I knew people who wouldn't give up no matter how great was the challenge before them, so I wanted to follow their example.

And follow it I had been… for over four hours now.

Facing the pot with the Mithril Arms Slime inside, I silently extended the thing in my right hand towards it. It was a thin rod less than a meter in length — a mithril wire. Mithril was their staple food, and I figured that trying to feed it wouldn't hurt.

I'd gotten the wire by asking Rubiella to go to the bazaar and buy it.

Now, she was at the counter, talking about something with the shop's owner.

"I've heard that the grandchild of the Luor Company's president got kidnapped by the Gouz-Maise Gang," I heard her say.

"Those scumbags still at it?" responded the shopkeeper. "How many times has this happened now? It's above one hundred, isn't it?"

I'd heard the name "Gouz-Maise Gang" several times while in this city. From what I could tell, they were a vile group that troubled Gideon and its surroundings by kidnapping children.

*What kind of person steals children, of all things?* I thought, pure disgust welling up within me.

"Ah…"

A moment later, the tip of the wire I'd extended got cut off and fell to the floor. I instantly concluded that she'd attacked in response to either my disgust or the attempt at feeding. Despite both the wire and the slime being made of mithril, the cut was impressively clean, making the tip of the wire as flat and sharp as a mirror.

I slowly brought what remained of the wire closer to her, causing her to repeatedly sever more and more of it. The way it gradually got smaller reminded me of a certain stick-shaped sweet.

It didn't take long for the wire to be reduced to nothing but pieces of mithril scattered on the floor.

"This thing cost me 2,000 lir," I sighed before finger-throwing the last bit of it towards the slime. It, too, got split in half the moment it entered her "personal space," so to speak.

"You seem to be having a hard time," said the shop's owner.

"I can't deny that," I replied. "Just as you told me, it becomes really difficult after you get her into a tamable state."

"Hm? You're there already?"

"All slimes are female, after all. Male Temptation works on them just fine, so I didn't have much trouble making her tamable."

Indeed, there had been no problems on that front. However...

"But when I reach for her to form a contract... she cuts me." I looked at the pieces of mithril on the floor and the countless shallow cuts on my hands.

"Among the Tamers who attempted to tame it was one who tried to do it while wearing mithril gauntlets," said the shopkeeper. "He still got his hands cut off." *So, not even properly processed armor-tier mithril can withstand these attacks, huh?* I thought.

"Armor made from Mythical metal... hihi'irokane... might protect against these cuts, though," he added. "Should we get some?"

"No, thank you," I shook my head. "I doubt my level's high enough to equip such things. Also, I don't think that's the right answer here." Relying on toughness and stats just didn't seem like the right way to go about it. If it had been, the Tamers that'd come before me would've already done it just because they had greater stats and equipment. The correct method of taming Mithril Arms Slimes had nothing to do with such things.

"You seem to be stuck, though," he said.

"So far, I've noticed two things," I responded while pointing at the pot. "First, her alertness. Rather than attacking automatically, she carefully considers each and every single one of her cuts. Over the four hours of doing this, I've noticed that the distance at which she starts attacking has a deviation of a few centimeters, meaning that she's not doing it with machine-like, automatic precision."

I pointed at the mithril pieces on the floor. Though they'd been cut by the same slime, their thickness wasn't consistent, which was proof of what I'd just said.

"I see. What's the second thing, then?" asked the shopkeeper.

"She *wants* to be tamed," I answered.

"Why do you think that?"

I showed him my open hands, which were covered in countless small cuts that the slime had given me. "All of these wounds are shallow."

"Well, I can see that much."

"Both the wire and my fingers entered her alertness zone. However, while the wire got cut apart, my fingers are still intact."

"Oh!"

She'd severed the mithril wire with ease, yet my hands — which were far weaker — were relatively unharmed.

"They're all little more than scratches, and the worst one among them is the one I got after carelessly pointing at her when I first saw the pot," I said. "As in, the one from before she was in a tamable state."

I raised the index finger of my left hand, and sure enough, the cut on it was the deepest one, if only by a few millimeters. Which was why I could infer that...

"She's holding back against humans. And she's been extra careful with those that have gotten her into a tamable state, reducing her attacks to nothing but warnings. It's clear that she treats us differently than inorganic objects."

"But the Tamers that came before you—"

"Yes, they had their hands completely cut off. I think the same would happen to me if I reached a little farther," I said as I extended my hand towards the slime's alertness radius.

Though her attacks put more small cuts on my fingers, I didn't retract my hand. Naturally, she continued attacking. After confirming that all the wounds were shallow, I took my hand out of her radius.

"See?" I said. "When you consider how differently she treats the mithril wire and my hand, it's clear that there's more to this than just distance. She's probably acting according to some simple rules."

"So you think you'll be able to tame her when you figure them out, eh?" asked the shop's owner.

"Yes, but figuring them out might be troublesome. I need a clue, and..." I stopped talking before I could finish what I was saying.

The shopkeeper looked at me with a puzzled expression, but I couldn't care about that. After all, something that I wanted to be oblivious of had entered the edge of my vision. Next to the pot, there was a small animal — a single *mouse.*

"Oh, a mouse," said the shopkeeper. "Guess the barrier keeping them out got broken."

The moment I saw it, the mind controlling my body went blank.

The mouse was so weak that it didn't even count as a monster. There was a hole in one of the walls, which was probably where it had come from.

It noticed our presence and ran away, passing by the pot in the process.

All of that entered my vision, and I properly processed it. However, at the same time, my body reflexively screamed. "Mouse mouse mouse mouse mouse MOUUUUUSE!"

I entered a state of absolute panic. As my brain tried to understand the situation, my mind was overwhelmed by memories of a certain event. Training, an old mansion, broken floor, falling into a room with countless mic—

"MOOOUUUUUUUUUUSSE!" Losing control of my body, I became even more panicked.

However, before that reached its peak and made me lose consciousness…

"It's okay. Don't be afraid."

…I was embraced by Babi.

"There there, Rook. There's nothing to be afraid of," she said, comforting me and patting my back.

Strange as it was, that was enough for me to slowly regain control of my panicked mind and body. It was just like when my mother had done it to me.

After about five minutes, I had completely calmed down, and the panic was gone as if it was never there.

"Sorry you had to see that," I apologized to the shopkeeper and Rubiella.

I knew that my behavior had been unsightly. Panicked as I was, my mind was still somewhat functional. However, I could almost feel a wave of other thoughts overwhelm me.

Sober as I was now, I concluded that this was how most so-called "traumas" were.

"No need to apologize," said Rubiella.

"Everyone has things they can't handle, after all," added the shopkeeper. "But why do mice make you so… Oh, I won't ask."

He must have noticed how I reacted to the very mention of the creatures and — out of consideration — refrained from asking me for the reasons.

It was good that he did, for I wasn't too sure how I was supposed to answer that. I'd been wanting to get rid of my phobia of rodents ever since I was a child, but it still showed no signs of going away.

*All right, that's enough about mice,* I thought.

There was something far more important.

"I found out the slime's rules, so I'll tame her now," I said. The thing I'd seen while panicking had given me the final clue I needed. All that was left was to test my theory.

"Really? What's this, all of a sudden?" asked the shop's owner.

"This incident wasn't all bad," I said. "Thanks to it, I figured out why I couldn't tame her."

"…You could do that in *that* state?"

*Well, I've been taught to analyze my surroundings no matter how confused I may be,* I thought.

Anyway, testing my theory required some preparation.

"Excuse me, keeper, but can I borrow an empty Jewel?" I asked.

"I don't mind," he said as he took one of the Jewels from the counter. It was the same type as the one I had, only completely empty.

As long as the owner allowed it, it was possible to transfer monsters from one Jewel to another by simply making them touch.

"All right, then..." Taking the empty Jewel in my left hand, I closed it in to the one on my right. And just like that, I transferred Marilyn and Audrey into the empty Jewel.

"KIEEE?!" ("BOSS?! YOU'RE SELLING US?! WHAT THE FUCK!")

"MHOOO!" ("C-C-C-C-Calm down! I-I'm sure he has something in mind!")

*Oh... they seem really startled,* I thought. *Now I feel kinda bad. I should've warned them...*

"The Tri-Horn Demi-Dragon is 2,400,000 lir, while the Crimson Roc Bird is 3,200,000," said the shopkeeper.

"KIEEE!" ("Take that, bitch! I'm more expensive!")

"MHOO!" ("Now's not the time to be happy, you birdbrain! Also, the reason you're more expensive is because they already have my kind here!")

*Does difference in price really mean all that much to them? Wait, that doesn't matter right now,* I thought.

"No, I'm not selling them. I just needed to momentarily move them. Babi, hold on to this for a second," I said as I gave her the Jewel with Marilyn and Audrey inside.

"Okaaay."

"All right, then," I muttered as I began taking off my clothes.

I removed everything that counted as equipment.

"Hmm, that should be enough," I said, clad in only a tank top and underwear, inner clothing that gave no bonuses to stats or anything. "I think I'm ready now."

"Rook, what are you doing?" asked the shopkeeper, and I responded with only a smile, leaving the proper answer to the results of my theory.

While distancing my left hand — which had the Embryo crest on it — away from the slime, I extended my right — the one with the Jewel — towards her.

Unlike before, the way I reached for her had no hesitation. Soon enough, my right hand passed the edge of the danger zone without getting hit by a single warning attack.

I continued moving my hand further, into the area beyond which countless Tamers had theirs cut off. However, my hand went through without getting a single scratch on it, and I reached the edge of the pot.

As I heard the people behind me gasp, I placed the back of my hand on the top of the pot and waited for her.

"Come," I said, not sure if she would understand me.

A few moments later, the Mithril Arms Slime crawled out and touched my palm.

It was hard to tell how long it had taken, but eventually, magic began flowing between us and the taming was complete.

"Your name is Liz… Liz the Mithril Arms Slime," I smiled as I rubbed her shiny, silver body. "Let's get along, Liz."

In response, the Mithril Arms Slime, Liz, shook in a happy manner.

Thus, my theory was proven to be correct.

I turned around to face the store's owner.

"I've tamed her," I said.

"...How did you do that?"

"Exactly as you saw me do it. I momentarily moved Marilyn and Audrey to another Jewel and took off my equipment."

"How does that connect to you becoming able to tame the slime?" he asked.

My explanation was probably a bit lacking, sure, but the truth was actually really simple.

"Liz... or, rather, Mithril Arms Slimes in general... are very cowardly," I said while petting Liz, who was crawling all over my body. "Even if you get them into a tamable state, having them recognize you as worthy, they're still afraid of other things."

"Such as?"

"The other monsters in the right hand extended towards them."

"Ah!"

Anyone who tamed and used monsters kept them in the right hand's Jewel at all times, even while taming a new monster. Also, not a single Tamer wore a Jewel without any monsters inside. Those were the reasons why no Tamers before me had been able to tame Liz.

"Also, she first attacked my left hand," I continued. "That was probably because she was afraid of the crest — the thing that channels the powers of Embryos. And the fact that she attacked mithril gauntlets and wire made it safe to assume that equipment scared her, as well. That's why I tamed her after removing everything she was afraid of."

Those seemingly-simple reasons were why I had removed my equipment and distanced my left hand away from her.

"Isn't that just circumstantial evidence?" asked the shopkeeper.

"Yes. However, I became completely certain of it when I saw th-the mouse," I answered. Merely using the word made me feel unpleasant, but I still continued the explanation. "That mouse was *just* a mouse — not even a monster. And it didn't get attacked even when it was right next to the pot and passed by it while I lost myself."

Though I'd been panicking, I'd clearly seen how the mouse had acted. Despite being so close to Liz, it hadn't been attacked once. That was because the mouse wasn't even a monster.

"So it came to me that I might be successful if I had nothing on me and didn't scare her. After all, the wounds she gave me were small, making it seem like she was being considerate of me."

Her attacks had been warning shots. But they hadn't been directed at me; they'd been directed at the monsters in my right hand's Jewel and the Embryo crest on my left.

"Did you consider what would've happened if your deduction was wrong?" asked the shopkeeper. "You could've been sliced apart, you know?"

"I had confidence," I said before pausing for a moment. I added honestly, "Also… if I was wrong, it would've been fine for me to die."

My father often told me words that he'd gotten from his own father: "When making deductions that might change other people's lives, always bear responsibility for your words. Bet your life on them and do your best to never be mistaken."

When other people were involved in your deductions, you had to make sure you had the resolve to carry that burden.

Suddenly, I noticed that the shop's owner was looking at me with a shocked expression.

*I guess that's to be expected, considering what I just said,* I thought.

"Oh, but I'm a Master, so I can't really die here," I said with jest as I finished my explanation.

"..." ("Are you okay?") At that moment, Liz — who was still crawling all over me — worriedly asked me that while looking at the cuts on my hands.

"Yeah, I'm fine, Liz," I replied. "The wounds are shallow, and your cuts were so clean that they don't even hurt. I'm not mad at all."

By default, *Infinite Dendrogram* had no pain, but I was confident that it wouldn't have hurt even if there had been.

"Rook," the shopkeeper addressed me. "You can talk to slimes?"

"I can understand them by looking," I nodded. "Animals communicate more than just by words, after all." In fact, I found animals to be easier to understand than people.

"Is that a skill?" he asked.

"No," I shook my head and momentarily fell silent. "It's a technique that my parents taught me."

After saying that, I took a moment to run my mind through those memories.

After that, I bought Liz for 5,130,000 lir, paid by installments.

According to the shop's owner, the Mithril Arms Slime taming method I'd discovered was worth more than 10,000,000 lir. Due to that, he'd wanted to give her to me for free, but that didn't sit right with me, so I'd chosen to pay at least half of her original price.

My mom had always told me that "Taking too much free stuff is best left for stealing," and it wasn't like I wanted to steal from the shopkeeper, so I was satisfied with the outcome.

Also, instead of having her join the other monsters in the Jewel, I had Liz use her Camouflage skill — common among slimes — to turn into clothing for me to wear. The clothing's appearance was still metallic, but there already was a piece of equipment known as "Mithril Coat," so I didn't really stand out too much. Also, when people with a low Identification skill level looked at her, they would see nothing but "Mithril Coat (Custom-Made)."

The only problem I had with this coat was the fact that Liz's fear of the crest caused the left arm's sleeve to be a bit shorter than the other, but that wasn't a big deal. She also moved in an unnatural manner every once in a while, but most would simply assume that it was just the wind.

Anyway, we were now gathered outside Gideon's north gate to see off Rubiella.

Apparently, while I had been busy taming Liz, Catherine had returned to the capital, and Rubiella was about to go after her.

"Thank you for your help, Rubiella," I said.

"I am humbled to have you thank me, Master Rook. I, too, am thankful for your giving me an interesting story to tell Milady."

"Speaking of Catherine, I really wish I could've thanked her before she left." After all, it was thanks to her that I'd met Liz.

*She really helps me out a lot,* I thought.

"I will make sure to pass over your gratitude," she said.

"Thank you."

"Now, then. Master Rook, Babylon, Marilyn, Audrey, and Liz," she said. "I hope we can meet again."

"How will you go the capital? Dragon Carriage?" Babi asked, making Rubiella silently chuckle.

"This body of mine will be more than enough," she said, and a second later, two large wings sprouted from her back.

As soon as I noticed that they were draconic, she flapped them and rose up to the clouds, where her appearance suddenly changed. She was now a large dragon emitting a crimson light that I could easily see from the surface.

Rubiella, the crimson dragon that could use Anthropomorphization, waved goodbye to us by spinning in the air and then flew off towards the capital, looking truly majestic in the process.

"KIEEE!" ("Hey, turtle. I'm gonna try and get Anthropomorphization, too.")

"VAHMOO!" ("What a coincidence. I was thinking the same thing.")

Audrey and Marilyn seemed to be quite impressed by what Rubiella had just shown us.

"Well, what do we do now?" I asked. "The meeting with Marie is the day after tomorrow, Ray doesn't seem to be online yet, and I don't really have any plans."

My only personal business for today had been to say hi to Catherine and get a new tamed monster. Needless to say, I'd already done both of those things, leaving me with nothing to do.

"Then why don't we go and level up?" asked Babi, to which I replied with a nod.

We had yet to fight with Audrey and Liz in the group, so that was a really good idea.

Also, I felt that our party would end up fighting some truly great foes in the future, so I wanted us to be useful when that time came.

"Good idea," I said. "I want to become stronger, so let's go get some levels."

Audrey cried, "KIEE!" ("Boss! I know where to find the prey around these parts!")

Audrey had originally been the mount of Gardranda, a creature that lived around the Nex Plains, so it was only obvious for her to be familiar with the surroundings.

"Can you show us, then, Audrey?" I asked.

"KIEEEE!" ("Sure thing, Boss! Hop on!")

"So, Marilyn, you'll have to go in the Jewel for now," I said. "We're hunting once we get there."

"MHOOO." ("Understood.")

"Will you protect me, Liz?" I asked.

"…" ("Of course. Don't you worry.")

"Babi, are you ready?" I asked.

"Always am!"

And, of course, I was fully prepared, as well.

"Let's go, then."

"Yes, Master!" they all replied in perfect unison as we took off.

[ROOK STORY, END.] To Be Continued in the Next Episode…

## Side Story A Day Off in Gideon — Noon

*Journalist, Marie Adler*

"Here are your luxury box tickets for tomorrow's event," the tian scalper told me. "100,000 lir each makes 300,000 lir. Instant payment."

"Okey dokey," I replied as I gave him the money. I'd already confirmed the legitimacy of the tickets by using my Truth Discernment and Identification skills.

I paid from the reward money pool the three of us had decided to split as a group yesterday.

"A pleasure doing business," said the scalper. "You're in luck, lady. Those are the last box seat tickets I had."

"Quite a popular event, isn't it?" I commented.

*Not every show can get scalpers to sell out while pricing their tickets at three times the original cost,* I thought.

"Well, obviously," he nodded. "After all, the thing going on at the central arena tomorrow has never happened before."

"True," I agreed. "It's only to be expected for a battle between Superiors to get this much attention."

The tickets in my hand had the words "The Clash of the Superiors" written on them. That was the name of the main event that was happening at the central arena tomorrow.

The participants were two Superiors.

One was a Superior of the Kingdom of Altar and the undisputed champion of the central arena: Over Gladiator, Figaro.

The other was a Superior from the hermit Empire of Huang He, summoned here to participate in this event: Master Jiangshi, Xunyu.

The idea of seeing a match between such distinguished personalities excited both players and tians alike.

Despite *Dendro* having hundreds of thousands active players, the total number of Superiors didn't even exceed a hundred. Due to that, opportunities to see two Superiors fight were few and far between. Since none of Altar's Superiors had participated, not even the war with Dryfe had had such a fight. Though Figaro's battles were a common sight at Gideon's arenas, all of his opponents so far had been either tians or non-Superior Masters.

As far as I was aware, Superior fights involving the kingdom's Masters had never gone beyond rumors that the furball (AKA The King of Destruction) had fought Caldina's "Magically Strongest" (The Earth), and one of the Great Seven Embryos of Granvaloa. Those fights were said to have happened in a secluded mountain area and in the middle of the ocean, meaning that there were few people who had seen them. Due to all that, this event was a golden opportunity for people to witness and find out just how intense Superior fights were. It was only natural for the tickets to get sold out. In fact, when they had officially gone up for purchase two weeks ago, they had been snapped up in less than ten minutes.

I silently looked at the ones in my hand and tried imagining what would happen if either of the participants boycotted the event. Count Gideon, the one managing the arena, would surely flip. Of course, considering that I'd spent most of the reward on these tickets, my situation wouldn't be too good, either.

*I really hope the event happens without much trouble and that Ray and Rook enjoy it.*

"Take care, now!" I said.

"You too," replied the scalper. "Come to me any time you need a ticket for something."

Silently praying that the event would start as intended, I left the scalper.

It was now past three in the afternoon, and I no longer had anything to do.

My job as a Journalist wouldn't start until tomorrow's event, while my *other job* didn't have any activity at all right now. I checked my friends list and found out that Rook was offline, while Ray was somewhere outside Gideon. I didn't have any other friends here in the kingdom.

Even if I wanted to do some observation and kill time while on a basic party quest, I couldn't get one because they normally rejected all Journalists. The job was of no use in battle, after all. It was a wonder why Ray had even accepted me.

Not having anything to do, I walked around the fourth district's bazaar while eyeing the wares with Identification. Every now and then, you could find some real bargains here, but nothing I saw today really caught my eye.

After a while of such walking, I saw the shop belonging to Alejandro, the man we'd met during yesterday's quest. I considered stopping by and saying hello, but the building seemed to be ridiculously crowded. From what I could hear the people say, the gacha machine there had just dropped an MVP special reward, causing many who were feeling lucky to try and hit another one.

Having only two special rewards in my possession, I could fully understand what drove them.

Yesterday, Ray had happened to become the MVP in a UBM fight when we'd run into Gardranda. But it rarely went as smoothly as that.

Encountering UBMs was rare even if you searched for them, and even the Epic-tier ones were really tough. Masters with high-rank Embryos and jobs would have to form a proper party just to stand a chance, and it was unthinkable to take them on solo without having a Superior Job. Even then, battles against Legendaries and Ancient Legendaries would be truly challenging.

Indeed, getting a special reward was no small task. Soloing UBMs while being like Ray — a high-rank job with a low-rank Embryo — was nearly unheard of, and it happened mostly because of luck and compatibility.

Nemesis's abilities were heavily focused on battle, countering, and giant-killing, making me quite excited to see how they'd grow.

Anyway, with the store being so crowded, going in just to say hi would probably make me nothing but a nuisance, so I decided to leave it for another day.

"I'VE WASTED A MILLION! AAAAHHH!" I heard someone scream as I slowly distanced myself from the shop.

As I aimlessly walked around and began thinking about killing time in some shop popular with cute boys and girls, a certain sound entered my ears.

A young girl was shouting something from behind the corner, in a secluded back alley between the buildings. With my curiosity piqued, I approached the source of the voice, stuck my head out to take a look and was presented with one of the most cliché scenes ever.

Four vulgar-looking men were surrounding a girl who didn't even seem to be ten years old. Though the blonde, coiled, drill-shaped hair made it obvious that she was Western, for one reason or another, her face was covered by a Japanese fox mask.

"Let's take this brat. She looks noble. Selling her off will get us some serious gold," said one of the men as he grabbed her wrist.

"Unhand me, you insolent cur!" the girl shouted as she did her utmost to struggle, but she simply wasn't strong enough to resist.

*How cliché,* I thought. *Truly the most of generic of incidents.*

It was even embarrassing to interfere, since that would make it even more cliché. However, that was exactly what I did.

"Now, wait just a moment, fellas," I said as I walked out from behind the corner. "Are you seriously trying to take this helpless loli away? Should I be concerned?"

"The fuck are you?!" one of them shouted.

"Just a passing Journalist," I answered while getting a better look at the men's faces. "Yep, those are the expressions of true criminals. Could you morbid-looking folks leave the loli alone and go home? Or would you like to go straight to jail?"

As I expected, my provocation made one of the men's foreheads twitch as he charged at me with a raised fist.

"A Journalist?! Who do ya think you're talking to?! C'mere and I'll...!"

"Aaand... there." I grabbed the man by the wrist and did a one-armed shoulder throw on him.

Hitting the stony path below instantly made him lose consciousness.

*As always, this move is very useful against tians who don't know about judo,* I thought. *They can never land safely.*

Of course, it would probably do little good against those who were aware of martial arts or simply had high stats. But these hoodlums weren't much better than the usual newbie.

"B-But she's a Journalist!" one of them exclaimed. "How can she fight?!"

"Oh come now," I said. "Journalist or not, everyone is capable of throwing people."

*Not to mention that I'm… Oh, there's no need to say it,* I thought. Then I repeated the same thing with the other three.

As a result, the four hoodlums who had been about to kidnap the girl were all spread out across the alley.

"Heh," I chuckled. "Once again, I went and threw something worthless."

"Amazing! You're so strong!" said the blonde girl as she looked up at me. The blue eyes I could see under her mask seemed to be gleaming. How adorable.

"Y-You bitch! We're not done yet!" Staggering, the hoodlums stood up and were about to charge at me, but…

"Hey! It's time to get paid! Stop messing around!" another hoodlum from outside the alley called.

*There were more of them?* I asked myself. *Five hoodlums, huh? Why couldn't it be five heroes, instead? That would've been far better in every possible way. Also, "paid"? Are they the underlings of some mafia or something?*

"Crap… We'll let you off this time! I know your mug now! Remember that!" one of them shouted a particularly stale phrase as they all ran away.

"Do they have some debuff that forces them to keep saying overused phrases?" I said as I casually waved them goodbye. I really didn't want to see them again. Not only were they awful as characters, but they were far too basic to be *useful* to me.

"Wow, that crest is the sign of a Master! I know why you're strong now!" said the girl upon noticing the back of the hand I was waving.

*Oh, the purity in her gaze is far too dazzling for a creature like me,* I thought.

"Oh no," I said. "That was just judo. Anyone can learn how to do it. Even you."

I'd only taken a few real-life classes, for instance. For a while, I had dabbled in a lot of various martial arts for my work. I was now unemployed… and dropping such sports certainly wasn't good for my weight.

"Truly?! I can learn that?! Could you teach me?!" asked the girl.

"Of course. First, we…" Suddenly, I realized that a stony pavement definitely wasn't a suitable surface to teach judo.

*We should find a patch of grass or get a soft mat and…*

"We found her!"

"She's over here! There's a suspicious-looking woman with her!"

Before I could finish my thought, a few guards ran into the alley and shouted those things.

*How rude! I'm not suspicious-looking!* I wore a black men's suit, had a properly-tied necktie, covered my eyes with sunglasses, and always had a grin on my face.

*All right, okay, I look suspicious.*

"Oh no! We must escape!" said the girl as she grabbed my hand and started running away from the guards.

"And why am *I* being dragged into this?" I muttered as I realized that things could get really messy if we got caught. But I quickly decided play along with her.

I took the girl into my arms, faced the wall, and jumped upwards, instantly putting us on roof-level. Then I jumped from building to building to get as far away from that alley as was necessary before going down to street-level in a place where no one could see us.

"That was riveting!" said the girl, bright-eyed and looking like she'd just gotten off a roller coaster. "I felt like I became the wind!"

"Oh, it was nothing, really."

"Could you do it because you are a Master or because you are a Journalist?"

"The latter. Journalists are amazing. We can fly, carry buildings, and reverse time by making the Earth spin in the other direction."

"Wow!"

*Okay, fine, that's limited to a certain man who is particularly "super,"* I thought. "By the way, about those guards..."

As I was about to continue, I heard an adorable sound coming from the girl's tummy.

"Shall we eat something?" I asked.

"We shall!"

And so, I decided to help her fill her empty stomach.

Coming out as we were and letting the guards see us wasn't the best idea, so I had to do a little messing around. Using two of my skills, Disguise and Illusion, I changed her appearance, making her look like a plain girl of a normal upbringing. People with Truth Discernment, Reveal, or Mind's Eye skills would be able to see through the disguise, but it wasn't like every guard here had one of those, so it didn't matter too much.

As for me... Saddening as it was, I had to remove my sunglasses. With that, I was no longer a "shady woman in shades." Truly a shame.

We walked out of the empty alleyway and made our way towards the stalls on the main street. It was a popular place, so, naturally, there were food stalls, as well.

"Do you have anything in mind?" I asked.

"I want something I never get to eat!" she answered, and then noticed something. "There! I want those clouds!"

*Clouds...? Oh, the cotton candy,* I thought. *What an adorable choice.*

I went and bought some of the white cotton candy, which looked exactly the same as the ones we had on Earth. The only real difference was that they weren't covered in wrapping displaying some character.

"Enjoy," I said.

"Very well! Thank you very much!" she said as she took the cotton candy, took off the mask and began eating. "Such sweetness and fluffiness!"

"Heh heh. Glad you like... it...?" I paused.

Her exposed face was very cute, making it more than obvious that she would be a real beauty someday. But the fact of her adorability meant nothing next to the fact that her face was familiar to me.

I reached into my inventory and took out my Information Notebook, a must-have item for Journalists that allowed the filing and managing of info, and followed the index to a certain part of it.

Specifically, the list of this country's important people and the entry about the second princess, Elizabeth S. Altar.

It had all the information I'd collected about her and displayed her portrait photo, which showed a little lady bearing the exact same facial features as the girl right before my eyes, the one still eating cotton candy.

"Well, this sure smells like trouble," I muttered as I became fully aware that I'd gotten myself into something both exciting and dangerous.

"Hm? But it smells sweet," said Elizabeth as she smelled the cotton candy, making me momentarily discard the bad thoughts and merely enjoy the adorable presence of Her Majesty.

*A journalist and a princess... Reminds me of a certain movie,* I thought.

Anyway, we'd distanced ourselves from the crowds, and it was time for me to take in the situation.

I had been strolling around.

A girl had been about to get kidnapped, so I'd helped her.

She'd gotten attached to me.

I had been about to be caught by the guards.

I'd taken the girl and ran.

The girl was actually the second princess of this country.

And that was the jist of it.

Conclusion: I was now officially a kidnapper of not only a child, but an extremely important person.

*Oh, dear.*

"In the worst case scenario, I might even get sent to the gaol," I muttered.

"Gaol?" the princess tilted her head to the side.

The gaol was a separate area where players were sent if they committed one too many grave *Dendro* crimes. Grave crimes in *Dendro* were primarily those against tians. Player killing and the like didn't count, and for me that was nothing but good news.

Going in and out of the gaol was completely impossible, and so far, not a single player had left it. According to what those who were sent there wrote on discussion boards, the gaol had equipment and dungeons, just like the rest of the game, allowing them to have a proper *Dendro* experience.

However, leaving simply wasn't an option.

No one knew its location, making many assume that it was the only separate *Dendro* server besides the worldwide one, but the truth behind it was still unknown.

Anyway, it took more than grave crimes to send a player to the gaol.

When criminals got on a country's wanted list, they could no longer use its save points. Save points were places such as the fountains here in the Kingdom of Altar, and they existed in all the cities, towns, and villages of all the seven countries. After getting a death penalty, players respawned at a save point they'd already "marked."

Getting a death penalty while not having any available save points would have the player respawn at the gaol.

I found that to be completely reasonable.

We Masters could get the death penalty, but besides that, we were completely immortal. The system needed a way to deter players from repeatedly committing crimes every time they respawned.

Mind you, for the wanted lists to work, the tians had to know the offenders' names, faces, and crimes. Also, even if they were put on a wanted list of one country and died there, players could always respawn in any other country, provided they had marked save points there. Such "escaping" was currently being used by Goblin Street — the clan responsible for besieging the west side of the capital, and the only group that had gotten on the wanted list because of it.

From what I'd heard, strong Masters who were criminals in some countries were sometimes kept as potential soldiers in case of a war by the other ones.

Now, some crimes were so grave that they got players on the wanted lists of all the seven countries at once, banning them from *all* the save points everywhere. Such cases were extremely rare, and few people had to worry about that happening. However, being someone who'd seemingly kidnapped royalty, I was now one of those "few."

*Oh, what am I to do?* I thought as I looked at the princess as she continued eating the cotton candy.

"Hm? What is it? Why are you staring at me so? Do I have something on my face?" she asked.

"Just a bit of cotton candy," I answered as I took it off her cheek and ate it myself. *It really is sweet.*

Anyway, for now, she was under the effects of my Disguise and Illusion combo. It wouldn't be easy for people to notice that she was the princess. I could've also used Presence Manipulation to make us stand out less, but that might've had the opposite effect due to stronger people realizing that something was off, so I refrained.

*All right, now why did the princess wander about the city all by herself?* I thought.

From the fact that the guards were searching for her, it was safe to assume that she had sneaked out for some sightseeing.

*Well, that would be another way this situation is similar to the one in* Roman Holiday*... I wonder if this city has a Mouth of Truth.* I'd do what they did in the movie, put my right hand inside and...

*No. I'm a tremendous liar, so it'd instantly get bitten off.*

"You haven't said anything for a while. What are you thinking about?" asked Elizabeth.

"Oh, nothing," I answered. "Just some things that might be slightly comedic to the audience."

"Comedic?"

*All right, now back to why the princess is here,* I thought. At this point, talking to her seemed like the best way to find out.

"Oh, we've yet to introduce ourselves," I spoke up, being careful not to make it obvious that I knew who she was. "I'm Marie Adler."

"I see! So your name is Marie! I am Elizabeth, the second princess of this country!"

...She actually had no intention of hiding it.

*Why the mask, then? Did she just want to wear it?*

"Umm, why were you in the streets, princess?"

"I was told that Gideon is an exciting place!" she declared. "However, my attendants did not let me go outside, so I escaped to have a pu-pleasure jaunt!"

And thus, it was confirmed that she really *was* just sightseeing. Not only that, but she'd done it without even trying to hide her identity, like any normal child just walking out to play.

*How bold of her.*

"That must've been quite the great escape," I said.

"Indeed! Timing it was hard."

*Would the timing really have been enough for her — a princess — to successfully slip through? Should I be worried about this country?* I thought. *Well, I obviously should, considering it's been on a decline ever since the war....*

"Today, I intend to spread my wings! However..."

"What is it?" I asked.

"When you found me, I was actually lost... Thus, I would appreciate it if you guided me around..."

It now made sense why she had been in that back alley.

As for her request...

If I stayed with the princess, they might assume that I'd kidnapped her and arrest me. However, the idea of leaving this adorable, socially-unaware girl all by herself was far more worrying to me than getting arrested. I also felt that there was more to this than it seemed.

"Why, certainly. I'll guide you around," I said.

"Really?!" asked the princess.

"Yes. I never lie."

*Apologies. That line itself was a lie.*

When asked about what kind of places she wanted to go to, Elizabeth said simply, "Anywhere that's riveting!"

As was natural for *duel city* Gideon, the most popular tourist spots here were the arenas, but I was quite apprehensive about bringing a little girl to a place so thick with the reek of blood.

Well, it wasn't like the arena barriers let any smells reach the audience. Also, no matter how severely damaged the participants were, they would come out completely unharmed once the battle was over.

*The barriers sure are useful and convenient,* I thought.

According to the setting, the barrier-equipped arenas hadn't been made by the kingdom's tians. All thirteen of them had been there since ancient times, and a city had merely happened to be built around them.

A barrier that could make the most critical of wounds simply disappear was extreme tech for both magic and science, and being able to replicate it would cause far too many people to take advantage of it. That was surely the reason why the devs had made it into a lost technology that no one could copy.

The barriers weren't the only pieces of such tech, either. There were the relics from the pre-ancient civilization and Granvaloa's underwater ruins, among many other things.

Anyway, with the arena being out of the question, I decided to bring the princess to the nearby plaza.

Just like on the main road, stalls were placed all across the area, but that certainly wasn't all. I could see street performers such as musicians, artists, and fortune tellers, as well.

"Wow! Is this a festival?!" the princess voiced her excitement.

"Many people with various impressive skills gather here," I answered.

There were the staples such as jugglers and people balancing on balls, but I could also see Masters entertaining people by using their Embryos.

What I found particularly eye-catching — or, rather, ear-catching — was the musical ensemble. It consisted of four people — no, one person and three creatures. A man wearing a bird-like hat was swinging a conductor's stick, a centaur was playing a violin, a cat sìth was blowing into a flute, and a kobold was hitting a drum. Quite a peculiar band of performers, indeed.

What was even more peculiar, however, was the fact that, despite there being only three creatures playing, the resulting music was like that of a large-scale orchestra. Their act enchanted not only the passersby, but some of the other street performers, as well. Indeed, the music was downright beautiful, especially once you got over the fact that it was an orchestral arrangement of a classic super robot anime opening.

I felt like I was listening to an elementary-to-middle school orchestra contest or a Koshien cheering song.

"Such a powerful melody," said the princess.

"Indeed it is," I agreed. *It's* Mazinger Z, *after all.*

"Are those monsters and a horse-man?" she asked.

"No, I believe it's a Type Legion Embryo," I answered.

"'Legion'?" she asked.

Legion was an Embryo type that evolved from the base category of Guardian. Its main feature was the fact that it was basically multiple Guardians in one. That multiplicity was exactly what made the type interesting.

For example, you could have an Embryo that was basically a "We are the Something's Elite Four!"-kinda thing, where they were few, but strong. You could also have an Embryo that was hundred-strong swarm of weaker creatures. They both would be categorized as "Legion." Quality and quantity meant nothing for this type.

This band was definitely focused on quality.

My Embryo — Arc-en-Ciel — was Legion, but I wasn't quite sure what it was focused on. It could go both ways, honestly.

“So that is an Embryo,” said the princess.

“Yes,” I nodded.

“I always thought that Embryos were only meant for fighting.”

“Embryos are based on their Master’s minds, so they’re not always created with battle in mind,” I said. There were actually quite a few Embryos that didn’t have a single fighting-related skill.

It wasn’t particularly surprising, really. After all, they always reflected people’s personalities and experiences. However, with that considered, I couldn’t help but grin in self-derision at the fact that my Embryo was so battle-focused and what it implied about my mind.

The band was done performing, so after we gave them their due applause and money, we went to do other activities.

That included eating ice cream and scooping goldfish-like monsters, both of which were common things in the Japanese festivals I was familiar with and didn’t seem the least bit special to any common citizen here. And yet, the princess looked like she was having tons of fun, as though these seemingly meaningless activities were a true treasure to her.

“Let’s go to the painter next! I want to be drawn!” she squealed.

“Don’t you get portraits regularly?” I asked in response.

“I do! But they look too serious! Also, they don’t look like me! I’m not that scary!”

Apparently, the little princess had a little trauma going on.

*I guess that’s how most portraits appear to children,* I thought. *That Beethoven in the music room is a good example, but let’s not get lost in thought again.*

“I can draw you, princess,” I said. In fact, I was the only one that could. She was under the effects of my Illusion skill, so if we let a random street artist draw her, the person on the result wouldn't even be her.

"Hm? You can draw?" she asked.

"Yes. Not only that, but I'm quite confident that I'm better than the average Painter." That was a non-battle job that had Drawing within its skill repertoire. Its effect was technical support that helped Painters draw lines to form pictures as they desired. However, people who already had the skill in real life didn't need any support from such skills. I was one of them.

Skills such as Drawing and Cooking, ones that players could replace with any technique and flair they had in reality, were called "sense skills."

Another example of this would be the Detective job's "Inferring" skill. It allowed the user to understand the tricks, clues, and evidence surrounding various incidents. But people who were skilled detectives in real life had no need for it.

Not like I was aware of any such players, but still.

"Anyway, you can trust my drawing ability," I said confidently. "I'll make you look very cute!"

"Very well! I shall believe you!" The princess sat down on a bench in the plaza and straightened her back. That bearing made her seem truly princess-like.

"And you are very right to do so," I said as I reached into my inventory to take out a sketchbook and my drawing equipment.

The sketchbook was opened on the page with a shirtless dog-eared Ray sketch.

*...The princess must not see this,* I thought as I skipped a few pages.

I put a lot of effort into drawing her, so it took me about ten minutes even without coloring, but I was quite satisfied with the result. It had to have her likeness, but since she didn't seem to like proper portraits, I avoided making it too realistic and just used my usual art style.

"Well, what do you think?" I asked as I sat down next to her and showed her the sketch.

"Wow! It's so cute! Is this really me?" she cried.

"Yes."

With the original being so adorable, making the drawing cute was easy, and the result had come out very naturally.

"Marie, you're amazing! You beat scoundrels! Run on walls! And can even draw!"

"Oh no, I'm really not that impressive."

"Are you able to do this because you're a Journalist?"

"Ah, no. My drawing ability has nothing to do with my job."

"Why can you draw, then?"

*The reason for my artistic ability? Well...*

"I used to be a manga artist on the other side."

*Nagisa Ichimiya*

I began drawing manga — or, rather, simple illustrations — when I was in the later years of elementary school. It all started when a friend invited me to join an illustration club.

Naturally, the club had books that described the proper ways to draw manga illustrations, so I began reading them and put the knowledge I received to the test. As I repeated that, I eventually became able to draw manga in a proper format.

At first, I tried drawing a story that was far too grand for a newbie such as myself, and I ended up giving up after about three volumes' worth of pages. Two of those volumes were actually nothing but setting descriptions…

Despite my first work being so shoddy, I didn't give up on drawing manga, and after learning from my mistakes, I began drawing ones that were complete with just single chapters.

The only people who saw them were my friends in the illustration club, which became the manga association when we entered middle school. However, as I continued drawing those shorts, I eventually became good enough to have my friends suggest that I send my works to a contest.

Figuring I had no reason not to, I sent one out, and though it didn't make the cut, I didn't stop sending my contributions.

This continued for about five or six years, until the winter of my second year in high school, when a certain award chose the work I submitted.

It was the first shonen manga I'd ever drawn. My previous works had all been shojo manga heavily focused on love, and this shonen work had merely been something I'd drawn on a whim.

It had gotten put in a certain magazine as a non-serialized story, and, supposedly due to good ratings, the editorial department had approached and invited me to ask whether I'd like to serialize it. At first, considering that I'd drawn it on a whim, I didn't actually think that I could continue it. However, when I gave it a try, the drawing went so smoothly that I felt as though my pencil was moving on its own.

The story continued without a hitch, and by the time I graduated, instead of going into higher education, I decided to become a manga artist.

I was worried whether I'd made the right decision, but my parents were fully supportive of my choice. They told me to live the life I wanted and offered to help me whenever I needed it.

That moment made me cry a bit.

Thus, I became a manga artist with a series in a monthly magazine.

At first, there were a lot of things I wasn't used to, and adjusting to them was quite a challenge. I even had to do research for my work by getting into martial arts and buying airsoft guns. When my parents happened to visit me, they said that I was being very boyish, but that was one of my very dear memories now.

The serialization went smoothly for more than two years. My work was pretty popular, too. Not enough to be the magazine's flagship title, but definitely in the top five. I even had hopes that it could get adapted into an anime after a year or two.

And that was when the magazine's publisher went bankrupt.

The cause was a business failure in divisions besides the one responsible for manga. And yet, the magazine was canceled, forcing my first series to end with its first part.

I was absentminded for a long while after that. There were entire hours… *days…* when I was just lying around and whispering, "What do I do now?" to myself.

However, there was a silver lining, as I got approached by an editor from a different magazine, offering me to continue my manga there. With the publisher's bankruptcy, other magazines began competing for the newly-unemployed artists and their works, and my manga happened to be among those.

I asked the editor to give me time to think, but definitely not about the answer to the offer. The answer to whether I wished to continue my series was a resounding, "Yes! Of course!" But I had another major problem I had to consider.

It was the fact that I *could no longer draw it.*

I had simply become unable to continue my manga series.

Right after the forced end of its first part, my vision of the work's protagonist, Marie Adler, had gone completely still. No matter how hard I tried, drawing her just didn't feel the same as before. She seemed to have become completely inanimate. Forcing myself to draw her made me feel as if I was a puppeteer using strings to move a corpse.

I was going through a so-called slump. As though I'd forgotten something I could do as easily as breathing, I became completely unable to continue drawing my manga… Marie's story.

Eventually, this extended to any other stories I attempted, rendering me incapable of completing the simplest of one-shots.

I'd spent my entire life being absolutely serious about manga. I'd drawn my works with all I had. And yet, that had gone away in a flash.

I did everything I could to try and regain my touch. Thinking that it would help me gain a new perspective, I used my money to travel the world and made attempts to gain new skills, like cooking, handicrafts, and koryu. However, all of that failed me, making me more than aware that I could no longer draw stories as I was.

"Oh, God. Please give me a possibility that isn't my own. Let me draw her story… *Help me understand her,*" I prayed.

Almost the moment I began asking for that, I became aware of a certain game.

"*Infinite Dendrogram* will provide you with a new world and your very own unique possibility!"

A VRMMO that bore the promotional line, and that didn't betray it, *Infinite Dendrogram*.

I believed… felt… *hoped*… that a game which provided countless different possibilities and lives would help me find the continuation to my story that I'd seemed to have completely lost.

With that hope in me, I began *Infinite Dendrogram*.

I made my avatar's name the same as hers — Marie Adler.

I gave my avatar a similar appearance: long black hair, tall, pretty, and always wearing sunglasses.

I even went as far as to talk the same way she did — unique in tone and superficially polite.

I finished it up by matching my behavioral patterns to hers, becoming a proper Marie Adler roleplayer.

I felt like and hoped that doing so might help me notice something that could breathe life into her again.

A year had passed since then, and I'd yet to draw her story's continuation.

However, I could feel her breathing every moment I spent in *Infinite Dendrogram*.

That alone was enough reason for me to stay here.

*Journalist, Marie Adler*

"Nhh..." The princess stretched. "It's been so long since I had such an enjoyable time."

"That's good to know," I said.

After I'd drawn her, she'd continued to enjoy the many activities available in this plaza. Enjoying the food that she was likely unfamiliar with and the activities she never got to do, the girl had obviously had a very good time. Now, she was sitting on a bench while licking a candy that had the shape of a cute animal.

*Why are the stalls here so much like the ones in Japanese fairs?* I casually wondered.

"Gideon really *is* a lively city," she said. "Count Brittis was telling the truth."

"Count Brittis?" I asked.

"Yes. He often talks to me about how fun Gideon is."

"Oh?" *Shady.* "Well, he's not wrong," I said. "As you probably already know — or have heard from him — Gideon is quite a feature-plenty city."

It was a popular center for trade with the nearby nations of Legendaria and Caldina. The western port city was just a few days away on foot. Its arenas also gave it a powerful tourist industry, making a popular resort city for both rich tians and Masters.

Also, when it came to the kingdom's main cities, Gideon was the one that was farthest away from the northern country of Dryfe, so there was little fear of them endangering these parts.

"It's probably the most prosperous city in the kingdom," I concluded.

"Yes," said the princess. "Even the people's faces are more cheerful than in the capital."

*Does she manage such escapes in Altea, too?* I asked myself.

Seemingly remembering the state of the capital, the princess suddenly looked a bit down.

The people there had to live in constant fear of war, and the recent PK incident that had resulted in the complete immolation of Noz Forest surely hadn't helped at all…

"My heart hurts a bit," I muttered.

"Hm? What's wrong, Marie? Do you feel ill?" she asked.

"No, I'm fine. Also, you seem to be thinking about the capital's people, but I don't believe there's any need to worry. They should cheer up sooner than later. That's what the castle's people are working for, right?"

"…You're right! I'm sure my sister will take care of it all!"

"Indeed she will."

*…Not like I believe that,* I thought.

A good governing body was enough *only* when there were no international relationships to consider. When a country had a very clear enemy, not even the greatest ruler could do anything to take care of the people's fears.

I simply didn't have the heart to tell her that the capital's people's woes would continue for a long time. Thus, I told a comforting lie, and considering that it cheered her up, I was confident that I'd done the right thing.

"I will do all I can to help my sister in her work!" she declared.

"Excellent. Do your best, princess," I said.

"Mrrgh."

*Oh? Why did she suddenly turn sulky?* I thought. "Is anything wrong, princess?"

"That's what's wrong!"

"By 'that,' you mean…?"

"You've been calling me nothing but 'princess' for a while now! It makes you feel de…distant!"

*"Distant," huh?* I thought. *Well, I guess avoiding her name and calling her just by her position wasn't very friendly.* Also, the word "distant" was more fitting than she'd ever imagined. After all, I was full of lies.

"Very well. I'll call you 'Ellie.'"

She said nothing.

*Oh? Why the silence? Did I close too much distance?*

"Ellie," she muttered.

"Don't like it?" I asked.

"No! I love it! From now on, I am Ellie!"

*So she likes it.* "Good to know, Ellie."

"Heh heh."

My, what an adorable smile. I wanted to take her home, rub my cheeks on hers, and sleep with her.

*All right, no no no no. Not only would that be cause for concern, it would also be a kidnapping of an important individual.*

Remembering that she was important made me curious about something.

"By the way, Ellie, you said that you escaped the place you were staying at," I said. "Why are you in Gideon, in the first place?"

"To enjoy it, of course!" she answered proudly.

"Sorry. Poor wording on my part. I meant the official business." I was confident that I already knew the answer, but it didn't hurt to confirm.

"Oh, I came here to observe the arena event tomorrow."

Sure enough, it was The Clash of the Superiors. The event was an absolute first, after all. It was only natural for royalty to come in and make it even more prestigious.

"My elder sister should come tomorrow, too," she added.

"...Eh? Elder sister?"

"Indeed."

The elder sister of Ellie — second princess of the Kingdom of Altar. The only person that could be was the first princess and the current acting ruler of the country, Altimia A. Altar.

It didn't make sense. After all, a single member of royalty was more than enough to give an event prestige.

*...Is there something more?* I thought.

"So you and your sister entered Gideon separately, huh?" I asked.

"I acted as her representative yesterday. I met Count Gideon and we made preparations for tomorrow's banquet. It was very hard!"

I would prefer it if they didn't overwork such a little girl. However, that was probably part being royalty, so I couldn't really say much.

"That's why I'm very glad I got a chance to relax and enjoy myself today!"

"Well, and I'm glad that you enjoyed yourself, Ellie... Oh, I have something to take care of. May we go?"

"We may! I had enough fun here in the plaza."

I took Ellie's hand, helped her stand up, disposed of the stick from her candy, and began walking away. While doing so, I looked at one of the city lights — specifically, the image reflected on its metallic surface.

"We're being followed by... three people," I muttered.

"Did you say something?" Elizabeth asked.

"No, never mind, Ellie." After leaving the plaza, we entered Gideon's DIN office.

DIN, Dendrogram Information Network, was one of the news companies of the continent. Just like Knights got their job from the kingdom's knight orders and like Ninjas or Onmitsu got theirs from Tenchi's shinobi villages, Journalists got their job by becoming associated with one of the many mass media companies all over the world.

The protagonist of my manga, Marie Adler, was a journalist, so it had already been decided that I would take this job.

The news company I decided to join was DIN. It wasn't the biggest in the industry, but it was notable for having offices in every important city of each country. Then there was the fact that it also acted as an information peddler without borders, which I liked because it was very "manga-like."

Naturally, DIN had a branch office here in Gideon, as well. In fact, I had found out about the scalper that sold tickets for tomorrow's event by asking my colleagues here.

By the way, every single Master working for DIN was treated as a special correspondent. After all, we could travel all over the place.

I had started in Tenchi, and I'd already been to Granvaloa, Huang He, and Caldina before ending up here in Altar.

We Masters made great special correspondents because we had the dynamism, fighting ability and — most importantly — the power to survive after getting the required information.

Of course, due to the skill "The Pen is Mightier than the Sword" preventing all combat action, pure Journalists had extremely high death rates.

However, just like Paladin's Aegis, it was the type of skill that only worked while having a main job from that grouping, making it perfectly possible to fight after nullifying it by switching to a job from another grouping.

That was why many Journalist Masters chose to travel after switching to another job, changing back to Journalist to do the relevant work and then switching to a fighting job when traveling again.

The problem with that was the fact that job switching could only be done at save points, which only existed at towns and cities.

Sure, there was also the option of using Job Crystals, which allowed the user to instantly change their main job no matter where they were, but they were both expensive and disappeared after one use.

There were pluses and minuses to both staying a Journalist and constantly switching jobs. That was why I'd chosen neither.

But enough about that.

Once we entered the office, Ellie looked like an elementary schooler that had just gone through an educational field trip. Well, not like anyone could tell, considering that I'd had her wear a mask. Many of my fellow Journalists had skills that allowed them to see through Illusion's visual trickery and Disguise's fake stats, so I did it to make sure no one realized who she was.

"I didn't know news companies were so active," she commented.

"They're really busy with the preparations for tomorrow's event," I said. "Even I got a job."

Once I thanked them for telling me about the scalper, they'd given me many various data devices. They'd wanted me to make the best of my special seat and get the best recordings I could.

Some might think it unnecessary, considering they'd reserved the media seats, but I could fully understand wanting to have shots from many different angles. It was especially important in fighting matches. I used many such photos as references when drawing my manga.

We didn't stay in the office for too long. I merely said hi, asked for two sets of information, and left.

The information I got was everything concerning two noble families.

The first family was the rulers of Gideon: the Gideons. The current head of the family, Count Aschbarray Gideon, was a fifteen-year-old youth.

He'd inherited his position from his late father, who had lost his life to an illness about two months ago. However, his coming-of-age ceremony had been only a month ago, so there was a bit of a lag until he officially inherited the title and became acknowledged as the count.

Speaking of coming-of-age, the Kingdom of Altar had a custom where the ones to be sent to war weren't the current heads of noble families, but their heirs. Many would assume that it should've been the other way around, but apparently, they believed that the ones who lived through such pain and trials were the ones who were truly worthy of becoming the nobles of the next generation.

However, the war had happened half a year ago, when Aschbarray hadn't been of age, so he'd ended up avoiding having to participate in it. The military officer the Gideon family had sent to represent him had died in the war, so it was safe to say that the Count was quite lucky.

Still, it wasn't a bed of roses for him.

The city of Gideon was still being terrorized by serial kidnappings at the hands of a group known as the "Gouz-Maise Gang." They had been happening since the rule of the previous count, and even after Aschbarray took over, it still didn't seem like it would be taken care of anytime soon.

The continuation of this terror made the people question the young count's ability to manage his lands and keep the peace. Apparently, the more critical nobles were talking about leaving the rule to someone else.

However, the first princess and the nobles who had a say in national politics trusted Gideon's name and had no intention of relieving him of his duties. That might change if the Gouz-Maise Gang continued its activities for longer than they could tolerate, but for all we knew, someone could just pop out of nowhere and simply take care of them.

In any case, the other family was the one bearing the name "Brittis." They ruled the area between Gideon and the port city facing the West Sea. The head of the family was Count Alzar Brittis. Though sixty years of age, he was still in good health.

Alzar had told Ellie about how fun Gideon was, but he had actually been on bad terms with the Gideon family ever since their previous generation.

They simply didn't get along. There were many reasons for that, one of which was the fact that, despite having similar amounts of land, the Gideons were far more influential simply because they had the duel city.

That was enough for me to find the situation suspicious.

It was odd that Count Brittis — who supposedly hated the Gideons — had told Ellie about how fun the city was. Most people wouldn't have anything good to say about those they hated, not to mention that a list of bad things about Gideon could have been pretty lengthy. And yet, Count Brittis had only told her the good things. That was enough reason to believe that he'd intended for her to become interested, walk out, and see for herself. I had my guesses, but I still wasn't confident about why he'd done that.

There was even more interesting info about him.

While getting up there in years, Count Brittis had had his first son. The man was an extremely doting parent and loved his son very dearly. Once his son came of age and became his official heir, he had naturally become excited about what the boy would become in the future.

Indeed, his son had gone through his coming of age ceremony. It had happened *before the war half a year ago.*

Following the custom, the son went to war to represent his father.

Good father that he was, Count Brittis spared no expense to give him the soldiers he needed to come back in good health. He also did some political maneuvering to have his son's army fight alongside the kingdom's strongest: the Knights of the Royal Guard. All so he would come back to him in good health.

And, after all he did for his son, all that Count Brittis got in return was a *right hand with the family's crest on it.*

Hell General, Logan Goddhart.

A Master sitting at the top of Dryfe Imperium's rankings, infamous for commanding numerous devils.

During the war, he had focused only on killing the Royal Guard's commander.

Naturally, the Brittis army, positioned near the Royal Guard, had been overwhelmed by the three thousand or so man-eating devils who had left barely any identifiable corpses. Thus, Count Brittis had lost his only heir — his beloved son.

The tragedy didn't end there, for not only had he spent great quantities of funds to gather the soldiers for the war, he also had to pay condolence money for those who'd lost their loved ones. To top it all off, the Brittis County got hit with a plague, causing the count to use the very last of his riches to prevent it from spreading all over the kingdom.

Though his efforts had been successful, they'd come at the cost of his county's bankruptcy. Count Brittis had bowed before the royal family and relinquished his territory to them. When managing a territory became difficult, it was rarely impossible to continue it, but I couldn't deny that the path to recovery would normally be harsh on the people.

Anyway, Count Brittis hadn't gone with that option. That could either have been because he wished to save his people by putting them under the royal family's wing or because — having lost his heir — he simply didn't have any attachment to his lands anymore.

Thus, Count Brittis became a noble without land, and he now worked at the royal palace as a common civil official.

I couldn't help but wonder what was going on in his mind these days.

"I must say, I'm impressed by the detail of their info on these nobles," I muttered to myself.

*As expected of a news company. They sure know their bigwigs,* I thought.

Anyway, all this info gave me a better grasp of the full picture. Still, if things really were as I assumed them to be, the plan really lacked thoroughness. It required a great bit of luck to produce the results he seemed to want.

"Ellie, what kind of person is Count Brittis?" I asked.

"Count Brittis? He's very diligent," she answered.

*Diligent, huh?* I thought.

"However, he sometimes seems to be very lonely," she added.

"Lonely?"

"I'm lonely, too, so I can see it," said Ellie. Her face fell, and she looked into the distance… in the direction of the capital.

"I have an elder and a younger sister," she continued.

"Yes, I'm aware."

"They both have it very difficult."

I had heard that her elder sister — first princess Altimia — was overwhelmed by her work as acting ruler, while the younger sister — third princess Theresia — was very sickly and could only live in a certain sterilized environment they had.

"My elder sister is much older than me, while Theresia is always in bed. We've never had a chance to play as sisters, and these past six months… we haven't even spent time as a family." Ellie breathed a silent sigh before continuing. "I always felt so lonely. I was no longer sure if I was even loved."

"Ellie…"

Before meeting her today, I'd believed that the second princess was a selfish little girl. Elizabeth S. Altar was said to be whimsical, excessively vigorous, really insolent, and so full of curiosity that it was troubling.

That wasn't really wrong. After all, she had escaped the place she was staying at just to go sightseeing around Gideon, completely neglecting to take any retinue with her. However, her actions could have been spurred by the loneliness caused by not having any family time with her sisters anymore.

"Today, however, I was very happy!" she burst out. "I had lots of fun playing with you, Marie! This was my first time partaking in such activities!" Ellie grabbed my hand in both of hers and gave me a smile reminiscent of a Sun peeking out from behind the darkest clouds.

"I'm glad you enjoyed it," I said.

"I enjoyed it very much! It was a wonderful time! Like from my magic picture books! However..." She cast her eyes down and momentarily fell silent. "However... this magical time is ending."

Ellie let go of my hand and turned her back to me.

"I think I will go back now."

"Are you satisfied, Ellie?" I asked.

"Very! Thanks to you helping me cheer up, I will be able to do my duties better." Still turning away from me, Ellie put her hands together. "Someday, when I become really good at my duties, I will take over for my elder sister and give her some time to rest!" she said before turning around and giving me a full smile. "Then, she and I will walk around Gideon, just like we did today!"

Albeit filled with determination, Ellie's words displayed nothing but the dream of a little child. Considering her and her sister's positions, it was really questionable that it could come true. However…

"Great. I'm sure you'll be able to do that."

That wasn't a lie, but my very own desire.

From the very bottom of my heart, I wished for this pure girl's dream to come true.

That was why I decided to help her.

*???*

"The target and the accompanying person are on the move. Likely heading for Count Gideon's residence in the first district… the place she is staying at."

"Our Magic Cameras got them on record. We have enough 'proof' to frame that Master as the culprit. The time is right."

"Inform the parties responsible for spreading false information all over the city. Once we gather, we will assassinate the second princess of the Kingdom of Altar — Elizabeth S. Altar."

## Side Story A Day Off in Gideon — Night

???

Come eventide, the two of us were walking through the dimly-lit streets.

The way we held hands might've made us look like sisters or mother and child, which was quite curious when I considered the fact that my avatar, Marie, was something akin to a daughter of my own.

As we walked, I chose to take us through a relatively empty alleyway. There were two reasons for that. The first was the fact that it would get us to our destination, Count Gideon's residence, about ten-odd minutes earlier, while the second was...

"Stop," I heard someone say, and I turned around.

A moment later, I felt something pass through my neck.

Then — after a momentary shiver — my head, separated from my body, fell to the ground.

*Leader of the professional assassin group "The Reaper's Pinky," Dead Hand, Roux Diene*

"Target secured," I said. "The accompanying person is confirmed dead."

Within my vision, I could see the now-headless Master woman turn into particles of light and vanish.

The target, the second princess, had fainted due to the sight before her.

"Hmph," I scoffed. "She's a Master, you know? Not like she'll die."

They were always like that. When driven to death's door, they just vanished and came back three days later as if it was no big deal. If that wasn't bad enough, they also had ridiculous powers, Embryos, in their arsenal. It was really bothersome for us that they had their own networks.

To us, a group that murdered by the request of nobles and other rich people, hunting immortal targets wasn't worth the trouble, causing us to ignore most such requests. However, in this situation, the fact that a Master was accompanying our target was actually convenient.

"You have the 'proof,' right?" I asked.

"We've recorded her walking through the town alongside the target," answered one of my subordinates as he took out a crystal used for visual recording. "After we kill the princess, anonymously giving this 'proof' to the right people will get her accused of kidnapping and killing the princess. That will get her on every country's wanted list."

Truth Discernment could reveal any fabricated evidence as fake, but what we had was completely legitimate, so there was no need for us to worry on that front.

The woman had used Illusion to make the princess look different, but that was a skill that only worked on the minds of living things, having no effect on the inorganic. She had also changed her status display by using Disguise, but that was unrelated to our cameras. Not to mention that I — being a skilled Assassin — had high-level Mind's Eye and Reveal skills, allowing me to see right through such tricks. Mind you, the fact that my low-rank job subordinates hadn't been able to see through it meant that her skills were very high-level.

It was a mystery why a mere Journalist had Illusion and Disguise at her disposal, but since those skills weren't battle-related, it was entirely possible that she'd gotten them from a different job.

"Killing royalty instantly gets you on all the wanted lists," I said. "Even if she revives, she'll be out in the gaol."

*She's as good as dead at that point,* I thought.

"This is going well," said one of my subordinates.

"Yeah," I agreed. "We only have to deal with a powerless woman and a child, so this is far easier than anything we originally planned."

We'd expected having to fight the Royal Guard or infiltrating the residence to poison her. However, for some reason, she'd gone outside all on her own and even ended up finding us a nice scapegoat. This situation was a windfall if I ever saw one.

"Marquis Borozel will enjoy this news," I muttered.

"Hmmm...? So it wasn't Count Brittis," replied someone who *wasn't my subordinate.*

A moment later, the subordinate holding the princess screamed as blood burst out of his limbs.

First, I realized that his tendons had been severed.

Then, I saw that the princess was no longer unconscious and that her eyes were wide open.

Finally, I noticed that she was holding a dagger of a sinister design.

Thus, I concluded that she wasn't the princess, but *an enemy.*

"Kill her!" I commanded my subordinates, who instantly and simultaneously threw poisoned knives at her.

However, the enemy bearing the appearance of the princess jumped backwards, moved behind the subordinate who'd lost his tendons, and used him as a shield. All the knives sunk into him and didn't even give him a moment to scream before he died.

"What a terrible thing to do," she said, still holding the corpse. "However, I say that such deaths are a given for fiends trying to kill an innocent child."

She then threw the body away and revealed herself, looking completely unlike the princess.

No longer bright and blonde, her hair had become as black as midnight itself. She was now clad in one of the so-called "men's suits," sometimes used in places like Dryfe and Caldina. Despite it being sundown, she also wore a pair of sunglasses. Her stature was completely different, as well, for she was now an adult.

The only things that were the same about her were the dagger in her hand and the fox mask she wore on the side of her face.

"I must say, Art of Transformation sure takes a toll on SP when you take the shape of someone with a very different physique," she said.

She now had the visage of the Master that we'd beheaded mere moments ago, and the shining crest on the back of her left hand proved that she was the exact same person.

"You…!"

"Oh? What's wrong? You look like you've seen a ghost."

*Why is she alive?* I thought stunned. *How did she transform? Isn't she a Journalist?*

As such questions went through my head, I used Reveal to take a look at her stats.

**Marie Adler**
**Job: Journalist**
**Level: 32 (Total Level: 33)**

Sure enough, I could see it. She was a mere Journalist who barely crossed level 30.

"What is it? It's rude to stare at people, you know?" she said.

"Did you come back to life using an Embryo skill?" I demanded.

*It will all make sense if she did,* I thought.

"Why would I need to come back to life if I never died?"

"Where's the real princess?" I demanded. "When did you replace her?"

"Replace her? But I've been here from the start, and—" Before she could finish her sentence, a subordinate positioned in one of the buildings to the side of the alley jumped out, got behind her and swung his blade at her neck. The moment it sunk into her body, she became particles of light and vanished.

At the same time, however, the subordinate who'd attacked her fainted and fell to the ground.

"And there was no one here but me," her voice reached my ears.

It came from the roof of the building the subordinate had jumped out of.

Looking up, I saw that her appearance had changed yet again. Her body was now shrouded in a dark mist, giving her form a vagueness that made it hard for me to make her out. All I could be certain of was the fact that she wore the fox mask, held a dagger in her left hand, and held a strange pistol in her right.

"...!"

Shock filled me as my Reveal skill — still active — gave me completely different results than before.

**■■■■■ ■■■■■**

**Job: ■■■■■ ■■■■■■**

**Level: ■■■ (Total Level: ■■■)**

I could no longer see her name, her job, or even get a glimpse of her stats.

I'd experienced this when I was training to be an Assassin.

That was how the results looked when my Reveal had a lower skill level than the person's Disguise.

However, I was an experienced Dead Hand — a high-rank job from the assassin grouping — and my Reveal skill level had already reached the maximum of 10.

*Is her Disguise above that?* I thought.

"It can't be," I muttered, yet I was hardly able to deny what I was seeing.

Another thing of note was the fact that my Reveal still got the right number of characters.

"It can't be," I repeated to myself, for it just didn't seem right to me.

The *main job level* — not the total level — was in the triple digits.

At the very least, it was obvious that it wasn't Journalist, for that was a low-rank job with a maximum level of 50.

The job and low stats I'd seen before were merely the result of Disguise or a similar skill, while this was her true form. The triple digits in her job could only mean two things — that she'd also reached the maximum on a high-rank job, or...

"What... What are you?!" I howled.

My question made her form a callous smile, making it seem as though she'd been waiting for it.

"'I am a shade,'" she spoke, each word thick with emotion. "'I am the reflection of all the wrongs you've committed — the mortal phantasm sent to pull you into the darkness...'"

Her tone didn't have any of the ridicule from before. It was cold and theatrical in delivery.

"'Into the Shadow,'" she went on with emphasis and grandeur, spreading her arms to the sides as if she stood before an audience.

"Credit for those words goes to Chapter 1 of Nagisa Ichimiya's hit man superpower battle manga, *Into the Shadow,*" she added, making as little sense as before, as her tone did a complete turnaround and returned to normal.

The fact that her stats were still Disguised and that she'd just killed my subordinates didn't change. Me and the rest of the subordinates still standing were intently observing her every single move.

"U-UWAAHHH!" screamed the new guy in our midst as he dashed towards her, unable to bear the pressure. It was a foolish thing to do, but if his sacrifice gave us an opening, then it would be worth it.

Not saying a word, the woman moved only her hand. With a snap of the wrist, she emptied the chambers on her revolver-like gun and loaded it with white and black bullets before pulling the trigger.

The muzzle was pointed in a completely irrelevant direction, but…

"GERGHGHGHGHGHGH!"

…what came out of it was a black and white, bullet-like creature that sounded a strange voice as it left the gun, changed its trajectory in an impossible manner. It sunk into the new guy's body.

Without as much as a groan, he collapsed to the ground and became unable to move a finger.

It was as if he'd been completely paralyzed.

Though alive, there was nothing he could do.

The woman had done this with barely any effort — by merely moving her hand.

"What's wrong?" she asked while looking down on us. "Getting cold feet? Cold sweat? Heartbeat too fast? About to break?" Her eyes were hidden behind both the mist and the sunglasses. "Is that how you become when facing something other than 'powerless women and children'?"

I could tell that the light in her gaze was still cold.

"I'm probably not one to talk, though," she said as she sighed. "When attacked by the land-warship, all I could do was run away. It was scary, and even though I was still in *Dendro,* I felt as though I could actually be killed… Yes, even I'm afraid of strong enemies."

Even as she spoke of something that had scared her, her expression didn't show a hint of fear. She was merely looking down on us, her gaze dense with coldness.

"That's why…" she continued. "…I'm only good at cleaning up 'powerless assassins' like you."

Following that proclamation, she made her move.

We tried to stop whatever she was doing, but the mist shrouding her concealed all her actions. A few of my subordinates threw knives at her again, but they all got deflected. Then, from behind the mist, she threw something in our direction.

It was an orb with a fuse on it — a bomb.

We tried distancing ourselves from it, but the fuse burned up far too quickly, blowing up and covering a part of the alley with an intense burst of… smoke.

It didn't take long for me to realize that it wasn't even a harmful kind.

"Don't panic! It's just a Smokebomb!"

Realizing that she might've used our reduced vision to kill us, we began to look around for her. I noticed her soon enough, but she instantly hid herself within the smoke. Thinking that she was using this smokescreen to get away from us, I got ready to do what I had to. However, a moment later, *five* silhouettes walked out of the smoke, all looking exactly like the woman.

Naturally, I was overcome with shock.

*An Illusion…? No, this is above that!* I thought.

"Get rid of the fakes! Throw!" I shouted my orders to my subordinates.

"Throw!" they said as they showered the five figures with throwing weapons.

It didn't matter if they aimed well. The knives would simply pass through the fakes, while the real one would block it. That would help us determine which one we had to focus on.

However, the result was completely unlike what I'd expected. Each and every one of the five figures moved in different ways to deflect all the throwing weapons heading in their direction.

"They... They're all real?!" I couldn't hold my surprise.

"Sadly for you, my Shadow Clone Technique creates corporeal bodies," she said.

*Shadow Clone Technique?!* I thought, shocked yet again. That was the name of a skill used by a Tenchi-exclusive job — Ninja.

*So when she took the form of the princess, she... I see! So she's...!*

"Ugaah...!" I heard my subordinates begin to panic, clearly because they couldn't tell which one was real.

The skill had created four clones that had the exact same presence as the original, making it difficult to tell which was the real one. Naturally, my subordinates were afraid of the person capable of this.

However, I was the only one who knew that her level was in the triple digits. If they were to find that out, their fear would become so great, it would hamper their ability to act. If that were to happen, I'd no longer have any chance of winning.

"Don't falter!" I shouted. "We have the numbers! Go two-on-one!"

"Understood!" they shouted as they charged at the clones.

A pair for each of them.

If logic applied, clones were weaker than the original. My subordinates should have a chance if they took advantage of their numbers.

Also, having them occupied like this gave me more options.

Or so I thought...

"Their levels sure are low," said one clone.

"Truly," agreed another.

"They don't require many of our tricks."

"Let's refrain from using Arc-en-Ciel, then, shall we?"

"Roger."

Even while fighting in pairs, they were still at a disadvantage against the clones. In fact, some had already lost their partner. Though supposedly weaker than the original, the clones were surpassing pairs of Assassins with a grasp of the trade's techniques.

Unlike me, they didn't have the high-rank job of Dead Hand, but they were capable Assassins nonetheless. And yet, they were getting disposed of so easily...

"Most people think that the biggest difference an Embryo makes are its unique skills," a clone spoke up. "I believe that to be both right and wrong. After all, even tians can have special skills if they get a UBM special reward."

Another clone picked up from there. "If you ask me, the biggest difference is their bonus to stats... and growth in general."

The third clone said, "The Embryo bonuses are what make Masters level up quickly and give us better stats. We're also immortal, so we can safely push limits tians can't. That creates a world of difference between the efficiencies of our growths."

A fourth one added, "That difference is great enough to have my three years here surpass your whole decades."

*Three years? She acquired these monstrous abilities in a mere three years?* I thought in disbelief.

"That's like a sick joke," I said. "If that's true, then to you Masters, all our training is nothing but fool's masonry!"

"Fool's masonry... that's an Altarian proverb, isn't it?" one of the clones responded. "It's based on the story of a man who tried to build a sky-reaching tower by hand, and it ends with it collapsing on him."

"But there *are* people who can build towers by hand, right?" another added. "Just like there are tians who have Superior Jobs."

"However, following that example, we Masters are building towers with heavy machinery," a third clone said.

They had basically said that there was a world of difference between us.

Many people equated Embryos with "talent" and "possibility," and the unfairness of it all made me grit my teeth in frustration. I just couldn't accept it. Ever since I was young, I'd been training with the organization to hone myself as an assassin, and it had taken me decades to become a Dead Hand. Due to that, I simply couldn't accept just how unreasonable Masters were.

A world where that woman was above me was a mistake.

I reached into my inventory and took out my secret weapon: a "Gem — Crimson Sphere." Just as it said in the name, it was a Gem which held the high-rank job of Pyromancer's ultimate spell, Crimson Sphere.

Its range wasn't particularly great, but its power was immense.

As things were, I would have no trouble having it hit that woman.

After all, my subordinates — the fools who had been able to do nothing against the clones even while in pairs — had been able to somehow able to keep them in place.

"Die," I said as I threw the Gem. It exploded right in the middle of the battle between the clones and my subordinates, covering it all in crimson.

There was no sound or explosion. There was only a crimson light and a heat that burned them all to nothing.

The woman, her clones, the subordinates fighting them, and the ones who were no longer capable of fighting all got engulfed in the light. A moment after I saw the shock in those guys' expressions, the skin on their faces became blackened ash, and their bones were soon to follow.

"Look at that… You useless shits were able to be useful, after all," I muttered. The crimson light also took out the woman and her four clones.

"Hmph," I scoffed. "So, just like Masters, clones become light when they die." With that, it was clear what had happened when we'd decapitated her the first time.

I stood around and watched them completely disappear. All that was left was to leave, find the second princess, and eliminate her.

"That woman sure was a pain," I muttered. "Covering the unexpected losses here will cost me a lot. I guess I shouldn't expect less from a Ninja — the eastern mystery high-rank job. Not like it matters now. She's the princess killer and she's going straight to the gaol. Hahahahah."

Entirely pleased with myself, I had my first laugh in a while as I played with the recording crystal containing the "proof."

A second later, I felt something cold sink into my back.

"Ah, wha—?" I voiced my confusion as the crystal fell out of my hands, shattered, and rang out with a high pitch. Looking down, I saw the blade of a dagger piercing out of my chest.

"Caught you off-guard, didn't I?"

I shifted my gaze forward, where I saw the very same five women that had vanished just a moment ago.

"You seem to have been misinformed about Ninjas. Allow me to correct you on two things," said one of them.

"One — Ninja is a low-rank job," a second one said. "The high-rank job would be Greater Ninja."

"First supplemental point: though 'shinobi' covers it all, there are different job groupings for different styles. Specifically, the ninja and onmitsu groupings."

"Second supplemental point: the ninja grouping's Ninja and Greater Ninja are for those who use the flashy ninja arts, like the ones that foreigners imagine them using."

"Third supplemental point: my job is one that grew from the onmitsu grouping, which gets the job done through hiding, sneaking, and confusion."

"And two — I'm not using a high-rank job."

Those last words were whispered to me by a sixth clone.

"Huh…? Gh…?" Bloody bubbles escaped my mouth as I turned around. There, I saw a mist-shrouded woman wearing sunglasses and a fox mask.

"Yes," she said. "I'm the real one. After making the smokescreen, I used Hidden Technique alongside Shadow Clone Technique to nullify my presence. Oh, and though you destroyed all my clones, I can easily make more by using the skill again, as you can clearly see."

She removed the dagger, causing me to fall to the ground. As I was lying there, the five clones and the woman all looked down at me.

There was a very clear difference between the woman and her clones. I couldn't feel her presence. Though she was right there before me, my five senses were denying her existence.

She had created several clones that had a physical presence while simultaneously nullifying her own presence.

*How is that even possible…?* I thought in disbelief.

"I hold the onmitsu grouping's Superior Job, 'Death Shadow,'" she said. "But you can call me the Superior Killer. I'm not revealing this as a parting gift, but that's what I am."

"A Superior Job… the Superior Killer…?!"

Superior Jobs were the ones above high-rank — the greatest of jobs. And "Superior Killer" was the nickname of the contract killer who, despite not having a Superior Embryo himself, had killed the Superior infamous for being "the greatest tian murderer of all time." It was the alias of the person who could kill Superiors — the ultimate hitman.

"O-Ooaagh…" I groaned, and not because of the pain. This girl, while being far younger than me, had surpassed me and all my years of assassin training, going far ahead into a realm meant for only a select few.

In terms of jobs and as a professional killer, she stood at a summit I couldn't hope to reach. That realization filled me with shock and emotion far greater than before.

"How… How can reality be so cruel…?" I muttered as the tears I'd thought had run dry began flowing out of my eyes.

"'Cruel,' you say?" she said with a hint of irritation in her voice. "You're a Dead Hand, right? That's a job you can only take after killing a certain number of people, isn't it? You tried to murder Ellie, and even sacrificed your subordinates as if it was nothing. You've turned so many people into lifeless corpses, and yet you're here crying after running into a little wall. That's really low, if you ask me." As she looked down at me, I looked up into her eyes. All I saw there was contempt. She wasn't just looking down on me; she seemed to feel the same scorn she would when looking at the usual problematic city-dweller.

I found that both humiliating and hard to stomach.

*But if she just kills me, those feelings will go away, and…*

"Anyway, I have to go pick up Ellie," she said while turning around, showing no intention to finish me off. "I put her to sleep and hid her, after all. Can't keep her like that."

"Ki—"

"No, I won't kill you. It would be a silly waste of effort." She made the clones vanish and began walking away.

At first, I didn't understand what she said.

A few moments had to pass until I completely processed her words, and their meaning made me burn with more rage than at any other moment in this encounter.

*I won't let her get away.*

Carefully, to make sure she didn't notice, I reached into my inventory and took out an item. It was a Gem — Crimson Sphere, just like the one I'd used before.

*I bet you weren't expecting me to have two of these,* I thought.

I quickly activated the Gem and got ready to throw it, fully intent on reducing her to ash. Then I would search for the second princess and kill her, too, making sure to make her death was as gruesome as possible. That would take care of the request, but I could no longer care about that.

The woman, so far above me, had looked at me with those contemptuous eyes. That made me want to reduce whatever she so wanted to protect to scrap.

*I can't wait to see her face when she revives and realizes that the princess is dead,* I thought, picturing the most amusing future as I threw the gem, and…

I threw it, and…

"...!"

Shock overcame me as I realized that I couldn't move.

"...?! ..." I tried to talk, but not even my tongue functioned.

*How? I wasn't shot like the new guy,* I thought.

"Oh, I forgot to say," the woman said calmly without turning around. "Like you saw before, one of the bullet types for my Arc-en-Ciel are paralyzing bullets, but I can actually do a similar thing with this."

Still facing away, she pulled out a dagger and held it so I could see it. That was the very same item that'd pierced me.

"A skill on this dagger allows me to cover the blade with slow-acting paralysis poison," she explained. "This thing is called 'Palsy Stingblade, Belspan.' That skill you've been hit with is actually from an Epic special reward, so — even though you're a high-rank job — its effects might be hard for you to resist."

*Wh... What?*

"I did say that killing you would be a waste of effort, but that didn't mean that I could let you act as you pleased. If you hadn't done anything stupid, you would've just stayed there for a day or two until the authorities found and took you away." She suddenly changed her tone. "I repeat — *if you hadn't done anything stupid.*"

In my hand, I held an already-activated Gem.

"H-hhhhh...!" I tried to scream, but only a whisper leaked from my mouth.

As I watched the woman casually wave goodbye to me — not even bothering to turn around — I was engulfed by my point-blank Crimson Sphere.

*Second princess of the Kingdom of Altar, Elizabeth S. Altar*

When I came to, Marie was giving me a piggyback ride. A moment ago, it had been evening, but now, the sun had completely sunk.

"Oh, are you awake?" asked Marie.

"Yes," I nodded. "Why am I being carried like this?"

"You got tired and fell asleep. It was a hectic day, after all."

She was probably right. This was the first time I'd ever played this much.

"We're almost at Count Gideon's residence," she said.

"Let me walk on my own feet, then," I said. "Piggyback rides don't befit a princess."

"Very well."

Though I'd enjoyed the ride, I didn't hesitate to get off her back and stand by myself. Count Gideon's residence was already in sight.

"This is far enough," I told her. "I can walk the rest of the way by myself."

"That's good," Marie smiled. "The guards would probably interrogate me if I got any closer."

"Marie," I said while gathering my resolve. "Thank you."

My memory told me that this was the first time I'd ever used those words. During my life, I had never been given a chance to express such simple gratitude to anyone.

"You're welcome." Marie gave me a smile as she took off the fox mask — that she was wearing herself, for reasons unknown — and put it on me. "This day will be one of my good memories in this world. Let's meet again someday, shall we?"

"Certainly! We… We shall meet again someday!"

And so, my day off in Gideon — a day I will never forget — finally reached its end.

Once I returned to the Count's residence, I got yelled at by a very, very angry Liliana. However, when I saw the tears in her eyes, the person I was now could easily tell that she was very worried about me.

"I'm sorry," I said, which made her look strangely surprised.

If today had made me different, that was surely thanks to Marie. I now had a very clear goal — to walk the streets of Gideon alongside my sisters Altimia and Theresia.

To achieve that, I first had to take care of the mountains of duties I'd neglected.

*Kingdom of Altar's Count, Alzar Brittis*

In the dead of night, I was doing work in the royal palace's archives.

I've been doing nothing but putting documents and numbers in order ever since I'd relinquished my territory after the war half a year ago. That was my job these days.

Compared to running a territory, the tasks I'd been given were by no means difficult, so despite not having any experience, I had little trouble doing them. However, this day in particular, I seemed to have overworked myself.

The light helping me work so late was made by a magic item that didn't use any fuel, but even if it wasn't a waste to keep it on, it was a good time to end it for the day.

As that thought went through my mind…

"Count Alzar Brittis."

…someone addressed me.

I looked to where the voice came from and saw a woman. She was wearing a black suit and — despite us being indoors — had sunglasses on her face, making her look questionable. Most would've assumed her to be an assassin sent to kill me, but I didn't believe that to be the case.

"I want to talk about Ellie… Her Highness Elizabeth… and what happened in duel city Gideon," she said.

"I'm listening, dear guest," I replied.

Thus, she began telling me about the day's events.

The second princess had run away from where she was staying. She'd encountered street ruffians and then met the woman before me. Together, they'd walked around enjoying whatever Gideon had to offer. And finally, the woman had fought assassins that had been hired by another noble, one who'd probably wanted the rights to Gideon and the surrounding lands.

"So that's what happened…" I said.

*What a curious turn of events,* I thought.

"At first, I thought that *you* were the one behind it all," said the woman. "Everything from her escape to the assassins."

"Why did you come to such a conclusion?" I asked.

"You were the ruler of the Brittis County, and it's well-known that you had a bad relationship with the previous Count Gideon — whose territory is right next to Brittis." she explained. "Also… in the war half a year ago, you lost your heir — your one and only son." Correct. All of that was nothing but the truth.

"Your son was fifteen years old at the time. Being of age, he was sent to the war as one of the kingdom's nobles," she went on.

Indeed. My son had participated in the war and lost his life.

"What went through your mind back then?" she asked. Though she was wearing sunglasses, I could feel her staring directly at me. "Unlike your son, the son of the current Count Gideon didn't participate in the war because he wasn't of age. As a result, the one that died was just the military officer that represented him. And thus, while Count Brittis lost both his heir and territory, Count Gideon continued into the next generation, ruling the most prosperous region in the kingdom. What did you make of this situation?"

She stopped for a moment, then took a breath before continuing.

"'Count Gideon is blessed with a prosperous territory and has a son he can bequeath its future to. I also gave my all for the sake of the kingdom. Why, then? Why am I the only one who lost everything?!'"

As if standing before a theater audience, she spoke those highly familiar words that I had said many times.

"Not many people could blame you for thinking that," she added.

"You talk as though you've seen me say that," I said. "We haven't even met before."

"That phrase is merely the result of the personality picture I've formed based on the information at my disposal."

*I see. That's some impressive imagination,* I thought.

The words she had spoken were more or less the same as mine. Indeed, there was a time when I'd thought those things and lamented in a similar manner while closed in my personal quarters.

It all made sense. That line of thought was more than enough to conclude that I had been the one behind the plot.

"That's correct," I admitted. "I was angry with everyone. The royal family, especially that foolish king, started the war that took away my dear son. The Royal Guard, despite being right next to him, failed to protect anything. And even though I went through such loss, Gideon still had everything… That made them all targets of my rage."

That was why I had begun plotting revenge, which consisted of…

"However," said the woman, "you were aware that those feelings of yours were unreasonable. A part of you thought that it was a mistake to direct your grudge at them."

*Oh, so you can see that much?* I thought.

"Am I wrong?" she asked in confirmation.

Out of all the ways I could've responded, I chose to be direct about how I felt.

"I was considering revenge against the royal family, the Royal Guard, and Count Gideon," I admitted. "However, just as you say, I knew that my grudge was misplaced."

Still, I had felt that I had to do something. My chagrin was far too great to let me stop.

"Thus, I chose to leave it all to the hand of fate," I continued.

"I can tell. That was why your plot had those intentional holes," she said as she put up three fingers. "Three main points. First, there was the question if telling Ellie about the greatness of Gideon would really get her to escape and abandon her duties. Second, it was a test to see if the Royal Guard was really incapable of doing what they had to when faced with such incidents. And third, there was the question of whether Count Gideon's city was safe enough for a girl like Ellie to walk around in all by herself. If they behaved in a way that cleared at least one of these three, they — just like you — would merely have been doing their duties to the best of their ability, which would mean that all the misfortunes you've faced were only your own fault. That's what you were thinking, correct?"

Correct.

I had talked to Her Highness Elizabeth, the most brazen of the three princesses, and given her an idealized image of Gideon.

Then I had intentionally provided the Royal Guard with the wrong documents — ones that would get in the way of their protection duties.

Those two acts had increased the chances of the princess escaping the residence, and that was the extent of what I had done.

"The only problems would've occurred if there were failures on all three points," said the woman. "If Ellie — a part of the royal family — got hurt, it would've been the responsibility of both the Royal Guard and Count Gideon, and your revenge would've been complete."

I had let fate show me whether my grudge was misplaced or if there was anything more to it.

"It's hard to call this a plan, and I don't quite believe that it would've been their fault even if it went through… still, it was quite close," she said.

"But it didn't happen, yes?" I asked.

"Indeed. To the royal family, the Royal Guard, Count Gideon… and to Ellie herself, this is merely a case of 'the whimsical princess ran away and enjoyed a day in Gideon.' That's it."

"Thank you," I said in gratitude before I even realized it.

"For what?" she asked.

I had said the words without even thinking, so even I didn't know how to answer that. However, after a bit of consideration, I decided that words of thanks really were the most appropriate here.

"Thanks to you fortunately being there to save Her Highness's life, I have finally reached a conclusion." The things that had happened during this incident had given me the ultimate answer. "I… I was merely unlucky."

The death of my son, the poor state of my lands… it all boiled down to that word.

No one in the kingdom was at fault. The cause of it all didn't lie with anyone else. I had merely been unlucky.

"I can't resent anyone for these results. My son went to war and was merely unlucky enough to die, while my lands unfortunately caught a plague. No one is at fault here… and yet, unable to see that, I went and did something truly unjust."

"Indeed," said the woman. "I also have a thing or two to say about you using Ellie's life as a pair of dice."

And she was right to feel that way, for — though indirectly — I had tried to hurt Her Highness Elizabeth. Brazen as she was, the second princess was a very gentle young lady.

*I can't believe I used her as a touchstone,* I thought in self-disgust.

"However, again, this incident is nothing but 'the princess ran away,'" said the woman.

Thus, no one would be blamed for this. Her Highness Elizabeth would get scolded, but that was the extent of it.

"But then…" I began.

"If you feel guilty," she cut my words short, "work hard enough to make it up to her. Starting with this."

Saying that, the woman gave me three bundles of documents.

"What is this?" I asked.

"I've gathered the proof and records of the injustices committed by Marquis Borozel — the one who sent assassins after Ellie," she answered. "Just say that you found it while organizing your documents or something and get him the punishment he deserves."

Naturally, I was surprised, for the files she'd given me were like the ones found in a noble's most secretive safe. Apparently, after protecting the princess, she had gone straight into Marquis Borozel's territory, taken these documents, and then returned here to the capital.

"Anyway, my job here is done, so I'll take my leave," she said.

"Wait," I called out. "Just who are you?"

My question made her form a smile.

"I'm just a passing Journalist," she answered as she disappeared like mist in the wind or shadow in sunlight.

*Journalist/Death Shadow, Marie Adler*

The day after the one I'd spent with Ellie, I was sitting in a terrace seat at one of the more popular cafés here in Gideon.

"...I'm sooo tired," I muttered.

The reason for that was obvious — I was still drained from all that I'd done yesterday.

Ticket acquisition, the date with Ellie, taking care of the assassins sent after her, getting dirt on the main offender, Marquis Borozel, and then talking to Count Brittis... all of that had happened in a single day. The latter three had been after sundown, too.

Sure, I had a Superior Job, and yes, my total level was above 500. Though my stats didn't match those of Superior Jobs focused purely on fighting, they were extremely high nonetheless. My AGI was in the quintuple digits, and I could move at the speed of sound, making me a particularly super woman, if you'll pardon the joke.

However, HP and energy were different things, plus MP and SP had no connection to mental fatigue. I was so sleepy.

However, I couldn't let the Sandman take me, for it was the day of the long-awaited event known only as "The Clash of the Superiors." I had to wait for Ray and Rook, too, which was all the more reason why I couldn't sleep.

"Ray, huh...?" I murmured.

That was the name of the young man I'd met at Noz Forest, where I had been doing my work as a professional killer.

I was a roleplayer taking the role of Marie — the protagonist of my hitman superpower battle manga. To get properly immersed in her as a character, I simply couldn't do without the act of murdering people as a professional killer.

However, tians — just like living people — were intelligent beings. Due to that, I was wholly averse to the idea of killing them. Although ones like the assassins from yesterday were exceptions.

Anyway, that was why I'd chosen to become a professional killer focused solely on Masters — who didn't die even if they were killed. Unlike tians, they revived, and their lives would never be in any real danger. I had no problems killing them for my roleplaying purposes.

With that in mind, I'd spent my time in Tenchi taking and training in jobs from the onmitsu grouping, such as Onmitsu and Shadow. Eventually, I'd gotten the Superior Job of Death Shadow, and become a professional killer focused solely on PK.

I had chosen the onmitsu grouping's jobs because my manga's Marie had a similar fighting style to them, often using transformation and clones in her battles.

My success rate was very high, and the processes I went through to get my targets helped me learn to *draw* methods of assassination I had never thought of before. Being a professional killer was a valuable experience for both *Dendro* and my real life.

Once, my target had been the King of Plagues — a Superior who'd gotten on all wanted lists for indiscriminately killing tens of thousands of tians. The battle had been so grueling that I'd thought I was gonna die for real, but I had somehow been able to defeat him and send him to the gaol.

My most recent job had been the newbie PK hunt at Noz Forest.

I didn't know who'd requested it, but I'd been presented with a sizable sum of money for it. Though I'd been averse to the idea of indiscriminately killing almost nothing but newbies, the fact that I hadn't done such assassinations before had greatly intrigued me. Also, I had recalled that *Into the Shadow* had an event where apprentice assassins of a certain organization were one-sidedly massacred, which had made me think that this might help me revitalize the Marie that was lying dormant inside me.

Thus, I'd accepted the job, entered Noz Forest, and started killing all the Masters there, among which was Ray.

I found him to be quite interesting. Despite being a newbie, he'd been able to survive the first of my Embryo's attacks. Then he'd gone on to block the second one, and had still had the willpower to deflect the third.

In the end, I'd used bullet creatures made from a mix of Black Pursuit and Blue Dispersion to finally give him the death penalty, but what mattered weren't the results.

The important thing here was the expressions and emotions he'd displayed.

While struggling against the death penalty, he was *alive*.

Well, of course he was. That applied to me, as well, but that wasn't a big deal.

What I meant by that was the fact that he was giving his all to survive here in *Infinite Dendrogram*.

I didn't know whether he was aware of it or not, but he was actually doing his best to stay alive in this *game*.

Some players who had played as long as me became like that due to spending lots of time here. There were also people — like the cultists — who didn't think it was a game from the moment they entered here.

However, he was neither. Despite being a beginner — a rookie — he was more serious about living here than most of the countless players I'd encountered.

That fact had greatly intrigued me, making me believe that watching him would help me discover what I was missing and perhaps even revitalize the Marie sleeping within me. Eventually, after I figured he'd most likely revived, I had started looking for him.

In the process, I had gone through a ridiculous encounter with a battleship-riding furball — the King of Destruction — which had resulted in the complete immolation of Noz Forest.

I had survived that predicament, and I'd soon found Ray and his Embryo, Nemesis, talking to another newbie, Rook. Not missing the opportunity, I had pretended to be a passerby and ended up becoming a member of their party.

By the way, my job back then had always been Death Shadow.

The onmitsu grouping had a passive skill known as "Onmitsu Conceal." While having an onmitsu grouping job as my main one, it made the job display remove all the onmitsu grouping jobs and replaced the main job with the non-onmitsu job that had the highest level.

That was why the only jobs that showed up for others were Journalist and one other, while the stats appeared lowered, as well. I could choose to turn it off for my party members, but since I was kinda infiltrating Ray's party, I didn't do it.

Due to that, the Journalist passive skill "The Pen is Mightier than the Sword" gave me a bit of a problem.

Normally, it wouldn't have been a big deal, for it would've activated the moment I switched to being a Journalist. However, switching my job to one outside the onmitsu grouping would've disabled the effect hiding my total level, which was something I definitely didn't want. Thus, I'd stayed a Death Shadow and opted to fake the skill's effect by secretly using items that increased EXP gain for a certain amount of time.

It was hard on my wallet, though — 100,000 lir for every 30 minutes. Still, I believed that I had to bite the bullet and just bear having to make these expenses.

...After all, I'd made quite a lot of money from the newbie hunt.

Looking back, though I felt quite guilty about it and thought that I shouldn't have done it, the fact that I wouldn't have found Ray if I hadn't made it a bit complicated.

As our party had gathered and traveled to Gideon, we'd gotten involved in the battle against the goblin horde and their leader — The Great Miasmic Demon, Gardranda.

Gardranda had been a very strong UBM.

UBMs all had something talent-like to them. While Gardranda had a lower level than the two UBMs I'd defeated, I had felt that its latent abilities were not to be trifled with.

Its level might've been low, but it was still a far stronger creature than the newbies Ray and Rook.

Normally, even Epic-tier UBMs required Masters with high-rank Embryos at their disposal, and even then, their chances of victory would be only about 50%. When facing such creatures, incomplete parties of Masters with low-rank Embryos simply had no chance — *no possibility.*

Victory could've been ours if I'd taken off my disguises and gone all-out, but I'd chosen not to do that. Sure, doing so would've revealed who I was, but that definitely wasn't the primary reason for that. I had wanted to see... to observe how Ray acted in a situation similar to the one in the forest — when faced with a being far stronger than himself.

Thus, I had limited myself only to things that didn't go beyond the capabilities of a Journalist, making sure not to sully the purity of the actions he took.

He had ended up breaking all my predictions and expectations.

He hadn't run away.

He hadn't abandoned people — even if they were tians.

Even when beaten by a power far greater than himself and even when his plans had fallen apart, he had never given up.

Until the very end, he had searched for possibilities and seized the one leading to victory against Gardranda.

Sure, I'd helped him out at the very end, but that was a triviality. Having given his all and used everything at his disposal, Ray had won against Gardranda. The instant I'd seen him stand victorious had actually made my heart throb.

He was as alive in *Infinite Dendrogram* as he was in the real world.

At that moment, I'd concluded that I wanted to see more of him. As a Journalist, as a manga artist, as Marie, and as myself, I wanted to observe him.

"I'm using the word 'observe,' but it's more that I merely grew fond of him," I said to myself. In all honesty, I wanted to reveal what I was and apologize for killing him. I wished for us to become friends.

However...

"...Ray and Nemesis's current goal is to find and defeat me."

On the way to Gideon and during the party we'd held once we'd arrived, he'd told us of his first death penalty and his intention to win against the one responsible — me. Listening to him had made beads of cold sweat form on my back.

"Revealing myself would probably hamper their determination... and I really don't want their motivation to go down..." Nemesis's reaction when she'd believed that I'd been defeated by the King of Destruction made it obvious that they were quite fired up about the prospect of revenge against me. Also, more importantly, I found that Ray was coolest when he gave his all to break through whatever was happening right before his eyes.

Thus, I chose not to interfere with their immediate goal and decided to wait until they became stronger. Then I would appear before them as a mysterious PK, and — just as they desired — face them with all I had.

As such thoughts raced through my mind, I saw the two I was thinking of approaching.

I waved my hand at the now-familiar Master and his Embryo — the people that had me so enchanted.

[MARIE STORY, END.]

## Afterword

**Bear:** “The part after the midword is done, so now it’s time for the afterword! I’m the beary merry Brother Bear!”

**Cat:** “And I’m Cheshire — the one who didn’t really have any scenes in volume 3 outside of this corneerr!”

**Bear:** “Man, time sure flies, doesn’t it? We’re already at volume 3!”

**Cat:** “Thanks to all the support from our dear readers, the novels are coming out smoothly!”

**Bear:** “I remember when a certain someone at the first meeting said ‘if it doesn’t do well, I hope we get at least 3 volumes before canceling. That should be enough to cover Part 1.’ How nostalgic.”

**Cat:** “How they expected to fit all that into just 3 volumes is beyond me. As our dear readers can see, even when we got a bigger page number than usual, we still ended right as the main event began! There’s no way Part 1 could’ve fit into just 3 voluumes!”

**Bear:** “Not to mention the fact that Ray bearly had a role in this one.”

**Cat:** “He chatted, ate, chatted, ate, and then just watched a fight!”

**Bear:** “And the one doing most of the eating was Nemesis.”

**Cat:** “I wouldn’t have been surprised if the fang on the cover was shiining.”

**Bear:** "Anyway, if this had been canceled after 3 volumes, the readers would've been in fur a beary summary-like experience."

**Cat:** "They might've had to cut the entire Figaro vs Xunyu battle."

**Bear:** "Or maybe just end it with the labcoat's appearance and tie it all up with a 'Our battle begins…!'"

**Cat:** "That's not tying up anything!"

**Xun:** "Gotta thaNk the readers that it didN'T cOme to that, eh?"

**Bear/Cat:** "…Who's there?!"

**Xun:** "Master Jiangshi, Xunyu. Since it's apparently necEssary, I'm joining tHe afterwords from noW on."

**Cat:** "Oh, I see… So you're saying that I'm about to lose even more of my already-few roles?!"

**Xun:** "You even got yoUr role cut out oF the manga, diDn't ya?"

**Cat:** "Don't say that! Don't remind me that I only have a picture of me grinning on the cover!"

**Xun:** "The manga is beiNg distributed bY Comic Fire, by the wAY."

**Cat:** "You even took the advertisement I was supposed to do! First Figaro's organs, now people's turns… Just how much of a thief are you?!"

**Xun:** "Okay, no. The one in chaRge of thieverY in this work is someoNe else, you know?"

**Bear:** (…Man, Xunyu already seems comfortable here.)

**Bear:** "You were on stage and in the limelight on this volume's illustrations, and you feel the same way here, eh, Dhalsim?"

**Xun:** "What diD you just cAll me?"

**Bear:** "You fight by stretching your limbs, using fire and teleportation. You're beary much Dhalsim, from *Street Fi*—"

**Xun:** "I don't do yOga. Also, I'm a womAn."

**Cat:** "Well, a jiangshi woman brings up images of a certain other fighting game character!"

**Bear:** "By the way, the author noticed Xunyu's similarity to Dhalsim a long while after introducing her."

**Cat:** "Anyway, it's time for the familiar serious comment from the author."

Dearest readers, thank you for your purchase. I am the author, Sakon Kaidou.

My work has reached volume 3 and — thanks to your support — will go beyond that, allowing me to continue my writing without any worries. You have my sincere gratitude for that.

Anyway, this volume has two significant points the previous two didn't have.

First is the fact that there are stories which have people other than the protagonist — Ray Starling — as their main characters. I hope you enjoyed the stories you couldn't see with just a single perspective and that they gave you a broader look at my work's world.

The second point is that the current central plot didn't end with this volume. The Figaro vs Xunyu fight and the two side stories are concluded in this volume, but a certain incident is continuing from this one into the fourth. Though, some might be inclined to say that the hand of fate has been leading to this ever since volume 1.

*Infinite Dendrogram* part 1's greatest event will continue in volume 4, so please look forward to it.

Sakon Kaidou

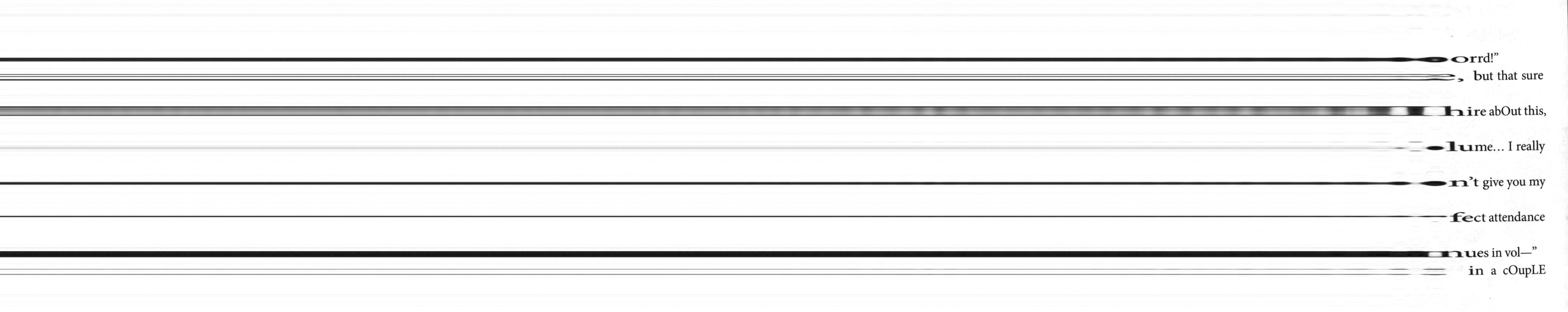
orrd!"
, but that sure
hire abOut this,
lume... I really
n't give you my
fect attendance
nues in vol—"
in a cOupLE

VOLUMES 1–
ON SALE NO
In Another Wo

**Cat:** "All right, it's time for us to end the afterwoorrd!"

**Bear:** "Ray's been a bit dormant in this volume, but that sure won't be the case in the next one."

**Xun:** "...Huh? Wait, I know I mAde fun of Cheshire abOut this, but whAt will I be doiNg in the next voLume?"

**Bear:** "Looking at how you ended up in this volume... I really have no clue."

**Cat:** "You just keep sleeping in the barrier! I won't give you my turns!"

**Bear:** "Well, my place is beary much secure (perfect attendance in the original webnovel)."

**Cat:** "Anyway, the story from this volume continues in vol—"

**Xun:** "Volume 4, which is sEt to come out in a cOupLE monTHs! Look forWard to it!"

**Cat:** "She stole it again!"

VOLUMES 1-7
ON SALE NOW!
In Another World With My Smartphone
©Patora Fuyuhara, Illustration: Eiji Usatsuka

# J-Novel Club Lineup

## Ebook Releases Series List

Amagi Brilliant Park
An Archdemon's Dilemma: How to Love Your Elf Bride
Ao Oni
Arifureta Zero
Arifureta: From Commonplace to World's Strongest
Bluesteel Blasphemer
Brave Chronicle: The Ruinmaker
Clockwork Planet
Demon King Daimaou
Der Werwolf: The Annals of Veight
ECHO
From Truant to Anime Screenwriter: My Path to "Anohana" and "The Anthem of the Heart"
Gear Drive
Grimgar of Fantasy and Ash
How a Realist Hero Rebuilt the Kingdom
How NOT to Summon a Demon Lord
I Saved Too Many Girls and Caused the Apocalypse
If It's for My Daughter, I'd Even Defeat a Demon Lord
In Another World With My Smartphone
Infinite Dendrogram
Infinite Stratos
Invaders of the Rokujouma!?
JK Haru is a Sex Worker in Another World
Kokoro Connect
Last and First Idol
Lazy Dungeon Master
Me, a Genius? I Was Reborn into Another World and I Think They've Got the Wrong Idea!
Mixed Bathing in Another Dimension
My Big Sister Lives in a Fantasy World
My Little Sister Can Read Kanji
My Next Life as a Villainess: All Routes Lead to Doom!
Occultic;Nine
Outbreak Company
Paying to Win in a VRMMO
Seirei Gensouki: Spirit Chronicles
Sorcerous Stabber Orphen: The Wayward Journey
The Faraway Paladin
The Magic in this Other World is Too Far Behind!
The Master of Ragnarok & Blesser of Einherjar
The Unwanted Undead Adventurer
Walking My Second Path in Life
Yume Nikki: I Am Not in Your Dream